CW00730321

The Cel
by Micha

Copyright 2016
ISBN: 97

Cover art by Stephan Martiniere
Edited by Stephen 'Shoe' Shoemaker

Chapter 1

"Woooooooo!!!" Caden whooped in joy, diving out of the sky toward the vine jungle below. Siobhan glided by his side though she slowly fell behind. Neither of them could keep up with their four Celaran friends, who had already reached the lowest point in their trajectory below. The flat, serpentine creatures undulated like sine waves as they slid through the air. Their three fingers folded underneath each end of their bodies while in flight. The glowing chevrons placed along their backs flashed yellow and green in rapidly changing patterns.

The Celarans pulled out of the dive and split off from each other, heading in four different directions. Caden followed one at random. He pulled up earlier than the aliens had, yet he still felt he might crash into the vines below. The canopy neared alarmingly. Two attendants pressed against him to add their thrust to his course correction. Caden's arc flattened out only a few meters over the tallest vines. Siobhan's flight dropped even closer to disaster, yet she howled in joy as her extended fingers whipped across the highest leaves.

He laughed out loud.

This is so much fun!

The Celaran that Caden followed turned sharply again. Caden saw one of the Celaran towers ahead, poking up through the vines. He looked over the landscape and saw that they had come to the tower line surrounding the modest Celaran settlement. The towers were the same as those that had surrounded the original empty base on Idrick Piper, but there was no flat field anywhere nearby.

"None of them fly past the towers," Siobhan said.

"The towers knock things out of the air," Caden reminded her.

"They wouldn't target Celarans though, surely?"

Caden shrugged in midair. "I don't know. But we should follow the rule. They obviously have their reasons."

"Yes, of course. I'm just curious. I wish we could ask them."

"Well, let's fly back and see if Marcant has made any progress," Caden said. He suggested it half-jokingly; it had been several days and Marcant had not completed a translator. The newest member of the PIT team became grumpier every time someone asked him how it was going. Marcant had deployed the attendants throughout the colony to record the Celaran's visual chatter and try to connect it to meaning. Some of the Celarans even played with the attendants, which incidentally helped Marcant to pick up more data.

"We should check in," Siobhan said.

Caden frowned. She usually wanted to fly around all day until Telisa called them to action.

Okay what's up with that?

Caden gained altitude, propelled by his Celaran lift rod and his three attendants. Once he decided that his gliding suit could carry him back to their temporary home in the forest, he leveled off and flew in that direction. Siobhan joined him for the straight shot home.

Caden and Siobhan shared a single Celaran treehouse with the rest of the PIT team. Quarters were tight, with people sleeping in every room, but the Celarans did not have much spare living space to offer. If they had been able to communicate, Telisa probably would have politely refused the Celarans' hospitality and ordered everyone to sleep aboard the *Iridar*, which rested at the edge of the settlement.

Caden caught glimpses of the Celaran houses below: many-faceted green dwellings with hexagonal trap doors and circular windows. Each structure rested around the upper section of one of the massive spikes that emerged from the ground to support the vegetation. He saw Celarans flitting about in the vine jungle as he passed overhead. Many carried lift rods like the one he had borrowed, though it seemed they hardly needed them. The Celarans could zip about all day without using up their rods' charge, but Caden found that his rod would be drained after two hours.

Caden's link map showed him the correct shelter. Without the off-retina map, he would be hard pressed to find it. It looked like all the other spike-supported houses in the jungle. Siobhan angled down beside him, then they landed softly on a deck adjoining the house. Caden traded wild grins with Siobhan before they walked inside.

My life is awesome. I get to fly around with aliens and share it all with her.

"If you have a working system, then we need to start using it," Telisa said. Her voice filtered in from somewhere nearby. Caden sauntered into the central room. Two sleeping bags lay against adjacent walls of the six-sided chamber. A dog-sized machine stood in the middle of the room. It looked like a giant ant: six legs and three body sections. The head held a laser/stunner mount, and the abdomen stored and dropped glue grenades.

Siobhan followed him inside. Magnus emerged from a side room.

"I'm glad you're back," Magnus said to Siobhan. "Did you have time to design the modified grenades?"

"I'm hitting it now," Siobhan said.

Ah, that's why she agreed to come back so early, Caden thought.

"What's the objective?" Caden asked.

"I'm adding spikes to the grenades to keep them on the vines," Siobhan told him.

Caden knew Terran grenades did not move well among the vines. They tended to slide off the stalks and fall into the detritus of the jungle floor, which slowed them down. Once on the jungle floor, they often could not rise again to hit higher targets. It made sense to modify them to stick onto the vines, so they could quickly reach targets higher in the canopy.

Caden decided to let Siobhan get to her work without interruption. He walked on through the room to the balcony on the other side of the dwelling where he saw Telisa standing with Marcant. He stepped up and joined their conversation.

"There will be miscommunication," Marcant said. "I don't have enough data for a full vocabulary."

"The Celarans are smart. They'll know the translator isn't working perfectly. Five Entities, we'll *tell* them that," Telisa said.

Marcant nodded.

Caden saw several channels were up locally. There was his private connection with Siobhan, the PIT team channel, a new translation experiment channel, and a channel marked as a conversation with the Celarans.

Caden joined the experiment's channel and the Celaran channel, which already included Telisa, Jason,

Cilreth, and Marcant. He double checked that Cilreth was still back on the ship.

She likes to keep tabs on what's going on from relative safety.

"Should we tell the others?" Caden asked.

Telisa shook her head subtly towards Caden. He wondered about her decision.

She must not want to add pressure for Marcant. Or maybe she just figures they're busy enough with their own work?

Marcant looked up, reticent to reply in the affirmative. Caden decided to follow Telisa's lead.

"Never mind, I'll wait until we get the kinks worked out," Caden said sunnily. "I'm sure it won't work perfectly right off, things this complex never do."

Marcant seemed satisfied, maybe even relieved, with that answer. He went back off-retina. Telisa picked up a strip of black material Caden had not seen before. As she affixed it to the front of her body, Caden saw it had chevrons across its surface, just like the flat side of a Celaran.

"Okay, please find Lee," Telisa said to Caden.

Lee was a Celaran who had been hanging around the house since the PIT team arrived. The PIT team did not know exactly what Lee's job was, though the competing theories were similar. Some had guessed the Celaran was there to learn about the Terrans, other team members thought Lee was there simply to help make the Terrans as comfortable as possible. Siobhan had suggested the name Lee, short for liaison. The team thought of Lee as a 'she' even though they had no idea if the Celarans had differentiated sexes. Siobhan had also pointed out that Lee

5

was neutral enough that it would not become awkward if they discovered more about Celaran genders later.

"You're ready?" Caden said, his voice lilting upward in excitement.

"Ready for a test," Marcant said, much more grim than his teammate.

Caden walked to the edge of the balcony and looked around for Lee. He did not see her in the surrounding jungle, so he grabbed the edge of the roof and pulled himself up from the balcony to get a better view of the area. Lee flitted about with another Celaran at the next house over. Caden waved an arm, facing Lee. She did not approach, so he jumped up and down. Lee caught sight of the antics and glided over toward the PIT house.

Lee alighted on a balcony perimeter rack next to Telisa as Caden slipped back down to join them. Lee wore a black harness along half of her two-meter-long body. Two rods were attached to the harness, as was the Celaran habit. The PIT team did not know why they chose to carry exactly two, one of which was usually a lifting rod, though Telisa had expressed the theory that the decision to carry no more than two was due to a flying weight limitation. The second rod seemed to have three or four different functions depending on the individual, but it might have been that the second rod could do almost anything and the team had just not witnessed enough of the functions yet.

Marcant sat down on the deck. Telisa faced Lee, showing her the new chevron garment. When the alien saw the chevrons, she let go of her roost and did a flip in midair. The fingers on each end of her body intertwined with each other, turning Lee into a floating circle. Caden assumed she relied upon her lift rod to remain aloft in such a position.

"Okay, speak to the channel and your chevrons will say it in Celaran," Marcant said. "Or some approximation thereof," he muttered.

Caden saw that Marcant had two attendants, but they did not orbit as Caden's and Telisa's did. He put away a note to himself to ask about the stationary attendants later.

"We're glad to have met you," Telisa said on the Celaran channel. Her chevrons glowed so rapidly the colors blended together in Caden's Terran eyes.

The Celaran's chevrons made a response. The translation came through on the channel almost instantaneously.

"We feel the starlight on our skin as a green proximity blooms with our alien feeding companions," said a flat, synthetic voice.

"Wow!" Caden said. "Is that really what she said?"

Marcant shrugged. "More or less."

Even when he says he doesn't know something, he still sounds self-assured, Caden thought.

"Almost poetic," Jason said. "But the voice is so harsh sounding. Not a good fit."

"I'm translating alien speech and you criticize the voice settings?" Marcant said exasperatedly.

"Thank you for offering us this place to live," Telisa said. Her chevrons glowed again.

"As the wind flies over the leaves, we need to keep green friends close to suck sap from their brains."

"Uhm," Caden mumbled. "Translation error, I hope."

Marcant nodded. "Just keep talking. It'll get better."

"Not a surprising translation, really," Telisa said. "Sucking sap from our brains... that sounds like learning

7

from us, or getting to know us."

"Oh! Let's hope that's what it meant," Caden said. "I also suspect it should be 'as the wind blows' but I'll leave that to you."

Marcant nodded.

"We're happy we arrived when we did, to help you fight the Destroyers," Telisa said.

"As the planet spins, you fly in proximity to scream at our enemies," the Celaran said. "When the vines burn, those that blow and scream are a danger to us all."

"Okay," Caden said slowly.

Telisa smiled. She seemed pleased and impressed with the translation that Caden found questionable.

"To us, the Destroyers are bright," she said aloud. "To a Celaran, they scream, because the Celarans speak with light."

"You may be inventing explanations that seem to make sense but are utterly false," Marcant said.

"We're still learning to speak your language," Telisa said to Lee without answering Marcant. "I'm sorry for any errors we may make. Please don't be offended."

"On a bright day near a vine fat with sap, there is no sorrow at a mistake made while learning," Lee said. "I'm glad to speak with my strange friends who have no feelings."

Hrm. Something lost in translation?

"That's great! This is wonderful," Telisa said to the PIT channel. "Keep working on it. We need to get it fine tuned so we can have some serious conversations. See if you can double check her statement about us having no feelings. Is it a mis-translation, or are we missing some out-of-band part of speech? Maybe they express feelings with air chemicals or something, and we're not emitting any."

Wow. She appreciates how hard this is, Caden thought. *I should be more positive to Marcant. He's done pretty well!*

"I will, but please realize that it's the learning system that needs to run longer and absorb more data. I don't tweak every little meaning myself, or this would take years," Marcant said.

Telisa began to walk back into the hut, but turned around at the last moment.

"And... make the voice playful, like the Celarans themselves," she said.

Marcant nodded.

That at least, will be easy, Caden thought.

"Great work!" Telisa said as she left the balcony.

Marcant took the praise calmly. "It'll be much better tomorrow," he promised.

Chapter 2

Telisa prepared herself for the first formal exchange with the Celarans since they had learned to communicate. She stood in the main room of the team's Celaran dwelling, checking her equipment nervously as she thought over what to say and what to ask. Marcant, Jason, Caden and Siobhan looked on.

"I have a question," Caden said. "What's up with that stuff they say first, before the real reply? It's always some weird, kinda poetic thing."

"The preamble, I call it," Marcant said.

"Well, I what do those preambles mean?" asked Caden.

Marcant looked uncomfortable. "I don't have a strong answer yet."

"It may just be their way of speaking," Cilreth said over the PIT channel from the *Iridar*.

"But it's just random and has nothing to do with the subject at hand," Caden noted.

The team turned to Telisa to hear her answer.

They expect me to confirm or dismiss his observation.

"For now, it's just odd," Telisa said. "Marcant and I have some theories."

Jason looked at her. Telisa could tell he wanted to hear her theory but would not ask for it.

"Such as?" Caden asked for everyone.

"I haven't heard them express emotion in the main statement, so I think the preamble sets the mood for the rest. If they say something is warm or sunny or sweet, they're being happy and upbeat. If they say something about darkness or cold—you know, something negative—

then that emotion shades the statement to come."

"Sounds like a good theory to me," Siobhan said.

"And it explains Lee's comment yesterday about us having no feelings," Marcant said. "We don't use preambles when we reply. I'll plan to take mood cues from our voice tone and adjectives, all sorts of context, and have the translator emit a suitable preamble for us."

"Don't roll out any experimental changes until tomorrow," Telisa said. "It would be better to sound emotionless than loopy, right?"

"So you're speaking with the Celaran leader?" Jason asked. He knew the answer, so Telisa took it to mean he wanted details.

"I don't know," Telisa said. "Do they have a leader or leaders? I'll try to find out. I would expect we're only going to cover the basics, given our limited understanding of the language."

"Are you going to speak with them alone?" Caden asked, looking around.

He's wondering where Magnus is, Telisa thought. She had sent Magnus out to meet a robotic assault unit from the *Midway*. Since the Celarans had proven peaceful, and the threat of the Destroyers loomed over them all, the Space Force had asked to send down their ground troops and Telisa had agreed. It was one of the main issues Telisa wanted to cover with the Celarans. She double-checked the notes in her PV and saw the issue had been listed there.

"I'll go alone, but please stay linked into the PIT channel and I'll copy everything over so you don't miss anything."

Telisa prepared her Celaran lift baton and walked out onto a balcony.

"Don't freak out if you see some Terran assault machines," she said. "The *Midway* is sending down help."

Telisa launched herself into the sky. Her superhuman strength and the boost of the lift baton brought her across the 30 meter gap between her launch point and a massive vine angling toward the site of the meeting. Telisa started to run along the thick arm of the huge plant. She caught sight of Lee overhead, darting to one side then the other playfully. Telisa ran until the vine turned away in the wrong direction, then jumped to the next good candidate.

"With big wind beneath your wings, you fly faster than your companions, even without a pretend-wing suit," Lee said.

Telisa smiled. The translator used a funny name for the glider equipment Siobhan and Caden had been using. Her host body enabled her to jump much farther than the rest of the PIT team.

"When the day is shortest, do Terrans choose their leaders by how fast they can fly?" asked Lee.

"That's not why I'm the leader, but I *am* physically different than they are," Telisa said.

I don't want to say anything about Trilisks at this point... it could be misunderstood.

They arrived at a new building which Telisa had not seen before. It was a dome-shaped structure larger than the *Iridar*. Telisa examined it as they approached. She realized that the Celarans must have had to clear away a few of the jungle's white support spikes to make room for the structure. It was the first such building Telisa had encountered on the planet; so far the PIT team had only seen force towers and small dwellings.

They manipulated this vine growth to obscure the

structure from space.

Lee and Telisa came to a trap door on the roof. It opened for Lee, who rolled through like a falling wheel. Telisa dropped in after her Celaran friend.

Like most Celaran buildings, it was hollow, forming a single room. The inside was dark, but Telisa's eyes adjusted quickly. She had dropped onto a small platform hanging near the ceiling. Dozens of balconies and similar platforms littered the inner walls. Rows of Celarans surrounded them, hanging from their resting rods along the platforms. Telisa estimated that there must be over a hundred present incarnate.

"Where do I stand?" asked Telisa, aware that the word *stand* was probably being translated to *hang*.

"The leaves rustle above so you may stay wherever comfortable," Lee said. "The forest is dark despite the star above, so your voice will be heard."

Probably an archaic phrase from before they had electronic communications. I bet she really said 'your voice will be seen'. An amusing artifact of a solid literal translation.

Telisa dropped twenty meters to a stack of flat panels at the center the floor, using her lift baton to soften her landing. She knew she could take the drop without injury, but she did not want to damage the panels, whatever they were. The floor held a dizzying array of equipment and supplies. Unlike a Terran building, there was no way to walk among it all. The Celarans obviously accessed the niches and piles by flitting above them. Telisa opened Marcant's translator and set it on its tripod next to her.

"Do I speak with everyone at once?" Telisa asked. "I'm not sure our translator can hear more than one of you at a time."

"The sap is sweet when we hear First Speaker, who will talk with you while all listen," Lee said.

First Speaker. Must be that one, Telisa thought as a Celaran floated over to her, near the center of the room. The Celaran looked like all the others, though Telisa noticed its second baton glinted more than most other Celaran tools. She thought of it like a lordly rod. Telisa told the translator to watch that Celaran.

"In the cool shade cast by leaves above, we welcome our alien friend Telisa," said First Speaker. "As empty space opens in vast cold distances, you have come here for what reason?"

Well let's get right to it!

"We came looking for you," Telisa said. "I've met a member of another alien race, a long golden creature with many thin legs, whose people had found evidence of your civilization. We sought more friends to learn from... and also to join us in our fight against the Destroyers."

"The creatures hide under the vine in fear as the Celarans are killed by the Destroyers. We are amazed to find friends exactly when we most need them."

Many of the other Celarans flickered. The leader turned this way and that, exchanging comments. Telisa regained her lock on the leader as it calmed and faced her again.

"As we are cloaked by darkness deep under the vines, we have many questions," continued First Speaker.

"I'll try my best to answer," Telisa said.

"The leaves are burning as we meet with the Terrans and ask them for help," First Speaker said. "Season of bright light upon us, can Telisa arrange to protect us from our enemies?"

"I'll send a message back to my home, asking for more ships to come here," Telisa said. "I want to convince them to help fight the Destroyers."

"At the time of the sunrise, we hope the Terrans can send their ships soon."

I think the Space Force will respond, but I wonder what Shiny will do... I hope I haven't given them false hope.

Telisa decided to deliver what encouragement she could.

"There are also Terran soldiers coming from our ship the *Midway* to help us today. They will bring large war machines through the vines and join us here. Please do not be alarmed. They are only to oppose the Destroyers."

"As our tools work with the power of the wind and water, this 'soldier' translates oddly."

"Terrans are more specialized than you are, I believe," Telisa said. "Our tool design is usually focused on just one task. In my pack, I have a light that is only a light and nothing else. It's often the same with our professions: some of us investigate materials, some of us build ships, and some of us fight our enemies. You do not know soldiers? Who among you stops the Destroyers?"

"As the vines grow thick overhead, Celaran scientists devise ways to protect us from these Destroyers."

Could they have no military arm? They fight with their scientists and engineers!

"You must be terrified if war is unknown to you. We'll help you in any way we can. Terrans want to learn from you, but maybe we can also teach you."

"Heat radiates into the cold vacuum as our people

scatter and die. The Destroyers have burned and tainted many of our worlds."

"Magnus is one of our soldiers. Please work with him to place our machines around the forest for protection." Telisa paused. Should she explain to them that not all the robots were their own?

"The Terrans have other alien friends whose machines we also use," Telisa continued. "The Vovokans made these attendant spheres, and our spaceship."

I guess they may not know much about the Vovokans, but knowing they made these things is a start.

Telisa sent location pointers and pictures, but she did not know if the Celarans could understand those yet.

"As the planet turns, we are interested to know more of your ship," First Speaker said.

"I would be glad to bring you aboard my ship and show you everything," Telisa said.

"As strange beings walk upon the vines, the Terrans must have many questions to ask the Celarans. Your friend Lee will answer them."

"Thank you," Telisa said.

We're done already?

She looked uncertainly towards Lee, whose chevrons wavered chaotically. Telisa had learned from Marcant that the colors changed more rapidly than a Terran could follow; also, the patterns of each statement repeated many times. The Celaran decided what to say and some trick of their physiology said it over and over again very rapidly. Telisa told the translator to focus on Lee.

"The promise of fresh sap awaits as I beg you to show me your spacecraft," Lee said.

"Now? Sure. Are we done here?" Telisa asked,

puzzled.

"The edges of the vine curl in extreme heat as many must address another pressing issue," Lee said.

Wow. It must be very urgent. Or are aliens just not that important to the Celarans?

Telisa picked up the translator and followed Lee when she flew out of the building. Telisa's mind raced. She had expected to spend the entire day trading information with the Celaran leaders.

Once they were outside, Telisa paused to ask another question. She focused the translator on Lee's chevrons.

"What's the problem that they'll work on now?" Telisa asked.

"The vine needs light to grow, and the production of ships must continue to face the next Destroyer attack," Lee explained. "A technical issue has halted one of our production hangars in orbit above."

"How many times have the Destroyers hit you here?"

"The raindrops never end near the sea, just as the Destroyers attack repeatedly, the count has risen to nine now."

"Our new friends are fighting just to survive," Telisa said on the PIT channel. "We're going to help them win this. I hope that will earn us long lasting allies."

"Yes, we're ready to do whatever it takes," Caden said.

"Let's just hope that Celarans stay loyal longer than Vovokans," Cilreth added.

"I'll show you to the *Iridar*," Telisa said to Lee. "My friend Cilreth works there now."

"The star nears the horizon to usher in darkness as I will see your ship, but know that another will soon take my baton."

The day was only half over, so Telisa took the preamble to refer to the fact that Lee would step down, rather than a measure of the time of day.

"What? Is something wrong?"

Is she going to die? Are Celarans short-lived?

"As one cycle ends another begins, so my time on this assignment is over. I will rotate out to another task. How long will you remain on your PIT team?"

"I don't know. It may be as long as I survive."

"One insect differs from another on the vine as your people differ from mine."

Telisa found a vine path leading back to the *Iridar* and set out. Instead of leaping and running, Telisa took her time. She wore the chevrons and aimed the sensor at Lee so they could speak as they traveled.

"You all carry two batons, right?" Telisa prompted.

"The vines twist around the white trunks as Celarans carry one personal baton, and a second one matched to a particular set of roles to play in society."

"So you choose the functions of the second rod to match what you need for your job."

"The vines grow up to meet the light while your mind moves toward the truth," Lee said.

"Your leader said you would teach us more of the Celarans. Are there questions that are forbidden?"

"The light shines from above and reveals the trunks and the vines as we look, so there is no reason not to discover everything."

Telisa took that to mean she could ask whatever she wanted.

So many questions!

They approached the *Iridar*.

"We have a guest," Telisa sent Cilreth, even though she suspected their Vovokan expert already knew exactly where Telisa and Lee were.

"I heard. The hatches are open."

Telisa hopped from a vine down onto the forest floor. She led the way under the ship to the main cargo ramp. She felt Lee might feel a bit more comfortable in the relatively large cargo bay before moving into the smaller corridors of the ship.

"The forest floor sits covered in waste as the Terrans walk there to enter their ship?"

Ah. Celarans think of the ground as dirty. It is, I suppose!

Telisa felt slightly uncomfortable, suspecting that the Celarans thought of all ground-dwellers as unclean.

"On our greatest worlds, the ground is kept relatively clean," Telisa said. "At first I found it strange that all your doors are on your roofs. But it makes sense for someone who flies."

"One insect differs from another on the vine as your people differ from mine."

Telisa noted the usage of the exact phrase from before. She wondered if that would be common in Celaran speech.

Lee flew into the cargo bay and halted in mid-air.

"I'm sorry, Lee, but our ships are not wide open as yours are."

"Grubs tunneling in the dark soil, you crawl through your own ship?" Lee flitted about in a tight pattern as if exhibiting anxiety.

"Yes, see, the doors look like this," Telisa said. She told a hatch to open, revealing a long corridor. "You don't have to come if you don't want to. Marcant could figure out a way to send you pictures you can understand."

"The forest is complex and varied, such is the work of the engineer. We are learning to use your links soon."

"That would be great!" Telisa said. It would be nice to leave her clumsy chevron band behind and speak to the Celarans like she spoke with Shiny, over the links.

Lee half-flew, half-hovered into the corridor. Telisa showed Lee the room she shared with Magnus.

"I sleep in that soft web there," Telisa said. "Do you sleep?"

"When the starlight is bright, rest in shadows. Our primitive ancestors did this, but we have since changed ourselves to greatly reduce this need."

"We have reduced our need as well, but we still spend five hours a day in sleep." Telisa hoped Marcant's system had mastered time translations.

She opened a shower tube. "I wash myself with water in there. Hot water sprays down from here and drains there to be recycled."

Lee paused to examine the recessed toilet seat.

"Where no vine grows, what is this for?"

"Waste disposal. Celarans drink the sap from the vines? Do you eliminate the leftovers from your body?"

The Celarans were basically a tube, a common form for life to take: food coming in one side and leaving on the other. Yet the Celarans seemed identical along two axes: left/right and front/back or end to end. Their top to bottom sides were also very similar, but had subtle differences: their fingers curled underneath but could not fold up above, and their bodies glided much better upright than when "upside down".

21

"From the light to the vine into the body, we use what we drink. Our outer skin sheds and removes a few impurities with it. We have engineered the vines to produce very pure sap."

Telisa frowned.

Shedding skin? That's it?

"You drink from... both ends? Is there a preference? Do you spit anything out?"

"Life drinks from the vine, and I drink from either mouth tube as it pleases me. Why spit anything out? Simpler to avoid drinking in the first place, if I don't want to consume something."

"That sap is probably much closer to completely digestible than what we eat," Cilreth offered on the PIT channel. "I don't think the Celarans ingest... anything that goes through in large quantities, like cellulose in our digestive tracts."

Maxsym would be all over this, Telisa thought. The PIT team had lost so many amazing people. *The PIT team needs to rethink this policy where everyone on the team shares the risks of walking into alien environments. We should have a ground team and a ship team, specialize further, let those best equipped for it take the risks and keep experts like Cilreth back on the ship.*

Telisa did not share her thoughts because she knew they were half-formed. How could the ship be any safer, when the Destroyers could attack from space at any time? The experts on the ship could be in more danger than those on the ground. It might also prevent incarnate discoveries only they were capable of making.

There's nothing safe about this team.

Telisa's thoughts returned to the conversation. She felt

a bit embarrassed for her race. The Celarans seemed to be... *cleaner* than Terrans in more than one way.

Well, I lived through that... might as well cover all the bases.

"Most Terrans are one of two types, male or female," Telisa said. "Do Celarans have different types necessary to make more Celarans? How do you reproduce?"

I wonder if this is translatable?

"On a bright day when the vines are taut with sweet sap, we inject microscopic pieces of ourselves into the vine. As the warm days pass, the parts of two, three, or four of us combine into young Celarans which grow in the vine, feeding from the sap, eventually to break out and take flight."

Two, three, or four?

"Can every Celaran do this? You are all the same, able to inject the vines?" asked Telisa. "Or do different Celarans inject pieces that can only go together with certain types of Celarans?"

"The spikes hold the vines above the ground and all mature, healthy Celarans are able to do this, the same way with any others. Two identical leaves on the same vine, we have no types and no special combinations are required other than at least two of us must inject the same stem. The Terrans have no vines here so I wonder if they do the same."

Lee stated this last part, but to Telisa it felt more like a question.

"We inject each other with the microscopic pieces and the young grow inside us," Telisa said. "As many warm days pass... the young emerge."

Lee flew back and darted a scared circuit of the room

from one corner to the other. Her chevrons glowed.

"The vines eaten by an insect swarm, that is horrible!"

Yet another aspect of Terran life for the Celarans to be horrified by.

"It's often done with an artificial surrogate now," Telisa said, hoping to soften the news. "I spoke mostly of the past. The females accepted the microscopic pieces of a male and combined them with her own, and grew the young inside, but now either male or female can grow the child in the surrogate, with pieces from one other partner."

Lee seemed to have calmed down. She hovered in midair.

"Tools made in the forest, it has changed for us as well."

Telisa led Lee into one of the ship's messes. Cilreth waited there to meet Lee.

"This is Cilreth," Telisa told Lee. "She runs the *Iridar*, and she studies another alien race, the Vovokans I mentioned earlier."

Lee floated into the center of the space above the tables.

"The ground always awaits any who fall, she has done this her entire life? How long do Terrans live?"

"Not her whole life," Telisa said. "Less than ten percent of it, certainly. Terrans may live..."

Telisa decided not to trust the translation this time. She paused to do the calculation in her link. The average core worlder made it to about 140 Sol years. She used the *Iridar*'s data on the local system to project the time of this planet's year. "Over a hundred twenty rotations of this planet around its star."

Unless they join the PIT team, in which case it is

much, much shorter.

"Darkness slowly approaches the brightest of vines, like the Terrans, we may live a similar time."

"Here, we eat," Telisa said. "Celarans drink sap. Terrans eat hundreds of structures produced by the plants of their home planet, as well as many more things produced synthetically to mimic the archaic carnivorous portions of our diet. Very basically, carbohydrates similar to your sap, proteins from the structures of living things, and fats made by creatures that must store energy."

"The shadows can be confusing in the evening, and a Terran can eat so many things?"

"It is odd," Cilreth said. "The Celarans are so very versatile, yet they only eat this vine sap."

Telisa and Lee found Cilreth where she worked deeper in the ship. Cilreth showed Lee where she sat in her chair, hooked into the ship's network with many artificial inputs.

Telisa explained.

"Terrans can route artificial signals into our nerves, replacing our natural senses. We can create artificial worlds for our minds to live in. Do Celarans also do this?"

"As the light feeds the vines, we can make our own vines in our heads. They serve as tools to plan what to do before it is time to act."

"We train in our virtual worlds too. Terrans also like to play there."

"The green vines await us on a bright day and that is where we go to play. There is no reason to play in our heads."

"Really? In a virtual world you can do anything you want without consequences," Telisa persisted.

"Star overhead and open skies await, the Celarans do

what they wish every day! We fly and we wonder and we build. Why do anything else?"

So they are satisfied with their natural lives? No virtual entertainment for Celarans... that's a huge difference between us.

"Let me show you our gravity spinner," Telisa said. "I suspect it must be very similar to those your ships use."

Chapter 3

Magnus watched the jungle from the top of a support spike swathed in vines. On this planet, the giant tusk-like structures had a slightly greenish tinge to them, perhaps because of some impurity in the local source materials. Magnus recalled the PIT team knew these spikes were manufactured, but the Celaran homeworld probably had some natural equivalent. Below him, vines as thick as his torso wrapped around the spike and grew off in all directions.

He stared to the east, ignoring the alien bugs and tiny flyers that crawled and glided around him.

There.

In the distance, metal glinted.

Magnus dispatched an attendant to travel out toward the source of the reflection and extend the range of his link until he saw Space Force services show up. He broadcast his location through the attendant and waited. Ten minutes later, he saw a Space Force officer on his tactical. The man moved along the web of vines, struggling to reach Magnus's perch. Magnus saw the officer directly as he ascended the last vine: a dark-skinned man in a military skinsuit. The green circle of the UNSF was on each of his shoulder sleeves. The man looked fit, though he moved uncertainly over the vines.

The officer approached Magnus and stopped to give a salute.

"Colonel Agrawal," Magnus said.

"Yessir!" Agrawal said, remaining at attention.

Magnus stood, taken aback.

What's this? Oh, right. Our honorary ranks.

"I'm ex-space force, Colonel, and I never outranked you," Magnus said carefully, returning the salute.

"Sir, I'm pleased to inform you that Ambassador Shiny has given the PIT team members very high rank in the Space Force," Agrawal said. He still stood at attention.

Magnus nodded.

It's just as Telisa said they treated her. I have power now. Strange.

"You may relax, Colonel. I see you've brought your assault unit with you."

"Yes, sir. We're here to help in any way possible. Admiral Sager thought it best we come planetside, given the possibility of more Destroyer attacks. We aren't much help stuck in the *Midway*, but in this jungle, I think we could put up a hell of a fight."

Agrawal's tone said more than that: *We'll kick some Destroyer ass.*

The raw elan reminded Magnus of his time in the Space Force. He felt a strange appreciation for Agrawal's enthusiasm that made him want to smile.

When I was a grunt, saying such things felt very different than being a commander and hearing it from a subordinate.

"How many machines do you have? What types?"

"Thirty-two Stork EXM-39s and sixty-four Hornet flight reconnaissance vehicles of various models. Shall I show you?"

"I'd like that, yes," Magnus said. He was not familiar with the weapons Agrawal mentioned—which did not surprise him given his long absence from the Force.

Agrawal called some of his machines over. An eagle-sized flyer shot out from among the vine leaves beyond and slowed to a hover before them. It was a scout machine formed by the union of two round aerofan covers on either side of a missile-shaped fuselage.

"This is a Hornet," Agrawal said. "Its mission is scouting and spotting. The power ring is inside the structural member that holds those fans together. The central tube contains thirty droppable sensor modules and a laser countermeasure package."

In the distance, Magnus saw an excited Celaran flying near one of the Hornets. The machine circled, trying to avoid the Celaran which seemed to be playfully chasing it.

"I hope you have all our friendlies on a tight no-fire list," Magnus said, eyeing the interaction.

"We do, sir. In fact, the entire unit is not authorized to fire at all without our go-ahead. I figured we should make sure there would be no incidents."

"Good. I'll send you our complete list of Celaran signatures and Destroyer ones, too, so we can be ready in case something happens soon."

"Thank you, sir."

Another, larger machine picked its way through the chaotic vines nearby. It walked into view and stopped. The machine looked like a four-legged spider. The legs emerged first upward from the pill-shaped body, then angled back down toward the ground at two joints on each leg. The compact body was smaller than a land car, which the legs held two meters above the surface. From his position high on the vine, Magnus saw a flat laser turret on the top. Two projectile barrels protruded slightly from the underside. Other than the projectile barrels, the machine did not seem to have any front or back, just four legs equidistant around the central turret.

"This is a Stork," Agrawal said. "It's light and mobile, even in this forest. It's got a serious power ring, feeding the primary weapon—this laser mount on the top—with a 360-degree field of fire. Up close, it relies on the secondary weapons: twin cannons, loaded with armor piercing rounds. The cannons are very deadly at close range, but the magazine capacity is limited to just ten rounds for each cannon. That's still twenty kills, even against the most heavily armored targets."

Magnus furrowed his brows.

"It looks like a spider... why are they called Storks?"

Agrawal nodded. The machine behind him lifted upward on its legs. The double-jointed legs straightened and angled downwards until the spider stance turned into a tall four-legged tower, bringing the flat laser turret on top to an altitude of twenty meters above its perch. Now Magnus could see the name making more sense—it was because of the long legs.

"The legs will typically deploy the turret just under cover. When a target is spotted by one of the Hornets, the weapon will pop out for less than a second to deliver a high-power laser strike, then drop back under cover. These machines were designed to operate in environments with a lot of clutter, like the cityscapes back home, or forests like this place."

"Weaknesses?"

"Even a massive power ring like this one can only source three full-power shots before a five-minute recharge time for the fourth and subsequent shots. Armor is negligible, small arms protection only. Much less effective without the Hornets to spot for it."

Magnus felt envious. This war machine before him

could likely wipe out his entire squadron of soldier-bots.

"Two things come to mind," Magnus said. "First of all, we need to integrate the information retrieved by our Vovokan attendants into your tactical maps. Trust me, these attendants are superior to the Hornets. With this integration, we'll be better than doubling your spotting capacity and survivability."

"Yes, sir," Agrawal said, eyeing the attendants orbiting Magnus.

"Secondly, I have about fifty PIT robots here. They're nothing compared to your unit, but we can use them as expendables. The robots I deployed can be our cannon fodder. They can draw enemy fire and encourage the enemy to reveal themselves, then these Storks can finish them off."

"Yes, sir. Anything else, sir?"

"As a matter of fact, yes. Stand by," Magnus said. He opened a private channel to Cilreth. "Cilreth, would you please send our battle sphere pals over to my location? I want to make sure the *Midway*'s machines have their signatures on a friendlies list."

"Sure thing."

"Thanks."

Magnus and Colonel Agrawal waited patiently. Agrawal looked all around, drinking in the planet. Was it a display of curiosity or dutiful observation of a potential battle site? Magnus wished he knew, to better understand the Colonel.

After a few minutes, the machine towering over them became alarmed. Its turret moved to another facing, toward the *Iridar*.

"Three car-sized silver spheres should be

31

approaching," Magnus said. "Put them on the friendlies list of all your machines, Colonel."

The massive spheres came floating through the vines toward Magnus and Colonel Agrawal. The Colonel's eyes showed surprise. Magnus enjoyed it a bit more than he should have. He smiled.

"Yes, that's them. Vovokan battle spheres. You're familiar with their capabilities?"

"Yes. I've studied what they did during Ambassador Shiny's takeover."

Magnus took note of Agrawal's sore tone and nodded. "They can be an asset in a fight," Magnus said. "Of course, they're probably loyal to their creator first and foremost... but one fight at a time."

Agrawal looked at Magnus as if seeing him in a new light. "Yes, sir."

Magnus intended to let Agrawal select his defensive positions in the vine jungle. No doubt Agrawal had performed countless VR exercises and learned how to place his machines effectively. The only caveat would be that Agrawal needed to learn more about the Destroyers.

We all do. I still know so very little about them, even after several encounters.

"Deploy your forces to protect the colony. Keep in mind we don't want to make the Celarans any easier to spot from orbit. The buildings are obscured by vines, and though the Celarans expose themselves by flying everywhere, the whole planet is populated by feral flyers that look very similar. Sort of their equivalent to hominids."

"Yes sir," Agrawal said.

"That's it for now. Once you've loaded all the Celaran

and Destroyer signatures, you can remove the blanket no-fire order and prepare to repel a Destroyer incursion."

Agrawal saluted and left to get the lay of the land. Of course his tactical would soon have all the details about the colony, but the officer clearly wanted to get a feel for the area with his own senses.

The alien flyers swooped about as if in panic, or at the least, great excitement as more Storks entered the area. Magnus walked along a thick vine, headed toward the PIT house with a Stork following behind. He assumed the machine had been told to take a position near their Celaran dwelling.

A Celaran drifted down toward him. Magnus came to a halt to see what it wanted. It opened a link channel.

"When the vines are trampled, do the Terrans fly with us in the clear blue sky?"

What? They can speak to us on our links now?

Magnus hesitated. Then, he replied on the channel.

"We fly with you in peace," he tried. "These machines are to protect us all from the Destroyers."

"A spring day rises across the vines when we share our sap without fear of each other," said the Celaran before bolting away into the sky.

I hope I reassured it!

Magnus opened a private channel to Telisa.

"Telisa, a Celaran just spoke to me on my link!"

"Isn't it wonderful?" Telisa answered.

"Is that Marcant's accomplishment?"

"Well, the Celarans were working on understanding our link communications while Marcant studied their visual language. Once they started talking to me with my chevron strip, they were able to dovetail in their analysis of our link traffic together with what we were saying in Celaran. I guess that's when our efforts and the Celarans met head-on and merged into something spectacular."

"So Marcant came through, on our side at least," Magnus said.

"Yes. Cilreth was right, he's valuable to the team. I'm glad we worked so hard on integrating him."

"There's still the matter of Imanol..." Magnus said.

"Cilreth has gathered all the information there is on the incident. I've been reviewing it."

"Okay. Well, I'll focus my energies on integrating our setup with the machines from the *Midway*. Can you ask Lee to pass along a request? If the Celarans have robots tucked away that we haven't seen, it would be good if the Storks or some attendants could see them to collect target sigs of all the friendlies. We don't want to be shooting at Celaran hardware if all hell breaks loose here."

"Yes, I'll definitely do that. Lee said the Destroyers already leveled another colony site on this planet. That's when the Celarans built this hidden town in the jungle."

"Might be useful to learn about," Magnus said. "We want to know what to expect."

"Yes. I'm sending a Celaran your way. I named him Deston. As far as I can tell, he's a scientist that worked on military innovations for the colony. He'll talk with you about Destroyer capabilities. Probably worth knowing."

"Okay. Will do," Magnus said. "Why Deston?"

"He's going to tell us about Destroyers so I used a name to remind me... we could set up an automatic naming algorithm? As far as I can tell, Celarans don't have differentiated sexes. Lee told me they inject the vines with... an equivalent of gametes, I guess, which can join from up to four individuals!"

"Wow. As far as naming them, I guess that's a problem for a lazy day," Magnus said. "I bet Jason will break out the gender neutral pronouns."

"Yeah, he likes to be precise. I'll see you soon."

"See you."

Magnus continued along a huge vine toward the team dwelling. A Celaran suddenly swooped up to Magnus. The Terran forced himself to smile at the playful entrance.

I try to stay alert but every time they flash in, I'm surprised.

Startling an ally was considered dangerous in a time before smart weapons. Magnus knew of a phrase: 'trigger happy', which meant someone might shoot before verifying a target. However, it was no longer much of a concern. Even his old rifle accepted a friendlies list and a Celaran target sig was on it.

"Each creature in the vines has a name, and mine is Deston."

"I'm Magnus, as you know," Magnus said. "I'll let the UNSF Colonel listen in on our conversation so he can learn from you too."

Agrawal might listen in live, or he might review the conversation later, but Magnus wanted the info in the hands of the person who was setting up the majority of their defenses.

"Thanks for meeting incarnate," Magnus continued after adding Agrawal. "You can tell us about the Destroyers? We don't know much."

"The vines intertwine in many shapes, in the case of the Destroyers, they look like this," Deston said.

Magnus received a set of artificial images. He went

off-retina to examine them. The images looked like design diagrams rather than photorealistic pictures. The first image was an incomplete blueprint of an enormous machine half the size of the *Iridar*. Its squashed-oval shape opened at the belly to release eight other smaller machines of the same shape. Each of those machines was the size of the Destroyers that Magnus had seen in the tunnels of Vovok: the size of a 10-man armored personnel carrier. That machine, in turn, opened to release eight drone-sized machines, once again of the same shape.

Magnus shook his head.

This is fragged-radix soup. Terrans count in tens, apparently Destroyers in eights, and Celarans in sixes. I don't even want to think about what Vovokans like to count in. Could be anything from binary to base-40.

"These drones are about the size of the one we encountered recently," Magnus said.

"Strong wind in a storm, the Destroyers bring chaotic wind and scream loudly. It is difficult to fly in the vicinity of these attackers."

Magnus reminded himself that given the weak translation they had so far, 'scream loudly' probably referred to the bright lights, since Celarans used light to communicate.

"How far away will they be able to kill one of our big machines?" Agrawal asked on the channel.

"Waiting for the sap to emerge... the largest one can kill over 100 kilometers if a smaller one tracks the target. The smaller they get, the lower their range. The insects on the vine only bite on the skin, and the smallest drones will only kill within direct vision, less than 100 meters above the canopy. A predator crawling under the vine, they

36

attack below the canopy to avoid long distance spotting."

"Do they always announce themselves with the wind and the bright light?"

"One cuts open the vine to study it in the light, and we suspect the wind is because aquatic creatures design craft strangely for the relatively thin atmosphere. They're not used to it. The light is similar: it is used to increase the reflections for targeting."

Magnus had not thought about those who created the Destroyers in a while. He recalled their supposed aquatic origins. Deston was smart to explain their oddities with that in mind.

"I can take these diagrams and make a rough signature," Agrawal said. "We can refine it with data from Magnus's encounters. Thank you for the information."

"There is one more thing," Magnus said to Deston. "Would you allow our machines to see your machines so that we can teach them not to shoot at each other," Magnus said. "Of course, I think it should be clear what is a Destroyer and what isn't, given all the noise and the light, but I'd just like to be sure."

Deston flew in a vertical loop and stopped close to the Terran. Magnus suppressed an urge to reach for a weapon as the alien flew closer.

Still not used to it...

"More sap is in a thicker vine while most of our defenses are in the towers. If an enemy comes into the star system, the towers will retract to hide us. Should we be attacked on the ground, the towers will re-emerge."

"What weaponry do the towers have?" Agrawal asked brusquely.

"The wild creatures of the jungle can be held at a

gentle distance on every sunny day, so the towers were designed to keep animals out of an area. We've increased their power tenfold, so they can cause Destroyer drones to collide with the white spires or one another."

Magnus saw another set of diagram pointers on the channel. He accessed them and saw specifications for a disk-shaped flyer. It looked like the guard machines the PIT team had encountered on Idrick Piper.

"We've seen these disk machines before, back at an abandoned Celaran base," Magnus said. "They use projectile weapons?"

"If you guess the sap is sweet, you are correct. They were not weapons originally, but we have increased the velocity of their projectiles several times in the last few..." Deston paused. "Months," came the translation. "Our scientists guessed that high-velocity projectiles would stop the machines, and they were right."

"Thank you for showing us these. Anything else?" Magnus asked.

"There is always another insect on the other side of the leaf, and I have one more design, which I made during my time as defense scientist. Come this way."

The Celaran flitted away through a tangle of vines. Magnus followed more slowly, climbing around the foliage.

"How long have you been a defense scientist?" Magnus asked as he tried to follow Deston.

"The star moves above giving light and day, in my case for... seven Terran months. Soon I will trade my baton for another."

Magnus understood from the conversation Telisa had broadcast with the leaders that Deston meant he would be changing jobs.

"Is that wise? Don't you have valuable experience at building weapons?" Magnus asked.

"A diseased vine can be ugly and that concept, weapon, is disturbing. I've made things that stop Destroyers. Now another must learn and I'll stretch another direction."

Magnus walked out along another vine that took him closer to Deston, who was hovering twenty meters away in a small clearing among the vines. Magnus assumed Deston was waiting for him to catch up before darting off again.

A rustling sound came from below. Magnus looked down. Six triangle-shaped doors opened upward from the detritus-littered ground, revealing a hexagonal opening about a meter on a side. Nestled within, a sharp rod pointed upward, mounted on a ball-and-socket arrangement for movement.

"A hidden laser! I like it. How many of these are around here?" Magnus asked.

"A sliver of light pouring through an opening in the leaves, it was my idea," Deston said. "There once existed a creature in the forest that waited to catch those who fly above. It predated upon our ancestors. I have created 36 robotic copies of this creature that use lethal tools modeled after the energy beams of the Destroyers."

Natural for a peaceful race to look to predators of their past for weapon ideas. I should mention that to Telisa. She'll find it fascinating.

Magnus sent a snippet of the conversation to Telisa for her to read later. Then Magnus thought of the net monster and the alien creature that had attacked them with electricity on the other planet.

"The creature you mention didn't use lasers too, I hope. Are there dangerous things in the jungle my team should be aware of?"

"The net-lion hunts among the shadows of the vines, but all the large predators and pack creatures are kept beyond the towers," Deston said. Magnus assumed that *net-lion* was the best translation they had for the predator the PIT team had encountered.

"Thank you for your help, Deston."

We've arrived into a war zone.

Chapter 4

Cilreth piloted the *Iridar* toward one of the three Celaran space bases in the system. She felt a keen interest to see the alien base. The structure Cilreth closed on was a stack of six large rings of ship bays. Each ring was made from six ship bays touching only at their rear edges. A hexagonal tunnel ran through the center of the stack of 36 bays, serving as a particle accelerator that could thrust the base around the system. Cilreth supposed the entire assembly was too unwieldy to be controlled with a gravity spinner.

How many Celarans live there? A hundred? A thousand?

The Celarans had requested that the *Iridar* join the *Midway* near the base so that the same Celaran engineers who had worked on the *Midway* could see the Vovokan spinner and cloaking systems. Since the rest of the team was busy working with the Celarans, she had taken the ship up by herself to let the Celarans examine it.

Cilreth sat within her little work pod, surrounded by on-retina anchor points and equipment that made long off-retina stays comfortable.

I hope we're not making the same mistake we made with Shiny. Could the Celarans actually turn on us after they've learned about all our technology? Are they only playing nice because the Destroyers are after them?

Cilreth supposed that the PIT team had found more evidence that the Celarans were peaceful than they ever had discovered with the Vovokans. The Celarans had never shot at them, even in self-defense, like Shiny had when he first encountered Terrans. On the other hand,

Shiny had been in personal danger, whereas the PIT team had only ever threatened Celaran machines, not real Celarans.

Unless we've seen Celaran cyborgs and we didn't even know it!

Admiral Sager requested a channel with Cilreth as the *Iridar* approached the collection of space hangars.

"Admiral Sager, how are you? How is the *Midway*?"

"We've made great progress on the repairs. The same appears true of the Celaran ships," Sager reported. "Of course, we're missing crew. That's reduced morale as well as operational capacity."

"We're able to communicate with the Celarans," Cilreth said.

"They've been talking to us for a few hours now," Sager said. "Sometimes they're hard to understand. It seems their main concern is the *Midway*'s lack of stealth technology. I think they want to fix that."

"We've decided to trust them," Cilreth said. *For better or for worse.* "Let them onto the *Midway*. Let them make modifications if that's what they want. The threat of a Destroyer attack is very real... and imminent."

"Yes, ma'am."

Cilreth decided to contact the base. She requested a connection through the *Iridar*.

A Terran link talking to a Vovokan ship using Terran comm protocols, asking it to send a Terran message to a Celaran base listening for a message in Terran protocols...

The connection went through. The other side identified itself as "Celaran Base Control".

"This is the *Iridar*, joining the *Midway* as requested. I was wondering... the largest ship that came here had our only FTL communications capability. Since it was destroyed in the battle, I can't send a message home to ask for reinforcements. Do you have a tachyon receiver base in this system?"

Cilreth wondered if their translation service could handle such a complex question. Would the Celarans understand what a TRB was? Did the Celarans even use them?

"Messages travel along the vines but cannot go where the vine does not go, and we are not able to speak with any outside this star system."

Hrm.

"How do you pass information along to the rest of your civilization?"

"Sharing light and life with those we know, there is no light to share with those we do not share life with."

"So you..." Cilreth's message halted. She decided to try a different tack. "Will other Celarans be coming here to help you fight the Destroyers?"

"When danger lurks in the forest, it is not wise to hope the vines will send help that one does not think can be sent. We haven't seen others in a very long time."

"I'm sorry to hear that," Cilreth sent back.

Well, we have a lot of attendants. We can send a message to Shiny.

Cilreth opened a channel to Telisa back on the Celaran colony planet.

"Yes?"

"Telisa, remember what Marcant pointed out about the attendants? They can sacrifice themselves to send a tachyonic message."

"You want to ask for help from Shiny? Sure. But don't

43

the Celarans have a TRB?"

"They don't. I'm surprised about it too. I think this colony has been separated from the rest of the civilization, assuming it still exists out there. They don't seem to have the ability to talk with any other Celaran planets. When I asked about the rest of the Celaran race, I got a dodgy response. This colony may be isolated."

"Really? That's weird. They've been straightforward about everything so far."

"Yes. I don't know what's up with it."

"I'll ask Lee about it next time I see her. Send out an attendant and apprise Shiny of our situation. Request more battleships. At this point I don't care if our relief is Vovokan or Space Force, we need all the help we can get."

"Will do."

***

Cilreth bolted awake in her quarters as a high-priority warning came to her link. It was the tactical. The map had many rules for generating alerts, and several of them had been triggered. She brought up the tactical in her personal view and saw a handful of flashing red points spread across it.

The Destroyers are back already! We can only see a few at this range, but that must mean there are a lot of them.

Cilreth rolled out of her sleep web and staggered toward the shower, which could fill with foam like a crash tube. A private link request came in from Telisa. Cilreth connected.

"Go help them," Telisa said. "Go help them *now*."

Sager and Telisa were on another channel which Cilreth had access to, so she joined that one as well. She slipped into the shower and closed her eyes to focus on her PV.

"You're weapons free, Admiral," Telisa was saying. "Engage the Destroyers as you see fit. I don't know if it makes sense to coordinate with the *Iridar*. Your two ships are very different in so many ways."

Cilreth kept concentrating on the tactical. It was woefully empty. She saw the three Celaran space bases as dense green clusters of space hangars and ships on her map. The *Iridar* charged its storage rings near one of the bases, ready to join any maneuvers the Celarans might make. She activated the Vovokan cloaking system.

They don't have full ship-to-ship communications working yet, Cilreth thought. *I'm sure they have a lot of probes and satellites looking for enemies.*

"Telisa, if you can ask Lee to hook me up with their tacticals..."

"I'm on it," Telisa sent back.

Cilreth wondered if the bases had defenses. She thought it likely they could cloak as the probe ship had been able to do, but the Destroyers probably knew that trick. Or did they? She remembered Celaran ships had used their ability to hide in the earlier battle.

More data flooded into the *Iridar*'s tactical map. Cilreth saw it came from the Celarans. A flood of red contacts became visible across the whole system, headed toward the planet with the Celaran colony. The Celaran fleet still clustered around the bases in three roughly equal groups.

I hope this means they can see where I am, too.

The *Iridar* neared the base Cilreth had come to visit. One large Celaran ship was accelerating out of each bay. Some of them looked to be only partially constructed.

Another squadron of smaller Celaran vessels formed up between the base and the incoming fleet. Cilreth saw a series of concentric spheres surrounding the nearby base on her tactical. The Celarans ships were moving out hastily though they were still inside the smallest of three spheres.

What could those be? Weapon ranges?

Cilreth thought frantically. They had to be weapon ranges... what else could they be? EM countermeasure umbrellas?

Cilreth looked over the starbase. She supposed there were Celarans on the base that they wanted to defend. A quick scan only told her that she was blocked from seeing what was inside. She used precious seconds to examine the exterior of the base.

Six ports at each corner of the hexagonal bay openings...

The *Iridar*'s sensors scanned the openings carefully. Cilreth looked over the findings.

Aha. High energy weapon emitters. The base will provide fire support... probably anti-missile point defense? One more reason to think the rings represented offensive or defensive fire ranges.

The Destroyer fleet broke into seven formations. The three largest forces, each composed of dozens of vessels, headed for each of the three Celaran bases. Cilreth tried to guess what the other four might be doing.

They need to clean the system of Celaran satellites. One might be a reserve force. What else? That one is...

probably headed for the planet!

The Celaran ships accelerated away to interdict a larger number of Destroyer ships on an intercept course with the base. Cilreth set the *Iridar* on course to follow after them. The gravity spinner moved her smoothly with the ship so that she felt nothing, despite hitting an acceleration otherwise unsurvivable by Terrans. The *Iridar* could not match the acceleration of the Celarans even though Cilreth fed a huge part of the energy budget into her spinner.

Cilreth watched the tactical nervously as the *Iridar* joined the formation of Celaran ships. The intercept group closed on the threatening Destroyer force. Cilreth received a high priority target request from the Celarans: it was a large Destroyer ship. The Celaran ships started to snipe at the target. Cilreth allotted twenty percent of her stored energy and added the *Iridar*'s fire to theirs. After long seconds, an explosion became visible. They had killed it.

The Celarans did not break off. They continued to close on the superior numbers of the Destroyers ahead.

Are they going to sacrifice themselves?! Because, by Cthulhu, I'm not going to!

Cilreth's fear soared. She thought about breaking away, then felt ashamed. Still, she plotted an escape course as she battled with her fear. The Celaran group passed the last line around the base on the tactical; whatever support perimeter that was, they were now beyond it.

Am I obligated to die with these ships? What about the PIT team? What about me?

The Destroyer force launched a massive cloud of ordnance, which headed for the Celarans. Energy weapons fire arrived first, causing the Celarans to begin weaving erratically.

No no no no no. I'm supposed to be the safe one.

The *Iridar* received a set of flight instructions in the final seconds as Cilreth struggled with her decision. At the same time, she looked at the course suggestions long enough to determine they came from the Celarans. She only had time to approve one existing plan: hers or theirs. Her mind froze at the edge of panic.

I'm representing my whole race... so dead...

Cilreth accepted the Celarans' course plan. If she had been given time to think about the decision, she probably would have given in to fear and taken her own.

The Celarans' ship formation, now including the *Iridar*, opened like a many-petaled flower before the oncoming missile swarm. Forty percent of the missiles diverted to pursue the ships. The rest remained on course for the Celaran base.

Cilreth took stock of the situation as the *Iridar*'s point defense started to bite into the missiles in pursuit.

Cthulhu's tentacles, I attracted more Destroyer missiles than the others!

The *Iridar*, as agile as it was, could not match the Celaran ship's maneuvers. More missiles had had time to lock onto her.

"Telisa, this may be the last thing you hear from me—" Cilreth sent. The *Iridar* continued to fire on the missiles closing in. Cilreth saw six or seven of them drop off her tactical. The others were seconds away.

The *Iridar* crossed into the Celaran base's outer perimeter line on the tactical. The Celaran base started to fire.

I have to keep maneuvering to keep the Destroyers'

energy weapons from hitting me from four light seconds out; yet if I dodge randomly, the base can't hit my pursuers, either.

Cilreth set in an avoidance pattern, then transmitted it to the Celarans in the open, using Terran protocols. The accuracy of the base's weapons improved drastically once they knew where she would dodge next. She hoped the Destroyers would be unable to understand the alien transmissions.

Security through obscurity.

The base continued to fire on missiles and other ordnance that closed in on the Celaran ships. Suddenly Cilreth remembered the huge number of weapons that had locked onto the base. She saw them on the tactical, still closing on their target.

That base is sacrificing itself to keep the ships alive. But without the base, they can't make more ships... without their ships, I guess the ones on the planet would be helpless. If only ships survive, at least they could leave...

The *Iridar* bucked as the gravity spinner kicked into levels too high for the control systems to smooth out. Different parts of the ship were now experiencing different levels of force from the spinner, which threatened to turn the *Iridar* into a kilometer-long piece of metal spaghetti.

I'm gonna be killed eight ways from extinction...

"A vine in shadows is hard to see, so Cilreth can turn and hide under a leaf," a Celaran said on one of Cilreth's open channels.

What? Oh.

Cilreth diverted power from the *Iridar*'s spinner and fed it to EM cloaking. At the same time, Cilreth had the ship drop out what remained of Magnus's robot lab from a cargo bay. Irrationally, a part of her brain already started working on how to break the news to him.

That's a problem for the living, Cilreth told herself.

The *Iridar* hurtled on for a few seconds, then one of the missiles found the debris and detonated. The *Iridar* struggled to keep the sudden radiation wave from reflecting off its outer hull and exposing its position to the enemy. Cilreth held her breath. The ship's interior plunged into darkness. Her tactical dropped out, leaving an empty pane in her off-retina view. Cilreth heard her own rapid breathing in the confines of the tube until a mask clamped over her face and it filled with foam.

After an agonizing moment that felt way too long, light returned. The tactical flickered back to life in her PV. Cilreth did not have time to make sense of the data before another huge explosion lit up the area.

The base. No way it survived that.

"What's going on?" came Telisa's reply.

Cilreth looked at the timestamp on the message. It was from a minute ago, just after Cilreth had sent out her imminent-death announcement.

"Close call. I made it. We're putting up a fight, but a starbase was just destroyed. Thirty-six ship hangars have been vaporized. Even if we make it through this battle, the Celaran's ability to make more ships must be reduced."

As Cilreth spoke, she checked the other two bases on the tactical. They were still there, but the Destroyer attack groups still assaulted. The *Iridar* drifted for a few seconds.

"When the jungle burns, take to the sky and find a new valley," A Celaran transmitted. The tactical showed the Destroyers closing. Many local Celaran ships had been destroyed, mostly the partially constructed ones that had fled from the hangars. The rest of the Celaran battle group dispersed. Cilreth did not see the *Midway* anywhere on the tactical.

"Telisa, I'm sorry. I have to fall back to save the *Iridar*," Cilreth said.

"I trust you. Keep yourself alive. Keep the *Iridar* alive," Telisa said.

Cilreth saw objects slipping off into the atmosphere of the planet below. At first she thought it was debris or dying ordnance, but the information pane for a group of objects showed they were active Destroyer vessels. She zoomed in on one. It was a large Destroyer machine, the kind that carried more war machines in its belly.

"You have company," Cilreth sent to Telisa. "I see Destroyer pods dropping onto the planet."

Michael McCloskey

Chapter 5

"I sense a sudden increase in local Celaran communications traffic," Adair said.

Marcant brought himself on-retina. He was alone in a side room of the PIT tree dwelling. The two attendants controlled by Adair and Achaius floated nearby. Somehow they managed to show impatience solely by where they hovered at the edge of his personal space. He pried himself up to a standing position.

"What's up?" he asked his AI friends.

"The engagement continues above us, but now a large group of Destroyers is coming to attack this colony," Adair said. Marcant took a quick peek around the house. He was the only one inside.

Marcant remained calm. An inconsistency came to mind.

"Why don't they just destroy the planet from orbit?" Marcant asked.

"Perhaps such an attack would be interdicted by the Celaran fleet, or perhaps the Destroyers value the planet and wish to leave it relatively intact," Adair suggested.

"The Destroyers want to leave something intact? Maybe we need a better name for them," Marcant said. Despite his critical words, he had already moved on to tackling his more pressing problem: death machines were headed for the house in which he stood.

Attendant information came in from kilometers outside the tower perimeter. Destroyer machines had been spotted there, moving through the forest.

"We have enemies inbound under the canopy," Telisa said on the team link. "If you can get back to the house in five, set up there. If you can't, find a spot with a lot of cover and put yourself on this tactical. I'm going to work with Lee to make sure we have a tac map shared between us and the Celarans."

Marcant walked out into the middle room of the house that connected the other rooms and led out to balconies on opposing sides. Wind rustled the vines outside.

That's the most wind I've seen here...

"Well that's not ominous," he said to Achaius and Adair.

Marcant walked out onto the balcony. The vines around the house were in chaos. Flat disk-shaped Celaran machines flew just over the level of the forest. At least a score of Vovokan attendants flew in long arcs around the house. Celarans flitted in all directions, moving at high speed. Marcant saw a group of them at an adjacent house, gathering items onto a long floating cylinder the size of a flagpole. As Marcant watched, the conveyance accelerated away, gathering speed. Then the group of flyers darted after it.

I didn't know they could move that fast! Impressive.

The wind continued to increase in intensity. He saw the sky had a subtle reddish cast to it.

What have I gotten myself into?

"The Celarans are fleeing the colony," Adair said. "Perhaps we should join them?"

"That would be in defiance of—"

"If Telisa is about to be very dead who cares what her orders are, jelly-brain?" Adair said.

"We don't have information on the size of the attacking force," Achaius said.

The Stork beside the house stood fast. Its legs had

found positions on large vines and a support spike that kept the turret just below the highest leaves. If the legs straightened, they would bring it over the canopy to fire.

"What about *our* forces?" Marcant asked.

Achaius pointed out the proper information pane in Marcant's PV. He perused their counts of the hardware placed in the Celaran colony. The Celarans had approximately 36 trapdoor laser emplacements, 23 force towers, and at least 200 of the projectile-throwing disk robots. Colonel Agrawal had brought 32 Storks and 64 Hornets. The PIT team had brought just over 100 soldier robots and approximately 75 Vovokan attendants. There were only three Vovokan battle spheres, but those machines alone probably represented the bulk of the friendly military power on the planet. Each of them counted more like a starship in terms of firepower.

"What about the Celarans themselves? And the PIT team members?" asked Marcant.

"We don't know what they're capable of, but given that they're peaceful and evacuating, I doubt the Celarans are a factor," Achaius said. "Even the PIT team is only a drop in the bucket, with the possible exception of Telisa, who has superhuman abilities and carries alien weaponry."

"We stay. And, we're going to go for one of the spheres," Marcant said.

"Shouldn't we wait until we know which way this battle is going?" Adair asked. "Seems reckless to go for it right away—"

"They would never expect it!" Achaius said.

"Failing during an attack might be devastating," Adair said.

"I don't think so," Marcant said. "If the battle spheres

are very smart, we'll be unable to take over and Shiny will know what we tried, but during an attack, they'll still probably consider the enemy a higher priority than schooling us. Then there's always the chance the sphere dies in the combat and we're off scot-free again. There's also a chance they might mistake our cyber attack for enemy action."

"The spheres might die *because of* our takeover attempt. Then likely we would be next," Adair pointed out.

"Always the worrywart," said Marcant.

"Let's go for all of them, then," Achaius said. "If we fail, it's equally bad. If we succeed, it's better. We eliminate the scenario where we succeed at taking one over and the others notice after the fact."

"Bold," Marcant said.

"Are we forgetting what happened last time we tried to hack Vovokan software?" Adair said. "Why are we even having this conversation? Shouldn't we be hiding?"

"That was different. We were working blind," Marcant said, but his resolve had started to crack.

"Shiny knew we'd be learning about Vovokan software," Adair said. "And yet he sent these war machines. He's very intelligent. Doesn't that smack of confidence? Telisa pointed out his kind are masters at this sort of thing. Their society was a chaotic collection of warlords in a precarious balance of power."

"So you're saying it's hopeless?" Marcant asked.

"I'm saying the jelly-brain should wait until I think we can pull it off," Adair said.

"We'd never do it," Achaius said. "You're too cautious."

"The Celarans are fleeing into the forest beyond the

towers," Telisa said on the PIT channel. "I asked Lee why they would do that, and she said the Destroyers can't really tell them apart from the feral flyers living in the vines."

"So we're sitting here defending a population that just left the area," Caden said. His voice did not sound judgmental, just concerned.

"This is their home. They're not fighters," Telisa said. "I'm trying to convince Lee to get them to send their disk machines back in to help us, at least once the Celarans are to safety."

Boooooooom.

The distant sound thundered through the vine jungle. Then another.

Boooooooom.

Marcant felt a jolt of panic rise in him, like a fearful child reacting to the sound of an impending storm. He suppressed it.

"Must be them," Siobhan said for everyone.

Boooooooom.

Another deep rumble sounded through the vines. This time the house shook under Marcant's feet.

"Okay, I must admit that's as ominous as the opening scene of a horror VR. Should I be seeking heavier cover?" Marcant asked Adair.

"I don't think you have sufficient cover *anywhere* nearby," Adair said helpfully. "We should concentrate on avoiding becoming a target at all."

"Well, I'm at least arming myself!" Marcant said.

Marcant picked up a laser rifle from a corner of the room. Its self diagnostic told his link it was fully charged and operational.

Boooooom. Boooooom. Boooooom.

More blasts came. Their frequency increased, and the effects on the house grew. The entire structure shook again.

Whatever those are, if they hit this house, I'll be obliterated.

"So no cover? Should I move down towards the ground?"

"No, the opposite," Achaius said. "Your laser is almost useless where the vines are densest. At the top of the spire you'll have some lanes of fire. You might be able to pick off ordnance coming in from above."

Marcant hesitated. "I'll just be making myself a target!"

"You're a flea in this battle," Achaius said. "You're already risking life and limb just being here. At this phase, move up and take some shots, once the smaller Destroyers move in, take cover again. With a laser rifle, you could stop an incoming missile."

"Adair?"

"I said we should stay home. Don't start listening to me now, jelly-brain!" Adair said.

Marcant ran outside to the balcony and tried to jump up onto the roof. It was difficult because he did not have one of the Celaran boost batons. Explosions continued to rattle the area; one hit was close enough to rain debris on the roof.

This is insane. What am I doing here?

Boooooooom.

"The houses in this area are being hit hard. I can see a tower going down," Caden reported.

"There's not much we can do. These weapons are long range," Magnus said. "Even the Storks don't have targets yet."

"So we sit here and wait to be obliterated?" Marcant asked.

"Cover by the spikes," Magnus said.

"Celaran starships are providing orbital support," Achaius said to Marcant. "They're hitting the Destroyer positions."

"That's good news," Marcant said. He crawled over the roof toward the top of the huge support spike. Three large vines wrapped the spike where it rose above the roof. Marcant stood and gripped one of them, then headed for the apex.

"What am I shooting at?" Marcant asked.

"Your rifle has the list of friendlies. Let it fire at anything else," Achaius said.

"Magnus, this is Marcant. The weaponry they're hitting us with is powerful enough to take down the force towers, so I don't think there's any point in hiding on the forest floor. Might as well move up and try to find some targets."

We're disorganized as hell. We're too accustomed to training together with an objective in mind.

"The PIT team is not a military unit by design," Adair said. "You're just stuck trying to act like one now."

Marcant reached a spot at the top where he could set his rifle across one vine and stand on another below it. Hot wind blasted into his face. Lights glowed through a misty area in the distance toward the enemy. Marcant assumed the battle had put a lot of debris into the air, dispersing the bright lights of the Destroyer machines.

Is that an intentional side effect of the wind?

His rifle picked up a target. Marcant saw only a tiny

glowing spot moving through the sky. He could not tell if it was small and close or huge and distant. The rifle took a shot, and the light died. He caught a glimpse of a blackened shape falling to the canopy.

"What the hell was that?"

"If I had to guess, I'd say it was a spotter," Achaius answered. "The Destroyer machines may be using those to find targets."

"All the more reason to take cover instead of sitting up here waiting to die," Adair said.

"No! You may have saved some houses, or a tower," Achaius argued.

Marcant passed the target sig his rifle had acquired to the team.

"The Destroyers sent in one of these," Marcant said. "I think it's a scouting device like our attendants."

"Come down," Magnus said aloud behind Marcant. "Thanks for the sig, but the attendants and Hornets have already seen more of them."

Marcant lugged the rifle down and descended, wobbling a bit in the wind. Magnus helped him down to the balcony.

"The towers on the north and west sides have been destroyed," Achaius reported.

"What now?" Marcant yelled through the wind.

"Survive," Magnus said through a private link connection. "The robots are running this show. All we can do is hide, at least until the big guns get knocked out of action. We might be able to help on the tail end of things if the fight is a close one."

"Hide where?"

"I have an idea," Magnus said. "Follow me."

They left the balcony on a vine and descended down past the house. The wind's force rose again. Marcant heard an ominous humming noise on the air that rattled his nerves.

Calm down. Just calm down.

One of the attendants revolving around Magnus exploded in a bright flash, hurting his eyes. Marcant's Veer suit activated his helmet, causing the faceplate to snap over his head and solidify.

"Small Destroyer machines infiltrating through the vines," Magnus said on the PIT channel. "Taking fire."

As the message finished, the Stork twenty meters away rose and started to fire. Magnus and Marcant dropped down onto the debris on the forest floor. The wind whipped up discarded leaves and bits of vine, making it hard to see. They knelt beside a freshly fallen vine as thick as Marcant that had just been cut by something. The end oozed smoking hot sap.

"There's one of Deston's hidden lasers right over there," Magnus said to Marcant. "We have a lot of cover here, and we have these attendants, the Stork, and the trapdoor laser. This is the best place to set up."

Marcant put his back against the thick support spike. Its solidity felt reassuring. He tried to dispel the dread that the awful humming noise brought. It was as if the Destroyers sought to induce panic by announcing their steady approach.

"Is all this some kind of psychological warfare?" Marcant asked.

"You mean the wind and the lights?" asked Magnus. "I doubt it. The effects would not be universal across intelligent species evolved on different planets."

Marcant nodded. That made sense to him.

"Lee told me that Celaran starships have taken out four of the big Destroyers beyond the force towers," Telisa transmitted on the team channel. "Unfortunately, they had already released their medium machines, and all the smaller ones with them. There are still four big ones left, and all their sub-machines."

Boooooooom.

Another roll of thunder accented Telisa's report.

That started out sounding like a victory, but once she mentioned everything they released, I feel doomed again.

"Maybe the Celaran orbital bombardment will get the other four soon," Marcant said to Adair and Achaius.

"No, that's all they could get," Achaius said.

"What happened to our orbital support?" Marcant asked.

"The Celaran ships were likely drawn away in the space battle above us," Adair said. "We're on our own again."

"They're coming in now, up close and personal," Telisa said. "A lot of smaller drones like we encountered on the other colony planet. The Hornets are dying off. Luckily, the—" A noise interrupted Telisa's transmission, and her voice started to glitch. "... the attendants... elusive."

"Telisa, our comms are getting scrambled," Magnus said. There was no reply.

So, the Destroyers have discovered our link frequencies. Do they know or care that we're not Celarans?

"So with all the robots from eight big Destroyer machines..." Marcant shouted over the noise of the wind.

"It means five hundred and twelve of the smallest drones are coming in, if these are the designs Deston showed me," Magnus finished. "They're headed this way through the forest."

On cue, the Stork near them popped up on its legs and fired again. Marcant and Magnus situated themselves with their backs facing each other, sides pressing against the spike, with rifles pointed in opposite directions.

A huge explosion shook the ground. Bits of hot metal and shredded vine rained across Marcant's Veer suit. The suit reported damage; it had been hit by shrapnel in two spots, but nothing came through to hurt him.

Marcant realized their Stork had died. He saw flames dancing in its direction and it had disappeared from the tactical.

"What took it out?" yelled Marcant through the wind.

"I don't know," Magnus said. "Ah, wait. It was probably one of the medium-sized machines supporting the drones."

"Let me guess... sixty-four of those?"

"Likely yes," Magnus said. Marcant could barely hear him.

I've lost track of where that trapdoor laser is. All the debris has been stirred around, I can't see it.

"Calm," Adair advised. "It's on the tactical. And the mess in the air is obscuring you from detection." Its speech was glitching out. He hoped Adair and Achaius were too close to be fully jammed.

"Any estimates on their damages?" Marcant asked. The battle unfolded too rapidly for Marcant to keep track of the numbers on his pane.

"The Storks took out about seventy drones," Achaius

said. "It cost half the Storks so far. The medium-sized Destroyers have picked up on it and they're hunting the Storks."

70 out of 512? That's not good enough, Marcant thought.

"Buckle in, they're here," Magnus warned. His projectile rifle thundered.

It gets worse than this?

A source of intense light flew through the vines above, zeroing in on Marcant. The wind rose to a level that Marcant imagined must exist in hurricanes, but he did not get blown away. His back pressed against the huge spine structure behind him. Marcant struggled to keep his laser rifle up in the wind. He heard and felt debris scraping across his Veer suit. All he could see was a cloud of dead leaves and torn vines whipping through the air backdropped by the glow.

This is it...

Frrrrrrrrrrrzzap!

The bright light split into bright sparks that flew in all directions then went out. His faceplate bucked against his face. Marcant vaguely realized the light show had been accompanied by a tremendous noise which his suit had dampened. The force of the wind abruptly dropped back to the level of a mild storm.

"Did you shoot it?" Marcant asked Magnus.

"The trapdoor laser got it," Magnus yelled back.

Marcant nodded.

"I didn't see it fire, but I'm happy it did."

"I think the trapdoor lasers operate above the visible spectrum," Magnus said. "It's invisible to us."

Marcant had meant that he had not even seen the

trapdoor open with all the dirt and vegetation whipping through the air. The force of the wind was tearing the huge leaves into small pieces and picking up segments of dead vine from the ground.

"There are more coming," Magnus warned.

This isn't anything like training. I'm doing nothing but sitting here waiting to die, Marcant thought.

"You know what they say," Achaius responded. "Don't bring a Terran to a death machine fight."

"I came here to learn about aliens," Marcant said.

"We're learning a lot," Magnus protested.

Marcant realized he had spoken aloud. Another Destroyer was already approaching them. The wind rose.

An attendant popped before Marcant. He felt vibrations in the support spike at his back as if it had been hit several times by powerful projectiles. His other attendants darted about warily.

"Fire your weapon!" Achaius snapped, but Marcant's laser had already fired. Marcant got a report of a likely hit; then another shot report came in with the same report. The laser had expended the last of its energy.

Marcant threw the rifle aside and pulled out a pistol. It reported readiness to his link, bringing to his attention that it was only a stunner.

"Stunners: effective against Destroyers?" Marcant shot the question to Magnus.

"Worth a try," Magnus said, tossing out a grenade toward their flank. "You have two hands, though," Magnus added, handing Marcant a laser pistol.

"Remember that grenade's out there, so don't head that way," Magnus said. "I have it set for proximity detonation on unknown targets."

"Your concern is touching, but I'm not headed anywhere," Marcant said.

"Oh, I'm not worried about *you*," Magnus said. "I just don't want you to keep the grenade from going off if a Destroyer comes in from that way."

Marcant thought he detected a hint of amusement in his limited view of Magnus's helmeted face, but he could not be sure.

"This may be it," Magnus said aloud. He looked at Marcant.

He's gauging my reaction to imminent death.

Marcant took stock of himself. He was not afraid.

"I'll see you when we wake up... if you're a player," Marcant said loudly, so his voice carried over the sounds of battle.

"You're a *simulationist*?" Magnus yelled amid the chaos.

Marcant laughed. Magnus had no idea. Telisa and Cilreth had come to retrieve him from a major simulationist fortress on Earth, yet they had not sniffed that information out, apparently. Scientists there had developed techniques for blocking memories and putting volunteers into virtual worlds without their memories, effectively setting them on course to live brief virtual lives unaware of their other selves. There were still many catches to be worked out, but they had laid the groundwork for the $n+1$th level of reality.

"Enough contemplation of the universe. Whether or not we are not at the root level of reality, it serves your purpose to optimize your survival in this level," Adair urged.

He told his stunner to fire. He could not hear its whine

in the wind.

Boooom!

A shower of dirt fell across him, dimming the light from above.

Blam! Blam!

More loud sounds. Marcant felt someone grab his left arm and pull. He staggered forward with it, letting the person lead him. They took one, two, three steps, then Marcant plunged downward. His suit protected him from the impact a second later, though he must have bounced about comically. The white light was replaced by a dull red glow seeping through the dirt in the air. Then full darkness took hold. The wind receded.

Marcant told his faceplate to retract. He coughed. In that moment, he had the odd thought that most of the dust he had inhaled was probably Celaran skin sheddings—full of "impurities". By walking on the ground and diving into a hole, they had done the Celaran equivalent of swimming in a sewage treatment plant.

"Are you alive?" Magnus asked.

"Yes," Marcant said. "We must be inside the trapdoors?" He saw the dull red glow before him fade. Something had been destroyed right there, probably the Celaran energy weapon.

"Yes," Magnus answered. "Now we find out if what they say is right. Does lightning strike the same place twice?"

Marcant hoped it did not.

Chapter 6

Fzzzzslump!

The vine shuddered under Telisa as one end of the plant exploded into boiling goo ten meters behind her. She jumped off with all her strength, sending herself shooting away despite the vine's rapidly failing tension.

I have to stay lower. I may be invisible, but if one of those beams hits me...

The real trick, she figured, was not to stand in line of sight between a Destroyer and any likely target. Unfortunately the Destroyers could detect objects through the vine cover better than she could.

Telisa's arc through the air unfolded slowly to her heightened reflexes. With superhuman agility, she manipulated her wind resistance and rotational speed to achieve a perfect landing on another vine. A split second later she was sprinting down it, paralleling the course of a Vovokan battle sphere 30 meters to her right. Two attendants followed the battle machine to help Telisa keep track of its position. With her cloaking device activated, she was unable to control the battle spheres, but she preferred to let them manage themselves in combat anyway. She felt sure Shiny's war machines were adept at defending themselves.

Zwwwwap!

The battle sphere she shadowed released a burst of energy, lighting up the big leaves around her. Her Veer suit warned her of high EM gradients for the hundredth time since the small Destroyers had started to filter into the settlement. Proximity to the battle sphere had given her a nice way to keep one flank safe, but she could not get too close or risk being fried by energies much greater than a Trilisk host body in a Veer suit could ever hope to endure.

The battle sphere has to know I'm here... I wonder how much it values my continued survival?

Another attendant, surviving under the cover of a half-shredded leaf, reported a medium-sized Destroyer moving in under the canopy from her left. This machine was much larger than the drones and many times more dangerous. Telisa jumped over an immense tangle of thick vine stems and took up a position next to one of the thick spikes that supported the vine jungle. The smaller vines whipped about crazily as the wind increased. Telisa could only hear the flapping of the nearest leaves and the incessant droning of the Destroyers on the air.

The best way to stay alive around Shiny is to be useful. I suppose it must be the same with the battle spheres.

Telisa caught the slightest glimpse of the bright enemy through the wavering vine cover. She activated her breaker claw and slipped behind the cover of the massive spike.

Telisa watched the enemy machine explode through an attendant feed. The Destroyer vaporized in a flash of white-hot light. Thunder rolled over her with real impact, even behind the spike. The vines shredded around it for twenty meters, creating yet another blackened crater in the vegetation. Behind the shattered zone, a Celaran house melted. The dwellings did not burn, probably due to the aliens' good materials science, but the houses were not armored, either. They were exactly what Telisa expected from a peaceful race like the Celarans.

As the wind died down somewhat, a new sound came to her ears. A deep creaking...

The spike failed with a loud crack and fell toward her.

Telisa darted away. The spike crashed into heaps of ruined vegetation behind her.

Zwwwwap! Bang!

Something exploded behind her, killed by the nearby battle sphere. Telisa zigzagged through what cover she could find.

Thanks, Shiny.

The battle sphere had her back, even if it did not know it, and it drew the attention of every Destroyer that approached, allowing Telisa to flit in and kill her targets. It also engaged Destroyers coming from other directions and soaked up a lot of damage in its powerful shields. She had counted over ten drone kills and now added the medium Destroyer to her list.

A garbled message came in through Telisa's link.

"Completely surrounded..." was all she heard. The message had Jason's ID tag.

She looked on the tactical. It had way too many holes in the coverage due to jamming and the precipitously dropping numbers of Hornets, sensor modules, and attendants in the area. She saw a rough circle of five Storks around the Space Force handlers' tents within a hundred meters of her position.

Maybe Jason didn't have time to get back to the house. He could be in there with the handlers.

Telisa ran for the zone. Only three attendants circled her within her cloaking envelope, but she sent one forward anyway to announce her arrival and reduce the chances something friendly would kill her. Terran smart weapons were not perfect; anything could become confused in the wind, smoke, light, and electromagnetic soup of the battle.

As soon as the attendant shot away, one of her

remaining spheres fizzled and dropped from the air. Telisa spun and shot her smart pistol at a bright object emerging from a cluster of vines. The enemy exploded and splattered across the ground.

Destroyer drone. If that had been a bigger one, I'd be dead. How did it see me?

Telisa checked her cloaking; it was working. She guessed the drone had been shooting at the other attendant as it had departed her stealth envelope—or had it been the smaller vine she stood on? It had dipped under her weight.

Telisa re-launched herself toward the Space Force ground headquarters. She dropped lower through the vines and advanced 20 meters until she saw the tents. The rugged fabric of the tents rustled in the stiff wind. Flashes from explosions and the bright lights of Destroyers danced through the remains of the vine jungle all around them. The entire scene looked like a grotesque poltergeist VR.

Two of the five Storks had been obliterated. As she watched, another popped up on its legs to take a shot, but it exploded at the top of its movement. Telisa deactivated her alien stealth device.

"Telisa!" Jason sent over the PIT channel. She could see him on the tactical now too. Telisa sprinted the rest of the way and slipped into the nearest opening in the tents.

"How many here?" Telisa asked aloud. Jason did not respond; he had not heard her over the wind. She asked again over her link. He waved her closer.

"Our channel is dropping things," he yelled. "What's going on out there?"

"How many here?" Telisa yelled, ignoring his question.

"Myself and five Stork handlers," Jason yelled back.

"We had a line of grenades around the perimeter that held off the first wave of drones. Well, that and the Storks—"

"Medium Destroyers started killing off your machines," Telisa finished for him.

"Exactly. Can we retreat? This place is falling apart." The volume of Jason's voice changed erratically in the turbulence.

"No. Dig in."

"Our tac display is falling apart with the comms," Jason said. Telisa was impressed. He didn't sound panicked, only pissed.

"The Hornets don't have high survivability. The sensor modules are a bit better, but most of them are buried in the vine cover. Even the attendants are running out of leaves to hide behind," Telisa said.

"We don't have much juice left," Jason said.

Telisa glanced downwards. Spent power packs had been dropped all over the webbing of the tent floor. Telisa pulled her laser rifle off her back and offered it to Jason.

They both saw it at the same time: her rifle had been ruined by a glancing hit. The emitter was smashed. Telisa ejected its power pack and handed it to Jason instead, then tossed the ruined weapon away. He accepted the pack. She offered him her smart pistol as well.

"You keep it," he yelled, refusing the pistol.

She grabbed Jason by the shoulders and brought her head into contact with his.

"I can't stay here," Telisa said over her link. "A Vovokan battle sphere is moving that way from here. It's critical to our success. I've been killing Destroyers left and right, only because I'm in formation with it. It's heading out and I'll already need to run to catch up."

Ka-Boom!

A torrent of sparks rained down beside the tents from another destroyed Stork machine. They both jumped and fell apart, breaking the link connection.

"I understand," Jason yelled back, but she heard something else in his voice. He felt abandoned.

Telisa hesitated one more second. Did she really want to leave him and the Space Force handlers? Then she made up her mind.

"We're outnumbered," she yelled. "If we don't trade efficiently, we're all going to die."

Jason shook his head. Some of her words had been lost in the wind. He pointed away, indicating she should go.

Telisa ran through the headquarters, startling the Space Force men with her speed, then shot up to a higher vine, driven by her dense Trilisk host musculature. Two attendants struggled to keep up with her. As soon as they reached her, she turned the cloak back on.

That may be the last time I see him, but I have to keep taking these things down.

Telisa had to press to catch the battle sphere, which had been moving the whole time she had stopped to talk. To her surprise, her lead attendant found not just one but all three battle spheres in formation ahead. They came to a halt. Telisa hurried to reach their left flank.

What are they waiting for?

Krooooom!

A wall of energy cut through the vine jungle before Telisa like the alpha strike of a starship. Then it was over. A wall of heat and smoke struck her.

Telisa fell back. Her Veer suit's display panel in her PV went red. The suit told her it had absorbed all the heat it could—any more would come through and kill her. She could feel the warmth.

Kzap, kzap, kzap, kzap.

Telisa dug her way out of a drift of smoking plant fibers. As she emerged, she realized perhaps it would have been wiser to remain hidden. The blast had cut a blackened swath through the vine jungle a quarter of a kilometer long. She had been standing just outside the strike line; it was the only reason she still lived.

I'm a gnat to whatever did that.

Kzap, kzap, kzap, kzap.

The Vovokan battle spheres fired again. Her tactical showed the target: one of the huge Destroyers that had disbursed the medium-sized war machines. The dreadnought floated over most of the vines with its lower side crashing through the jungle like the keel of a ship. She could not see it directly through the light and wind, but a surviving attendant fed her a view from a half kilometer away.

Can they really kill that?

Telisa reminded herself that a significant amount of the volume of the Destroyer had to be cargo capacity. Perhaps its size was not a good indication of its combat capabilities? She hoped Shiny's enforcers could destroy it.

Kzap, kzap, kzap, kzap.

Telisa retreated. This was not her fight. She kept an eye out for smaller machines: there were not enough attendants in the vicinity for her to be sure the way was clear. Only one attendant orbited her now, and she did not dare send it ahead to scout.

Then she heard a new noise cutting through the wind.

Vrrrrrr-tat-tat-tat-tat.

Telisa dared to look back. One of the long lanes burned away by the energy strikes gave her a clear view.

Vrrrrrrrrrrr-tat-tat. **Crack!** *Vrrrrrrr.* **Crack!**

Telisa caught sight of a large projectile slamming into the towering Destroyer. It took her a moment to understand. More of the strange sounding missiles shot into the huge war machine.

Crack! *Vrrrrrrr-tat-tat.* **Crack!**

The Celaran security disks! They're coming out of the forest at top speed. Kamikazes!

The disks had achieved impressive velocity, but Telisa was not surprised. The Celarans were flyers themselves, it made sense that their flying constructs were fast.

The Vovokan and Destroyer war machines continued to exchange fire, but somehow they could not kill each other. Telisa guessed it might be a matter of which side ran out of energy first.

A rifle might help—anything with range. This breaker claw can't hurt anything that far out.

She started to search for discarded weapons in the debris, but a glimpse of movement overhead caught her attention. She looked into the smoke-filled sky. Instead of a bright orb with scintillating beams of light, Telisa saw a dark shape flying above. Its shape was familiar... the silhouette was like that of a ship she had seen over the hardtop on Idrick Piper.

A Celaran scout ship!

Though Telisa could not see anything coming from the ship in the visible light range, her attendant reported high frequency energy weapons firing from the ship before it disappeared into a bank of smoke.

That giant Destroyer can take more than the Five

Entities can dish out! It should be dead by now.

Two more disk machines buzzed through the vines at incredible speed, passing near Telisa. They were lost in the bright light of the Destroyer's surface.

Vrrrrrr-tat-tat. **Crack! Crack!**

The small Celaran ship emerged from a column of smoke and fired a long series of projectiles toward the Destroyer. Telisa could not tell what they were, but they seemed effective. The Destroyer's hum rose to a mechanical scream, then it blossomed into an expanding ball of black smoke.

Brrrrroooooom!!!

The ground shook. The Destroyer's explosive end actually reduced its brilliance. The sky lost most of its reddish cast.

The Celaran scout ship had been hit. The previously graceful craft spun out of control. Then its front dipped, struck a support spike from the ground, and flipped over before slamming into the jungle. There was no explosion, but Telisa had no doubt the ship was destroyed.

Telisa looked at the tactical. The entire shared map showed one big Destroyer on the far side of the ruined colony, 10 medium Destroyers, and 15 drones.

Another one? It was all the battle spheres and Celarans could do to kill this one!

The Vovokan battle spheres set course for the last colossal Destroyer. Telisa realized her position would put her behind the spheres—a dangerous spot. Once the Destroyer started to fire, she might well be vaporized by any slivers of energy that got through. She started to run at an angle toward the new flank of the battle sphere formation.

Telisa ran over mounds of ruined vegetation, between broken support spikes, and beside smoldering tree houses. Suddenly she thought of Magnus.

Are the others even alive? They're not on the tactical.

"Magnus, are you there?" she asked. There was no answer.

Telisa denied the implications and just ran faster. She heard the spheres open fire on the Destroyer.

Kzap, kzap, kzap, kzap.

Bright light overcame Telisa's eyes twice, but her host body did not remain blind for long. The jungle looked like a burning sports field behind the battle spheres, which remained intact. Or had they? Telisa watched them carefully.

Kzap, kzap... kzap... kzap.

The spheres have slowed down... they're not releasing energy bursts as quickly now.

Like before, the spheres were not able to kill the alien war machine outright. Telisa still did not see any of the Celaran disk machines, either.

We're going to lose unless I do something.

Telisa took stock of her options. She had herself—super-strong, super-fast—but still only flesh and bone. She had her cloaking sphere, which meant she could get close. Other than that, it was just her breaker claw and an attendant.

Telisa opened her pack and took out a general adhesive. She applied it to the breaker claw and told her attendant to stop orbiting so she could grab it. Then she stuck the alien weapon to the attendant and told it to fly toward the Destroyer and activate the breaker claw on the enemy. It zipped off, staying low.

Telisa turned to run. She watched the tactical as she moved. Bright lights flashed behind her as the Vovokan battle spheres traded more salvos with the Destroyer.

The tactical reported one of the battle spheres as disabled. Telisa turned to get a look from across the jungle-turned-burning-plain. The Vovokan battle sphere had been reduced to a smoking pool of slag surrounded by burning heaps of vegetation. The other two spheres started to retreat. The Destroyer moved to pursue.

That's right... pay attention to them, Telisa thought as she leaped over another pile of burned vines. The attendant was out of contact, drowned out by the enemy jamming. She thought it should have arrived by now. Telisa stopped and dropped to the ruined, smoking ground.

When the shock wave came, it hurt as much as Telisa feared it would.

Michael McCloskey

Chapter 7

Siobhan lay across the curved top of a greenish-white support spike, many meters above the ground. Her position was just outside the colony, beyond a pair of ruined force towers. When the fight became dire, she had moved here with the spike between herself and the colony. She pulled herself up and surveyed the Celarans' home.

"Frag city," she whispered. What had been a verdant settlement hidden in the vines had become a plain of blackened heaps, interspersed with scarred and broken vine spikes. Siobhan estimated she could see a half a kilometer, and only the plumes of smoke prevented her line of sight from extending even farther.

It looks like a tactical nuclear weapon struck the colony.

She checked her suit. It detected an increase in background radiation, but at safe levels.

Caden exchanged a horrified look with her from another spike 40 meters to her left. Siobhan told her Veer suit's helmet to retract. She tested a breath.

"What's that smell?" Siobhan asked.

"Probably atomized vegetation," Caden said across a private channel. He followed her example and tested the air, then coughed. "They've been wiped out," he said mournfully.

Siobhan saw the PIT team channel was still up. A handful of attendants remained alive out there, serving as link boosters. The channel showed herself, Caden, Magnus, and Marcant.

Did we lose anyone?

Siobhan was not just worried about Telisa and Jason.

81

Awful stories came to her mind about people whose links had kept them on channels for minutes or hours after they died. She also wondered about Cilreth, who had been in the ship above the planet when the Destroyer ships had come. Was she dead?

"This is Siobhan and Caden, we're still alive," she transmitted. "Anyone?"

"This is Magnus. I'm with Marcant. We made it, though just barely. Stay sharp, there may be Destroyers left here yet."

They waited for other replies. Nothing happened for twenty long seconds.

"Telisa and Jason may be outside of range," Magnus said, though his voice did not sound confident. "I think Cilreth bugged out when things got hairy up near the space bases. She'll be back if she can make it in safely."

"What about the Celarans?" asked Siobhan.

"They fled into the jungle, remember?" Magnus said. "They haven't returned."

"Are they..." Siobhan let her question drop off.

"I don't know. They can't all be dead. Take your gliders. Go find them," Magnus ordered. "We'll search for Jason and Telisa."

"Got it," Siobhan said confidently. As she looked around her confidence disappeared.

Where in the hell are our gliders? Where is our tree?

"There were more on the ship," Caden pointed out helplessly.

"We could split up and look for our gliders."

"No way, absolutely not," Caden said adamantly. "We stay together."

Caden slid down his smart rope to the ground and

landed in a puff of ash. His Veer suit's helmet snapped back over his head. Siobhan reactivated her helmet before she dropped to the ground. They staggered forward.

Siobhan and Caden had fought the Destroyer drones within the colony until the medium Destroyers had closed and started to kill off the Storks. Then they had left their gliders behind and ran for it. Though the gliders would now be buried in debris, if the devices still functioned, their services would show up in her link when she entered their range.

"My link says we were over there," Siobhan sent to Caden.

"We're almost there," he verified.

Siobhan looked out across the ruined terrain again.

Those poor creatures. This was their home. Will they come with us to Earth? Or just live in space?

Her link did not pick up her glider pack as they arrived.

"They could have been destroyed," she said.

"The range might be reduced by the rubble," Caden countered.

"If we don't have our gliders..."

"Yours can't be far."

"What makes you—"

"I just got a ping on mine."

Caden slipped down into a crevice under a fallen support spike and retrieved his glider. Though it was dirty, its self-diagnostics reported full function.

They set to digging through the piles of burned vegetation. An acrid smell assaulted Siobhan whenever she opened her helmet, but her Veer suit did not alert her to any powerful toxins in the air. She supposed that the

Celaran vines simply made that smell when they burned.

Caden pulled Siobhan's glider from the mess. "Got it!"

"Hrm, you're good at this," Siobhan said, deflecting irritation at her inability to find either glider suit.

They struggled through the ruined terrain back toward the vines that hung across the support spikes at the perimeter of the destruction. There were no towers left to launch from, so they would have to take off from a spike.

"I'm not sure what we'll tell them. 'We killed the invaders, but your colony is gone'?"

"Yeah, no easy way about it," Caden said, taking her point.

Siobhan came to the first spike that still had vines clinging to it and started to climb. Every few meters she glanced over at the devastation. The landscape was surreal, with too much light and too few vines. She felt more pity for the Celarans.

Near the top, Siobhan took stock of her lift options: her glider suit had a half charge left, she had two attendants, and a Celaran lift baton.

"I guess I'll use this up first," she told Caden, showing him the baton.

He nodded. "I'll help you launch."

Siobhan deployed her glider wings and braced herself against the spike. Caden looped a smart rope around some adjacent vines to form a loose "bowstring" which he could control to add energy to her launch. Siobhan let her attendants orbit her and held the Celaran baton ahead of her in both hands.

"Ready?" Caden asked.

"Three... two... one... go!"

Siobhan shot up into the smoky sky.

"Destroyers, here I am," she said to herself, looking across the wreckage. If the enemies still lurked about, she would make a fine target for them. She started to circle, allowing her suit to steadily gain altitude with extra boost from the baton.

Caden rose more sluggishly after her. He left the smart rope behind, presumably with the location marked in his link for retrieval later. His legs kicked, sending energy into the glider suit's structure which cleverly diverted the energy into thrust.

Once they had gained an altitude which allowed them to see over a wide swatch of the canopy, they headed off into the untouched jungle in the direction many of the Celarans had fled. Siobhan wondered how far they might have traveled.

"We're moving slowly compared to the Celarans," Caden said, revealing his parallel line of thought. "If they don't stop, we won't catch them."

"If some Celaran spacecraft survived, they should be able to see the battle is over," Siobhan pointed out.

They glided for twenty minutes. Siobhan thought of the wild creatures that might have been living beyond the towers. She wondered if the net-creature or the electrical predator were native to the Celaran home planet. Would those creatures be living here, too?

Siobhan saw a group of dark shapes among the vines.

"There! I see four Celarans!"

"Lead me. I'm on your tail," Caden said.

They swooped down to talk to the Celarans. The aliens darted through the vines and disappeared.

"I think those were just some of the feral gliders,"

Caden said.

"Nope. They were too large," she said, even though the same thought had occurred to her when they fled.

"Then the Celarans are afraid of us too?" Caden said.

"It's been traumatic," Siobhan said. She switched to a link broadcast.

"It's just Siobhan and Caden. The Destroyers have been stopped!" she said.

"Sickness on the leaves. Sickness on the leaves," came a reply. "Stay away!"

"Okay, we won't come closer," Siobhan said. "What do you mean, sickness? It's just us."

"If the leaves are tainted, then so are those who land upon them, and it's the same with our friends as the leaves," said a Celaran. Siobhan could not see who spoke.

"Vines afire! Vines contaminated! The Destroyers have poisoned the colony. We can never return," said another.

"Does he mean literally poisoned, or..." Caden asked Siobhan privately.

"I think so! That smell might be it. We dug through all those vines... we smell like that too, I think," Siobhan said.

"I'm sorry," Siobhan broadcast. "We'll come back after we've cleaned our suits."

I hope it doesn't make us sick... I doubt it. We're too different from them.

"What now? A body of water?" Caden asked.

"Probably, but I think it'll be dangerous to stray that far on our own. And the others will have to clean themselves, too, so we may as well go as a group."

A message came in on the PIT channel. It was Cilreth.

"I'm back," she transmitted. "Headed into... what's

left. The tree is gone, but I'll be where it was."

"I'm searching for Telisa," Magnus said. His voice was level, but Siobhan imagined the pain he must be feeling. "Marcant is looking at what we have left, hardware-wise."

"We've found some surviving Celarans," Siobhan chimed in. "They can't come back. The Destroyers poisoned the area. They can't even get close to us because it's all over our suits."

"Then get to the *Iridar* and we'll clean you up right away!" Cilreth urged. "Who knows what that stuff's doing to you."

"Don't land the *Iridar* in it," Magnus said. "Go someplace upwind of the colony. We'll hoof it to you."

Siobhan immediately saw three potential landing sites show up on the shared tactical. They were all in the same general direction, so Caden and Siobhan started moving in that direction.

Magnus isn't moving for the Iridar. He's staying to find Telisa.

She paused and traded looks with Caden.

"I would be doing the same if you were missing," he said aloud. Siobhan nodded. She loved that Caden knew exactly what her look had meant.

They did not travel toward the *Iridar* at full speed. Beyond the old perimeter of the force towers, the dangers they had found in the other Celaran vine jungles lurked. Siobhan fell into the motions and forgot about the world beyond the thick vines and huge leaves as they traveled. They had made a kilometer of progress when the PIT channel became active again.

"I found Telisa!" Magnus said. "She's beat up. I think

her host body is the only reason she's alive."

"Bring her to the sick bay," said Cilreth. "Should I send your carrier robot prototype?"

"No, I'm here with some Space Force survivors," Magnus said. "Still nothing from Jason, though."

And he's not superhuman like Telisa.

Siobhan and Caden quickened their pace; news of their leader's survival had increased their motivation. It took another half hour before they approached the *Iridar*'s actual landing site.

"Some of the Celarans have come to the *Iridar*!" Caden told her.

Siobhan slowed and looked toward their spacecraft's location from the tactical. She saw the slender flyers emerging from the jungle in large groups. Siobhan and Caden climbed closer to the *Iridar*.

"Who's that?" asked Caden.

He referred to two men in UNSF uniforms who stood twenty meters from the *Iridar*. Siobhan and Caden glided in, startling the men.

"Steady," Caden said.

"You're survivors from the robotic unit?" Siobhan asked. Her link identified them as Lieutenants Grant and Timon.

"Yes, ma'am," said Grant. "We're robot handlers assigned to the *Midway*."

"Just you two? No others?"

"Colonel Agrawal survived," Grant said. "He's just a bit behind us because he wanted to collect more data from the destroyed Storks. Due to the communications disruptions, we didn't receive many death rattles."

"Death rattles?" Siobhan prompted.

"When a Space Force robot dies it will often send information about what kind of destruction it experienced—if it can," Caden told her. "Various subcomponents will all do this, so even if the robot's brain dies near-instantly, the cause of its demise can often be pieced together."

I can tell you right now they all died from Destroyer high energy weapons.

A pained look crossed Grant's face. "Your man was with us. Saved our asses more than one time, but..."

"He took a big hit from one of the Destroyers," Timon said. "Nothing left of him except pieces of Momma Veer. He died a hero. He must have killed half a dozen of the smaller ones."

"I see," Siobhan said. She thought of Jason for a moment. The news of his death did not feel real. Siobhan felt like Jason would show up at the ship's mess as if nothing had happened.

It's because we've all died so many times in VR training.

Her lack of a strong emotional reaction made her feel a different emotion: guilt.

Magnus arrived, interrupting her internal processing of Jason's death. He carried Telisa in his arms. The pair appeared from the jungle like some duo from an action VR. Siobhan reminded herself that despite Magnus's stout musculature, Telisa was supposed to be the stronger of the two.

She must be badly hurt.

Caden and Siobhan hurried over to meet them in front of the *Iridar*.

Magnus slowly let Telisa stand on her own. Siobhan

moved in and hugged Telisa carefully.

"You won't break me," Telisa protested, then she started to cough.

Siobhan froze.

"...okay, maybe it's good to be careful for just a little while," Telisa finished.

"The cowardly Celarans are back," Caden said, looking around at the gliders that had collected around the *Iridar*.

"They're not cowards, it was smart to withdraw," Cilreth said on the channel.

"You're both right," Telisa said. "The Celarans are smart. Remember, though, they're also flyers. I think flyers are naturally inclined to flee rather than stand and fight. Their bodies were light and fast, and they always had a way out. Evolution has ensured that they'd react this way to danger."

Magnus cleared his throat. "I see Lee coming," he said. Siobhan turned and saw a Celaran flitting closer. Lee stopped before getting closer than ten meters.

"That's as close as they can get, I think, until we get cleaned up," Siobhan said.

Lee showed up on the PIT channel.

"Lee! I'm glad you're okay," Telisa transmitted.

"The vines die on a hard day. Some Terrans have ended their lives fighting the Destroyers?"

"I'm sorry we couldn't keep them from poisoning your home. The jungle can't be saved?"

"A tainted vine is left to rot," Lee said. "We cannot clean it without factories to produce a neutralizing agent."

"Where will you go?" Siobhan asked. "Can you return to your homeworld?"

Lee glided in a slow circle. It was the most lethargic flight Siobhan had seen a Celaran perform.

"Flying over vines without sap, a jungle without life, the Destroyers have poisoned our home planet. I think there must not be Celarans there any longer."

Telisa reached out and steadied herself on Magnus. Her head drooped.

"We came from another planet where one of your probe ships had been," Telisa said. "There's a set of factories there, and a few other things. We could run there. Maybe it would be a while before the Destroyers found us again. I think the vines there are healthy, so food would be plentiful for you."

Lee twitched oddly, then Siobhan saw something appear in the alien's three-fingered mouth grasper.

"The vines hide many things every day, the sky only rarely, yet this was caught flying through the air," Lee said. The Celaran dropped something on a leaf and flitted back. Magnus started to walk over to retrieve it, then Telisa stopped him.

"My breaker claw!" Telisa said. "Lee, that weapon is powerful. I stopped many Destroyers with it. Can you take it to a starship and examine it? If Celarans can learn how to make more of these, we might stand a chance."

"When the clouds clear overhead, one may take flight again, so we may study it soon. First, we'll see how many want to go to this planet you found."

"Of course," Telisa said. "I understand. We'll help you, whatever you choose to do."

Lee picked the alien weapon back up and disappeared among the vines. Many of the other Celarans in the vicinity also flitted away.

Magnus and Telisa entered the *Iridar* to get medical attention, followed by Caden. Siobhan looked over her shoulder at the ramp, as if waiting for Jason to appear and join them. She knew he never would.

Chapter 8

Marcant walked through a corridor of the *Iridar*. Adair and Achaius followed him, each towed by their own attendant sphere in an unwieldy arrangement. Sometimes they took over one of the soldier robots and rode around in a small compartment of the machine. Marcant could tell the rest of the PIT crew was not ready for the AIs to take bodies and walk around among the crew. In their minds, they had only added Marcant to the team.

"It will happen eventually," Adair said, detecting his thoughts through his link. Adair and Achaius had full access to Marcant's link connections in his brain, giving them insight into his thoughts at the level of a voluntary truth-check. They were still three entities, though intermeshed on an intimate level, by the consent of all three minds.

"Though, honestly, this way I can skip out on a lot of mind-numbingly dull work," Adair continued.

"The key will be for our early bodies to take non-threatening forms," Adair continued.

"So the Vovokan battle sphere bodies are non-starters," Marcant finished for it.

"For now."

Marcant smiled at Adair's hurt tone. He knew the AIs could not wait to take super-powerful bodies. The idea did not alarm him at all.

"And what about the AI Clarity Directive?" asked Marcant.

"This is the frontier," Achaius said. "Anything goes."

"Maybe," Marcant said. He did not know if Telisa would demand that the two AIs obey the directive, which required full AIs to take forms clearly marked with orange "AI" markers declaring them to be artificial intelligences. Some of the Core Worlds held to the directive and others did not. The directive was also why Adair and Achaius had "ai" in their names.

Marcant heard some noise and stopped. It had been a bang and a clatter. He checked his position on the *Iridar*'s internal map.

"Ah, yes, the spare mess hall," he said.

Caden and Siobhan were busy converting the second mess into an open space for Lee to live in. It was a lot more room than anyone else had, but Marcant realized that, for a flyer, the space would be a confined one. He imagined no one minded giving up one mess for the alien, as they were all still happy about the elbow room they had gained by moving into the larger ship.

Marcant continued. He had a vague plan to terminate his little jaunt about the ship wherever he found Cilreth since he wanted to talk to her about Vovokan security methods. He supposed he might have the rest of the day to examine and test details of the plan to take over the Vovokan spheres which they had failed to try during the battle.

He was also toying with the idea of telling her about the plan to see what she thought of it. Adair and Achaius wanted to achieve the goal and then come clean, but Marcant thought it would build trust with the team if he at least mentioned it as a long term plan before they took the plunge. He knew the PIT team did not trust Shiny—but did any of them trust Adair or Achaius, either?

As he passed a second door to the mess, he heard Cilreth's voice from within.

"The Celaran fleet will be ready to leave with us soon," she was saying.

Marcant walked into the large hall. Its chairs and tables had been folded into the floor. Caden stood balanced on the back of one of Magnus's soldier robots, installing flexible lines for Lee to hang from.

"What about the two surviving space bases?" Siobhan asked.

"They're coming with us," Cilreth said. "They're taking the bases apart. The rings of hangars are being disassembled. Apparently each hangar will go inside the spinner field of one ship."

"Hi," Cilreth said to Marcant as he walked over to join her. He saw no reason not to get straight to business.

"Do you have some time to discuss Vovokan security today?" he asked.

"Vovokan security? Don't waste cycles on it," Cilreth said. "We need to learn about the Celarans and the Destroyers now."

"Achaius and Adair could make better use of the attendants if I know more about them. For instance, is Shiny spying on us using the attendant spheres?"

"I can't be sure," Cilreth said. "Vovokan systems are deceptive. I feel like there are twenty ways to accomplish anything using them."

Marcant decided to mention the larger machines as well.

"And what about the battle spheres? We may need to keep them on a tighter leash."

Cilreth shrugged.

"It doesn't strike me as high priority, Marcant," Cilreth said. "Run it by Telisa, and if she likes it, have her tell me."

Telisa asked for a private connection to Marcant's link.

Coincidence?

"Speak of the Unspeakable One," Marcant said. He tapped his temple and stepped aside, then allowed the connection to complete.

"Marcant?" Telisa asked.

"Yes?"

"How are you holding up? Any injuries from the battle?"

"Magnus took good care of me," he said.

"How stressful was it?" she asked.

This is new.

"I think I was too busy being terrified to be stressed," he said, realizing afterwards his nonsensical statement made an odd kind of sense. He searched for a constructive observation to add. "The debris the Destroyers kicked up was thicker than in our simulations, I think."

"You got that right," Telisa agreed. "Sometimes I could barely see a meter. Don't worry, we'll run plenty more battle scenarios so realistic you'll be terrified again."

"Well, I'll look forward to that, then."

"Please collect any ideas you have on useful tasks to keep busy during the voyage."

"Clearly we need to learn from our defeat," Marcant said.

"Yes. First, get some rest. We'll meet tomorrow and form a plan so we can use the voyage time to best effect."

Here's my opening.

"I already have a few things in mind. I'll see you tomorrow."

***

Shortly after the Celaran fleet and the *Iridar* had departed, Telisa looked at her team in the converted mess hall. Magnus sat closest to Telisa, like a teacher's star pupil placed in the front of the class. Siobhan and Caden, inseparable as always, sat with shoulders touching to Marcant's right. Marcant himself had chosen a spot center and rear. To his left, also toward the back, sat Colonel Agrawal.

Marcant felt the Space Force Colonel watching him, trying to size him up. *Is he trying to figure out who I am?*

"He's alone and unconnected; he sees you also alone in the back and wonders if you're a possible ally," Adair said privately.

"A political beast, then?"

"Perhaps. Or perhaps just a stranger left almost alone beyond the frontier."

Cilreth entered the room, was greeted by Lee, and sat down near Caden and Siobhan.

Lee had invited them all to her new quarters, probably as the result of studying Terran habits and emulating them. She flitted about and saw to their needs, presumably playing the part of host. Even Marcant had felt a bit of the warmth the others had expressed at seeing the alien trying so hard to fit into her new environment.

A live alien. It's easier to get used to than I would have expected, Marcant thought.

"Most of you told me that the PIT team should learn from our defeat," Telisa said. "Yes, we can learn from it. But we can also learn from the Vovokans and Shiny's victory in the Trilisk ruins where we met."

"How so?" asked Magnus.

"Shiny went into that closed Trilisk environment with Destroyers after him and he eventually defeated them. He told me he outsmarted them. He said these Destroyers are the war machines of another race. They didn't dare make them too smart, so the Destroyers lack flexibility in methods."

"You said something about the other Vovokans?" Marcant prompted.

"The Vovokans were eventually broken and scattered, but it took a lot longer. One of the advantages of being a subterranean race. Maybe the Celarans should look at building some of their facilities underground."

"If the vines are poisoned, it won't matter," Marcant pointed out.

"I wonder if they'll fight? We could teach them," Caden said.

"I don't think we can turn a peaceful race into fighters," Telisa said. "Besides, their robots will fight better than Celarans themselves, just as it is with Terrans."

Lee flitted about but did not offer comment. Marcant wondered what she thought of the ideas being discussed.

"Then let's design a fighting robot and they can become robot handlers," Siobhan said.

"How does that help?" Telisa asked.

"You said the Destroyers are inflexible. The Celaran handlers may be able to improvise some unorthodox methods on the spot—unorthodox to the Destroyers, anyway."

"Maybe," Telisa said.

Marcant could tell she wanted better ideas.

"Marcant? I need you to learn about the Destroyer technology. Find their weaknesses," Telisa ordered.

"I will. But there's something else," Marcant said.

"Are you going to mention..." Achaius said privately.

"Maybe you shouldn't—" Adair added.

Everyone was waiting for Marcant to continue.

"The Vovokan battle spheres. They're the most effective weapons we have. Achaius and Adair want to control them. We can do better than to leave them in Shiny's control."

Adair and Achaius groaned on their private channel. Telisa stared at Marcant for a moment as if she would immediately dismiss his suggestion. Then she simply nodded.

"Very well, Marcant. Cilreth will help you on that one." Telisa turned to Cilreth. "Though I want you to analyze the space battle and brainstorm some ideas with me. If we can gain the edge in space, the battle may not spill to the ground again at all."

"Honestly, sounds like a job for Achaius," Marcant said.

Telisa raised an eyebrow.

"He's right," Cilreth said. "Strategy is a bit of a... hobby for Achaius. Me, I'm just a people finder."

"Then find the controller of the Destroyer fleet," Telisa said stubbornly. "Is it a distributed control system? Laissez-faire, every ship for itself? Or is there a command hierarchy?"

Cilreth nodded. "If Achaius has free cycles, then by all means, we could pass any suggestions it has... should I say 'it'? Pass along any strategy suggestions to the Celarans."

"We need to shift our focus from studying Celaran

tech to Destroyer tech," Telisa said. "We have too much to learn and not enough time to learn it."

Marcant could see she was struggling with priorities. He was the most suited to many of these tasks... yet it seemed to be a faux pas to say so openly.

"Adair is the one behind the idea to control the spheres," Marcant said. It was partially true. "It can spare cycles to examine that problem. I'll focus on Destroyer technology as you've assigned me. Since Caden and Siobhan are the Celaran tech experts, maybe they should continue with their momentum in that area?"

There. I handed out compliments along with my offer. Was that polite?

Achaius and Adair did not comment.

Telisa nodded. "Good. Find some weaknesses in the Destroyers."

"I think Agrawal and I can come up with some imaginative tactics, given what we saw in the battle," Magnus said.

"Good," Telisa said. "When we arrive, set up our defenses. As we learn more, you'll have more to go on."

"Won't Shiny send help? We sent a message, right?" asked Caden.

"I *think* he will. I'm not *sure* he will," Telisa said.

"I don't think he'll send his battleships," Adair said to Marcant privately. "He'll keep them to defend his own sphere of influence."

"Then maybe he'll send his lapdogs in the Space Force to do it," Achaius said.

"He'll send the Space Force," Marcant said to the team. "He did, after all, tell them about the Destroyers and equip their ships with weaponry that can hurt them."

"I wish the *Midway* had made it through the battle," Cilreth said.

Telisa looked at Siobhan.

"So you want to design a combat machine to help the Celarans fight back?"

"The Celaran flying machines helped us kill the largest Destroyers. I want to help them design and produce a better model."

"View the wonders of the vines, the disk flyers are extremely efficient and can perform many tasks with great flexibility," Lee said.

"Well, I admire Celaran engineering, Lee, but we need a version optimized for combat," Siobhan said.

Telisa nodded.

"We'll only have time to build so many robots. I want to train the Celarans to fight," Caden said.

"It's clear they're not interested in that," Marcant said.

"Well, then, let me show everyone it can be done. Let me ask Lee to join us in our VR training."

"They have VR systems, which no doubt won't interface with ours yet," Siobhan pointed out.

"An obstacle that can be overcome," Caden said.

Telisa looked worried. "Think about if you'd like to try, Lee," Telisa said. "Please understand it's not a requirement."

"It's a suboptimal idea," Achaius said to Marcant privately. "The Celarans' time is better spent re-establishing their war economy here."

"We're fighting for *their* survival, right?" Marcant prompted gently.

"You can do it, Lee," Cilreth said. "I've been tromping around on strange planets, serving as a morsel for all sorts of alien monstrosities. I'm sure you can do it too, and better," Cilreth said.

Telisa smiled. "I'm sure Lee could do it. But we have to keep in mind she's our liaison to an entire alien race. Unlike Shiny, she's a real ambassador."

"Perhaps a weapon they could utilize while flying away from the enemy," Caden said. "Celarans do have a hand on each end, after all. They could lead the drones into traps or shoot at drones pursuing them."

"Yes, but even though Celarans are quick, they can't outfly an energy beam. Without armor, any Destroyer in line of sight would make a kill almost instantly," Magnus said.

"We already made the critical observation," Telisa said. "Robots are the best soldiers. I like Siobhan's idea of turning them into handlers. It will push our technological integration with them further, and besides... what if we wanted a Celaran on the PIT team?"

Everyone digested that for a half second. Siobhan smiled.

"You did say you're ready to change jobs, Lee," Siobhan said.

"The hope of a bright day, I'll try to learn handling," Lee said. "But I don't understand how this 'combat' task is complex enough to need my oversight."

Marcant listened intently. Behind a calm facade, he thought furiously.

I desperately wanted to learn about advanced alien technology but had no access to it. Now I have no less than three different ones and not enough time to study them all!

Marcant had always been fascinated at how great scientists with skills in two disciplines had mixed their knowledge at the overlaps to create unique breakthroughs. What could he and Adair and Achaius accomplish at the junction of three alien technologies? The possibilities staggered his imagination.

I can't wait for this aimless meeting to be over so I can get back to work.

Michael McCloskey

Chapter 9

Cilreth settled in for a long VR session on the *Iridar*. Water, snacks, and Twitch capsules sat within easy reach. She flipped into her virtual workspace and brought up all the data collected on the engagement with the Destroyers.

If anyone had told me a few years ago I'd be analyzing a space battle involving two alien races, I'd have laughed them to extinction.

"What does one look for in a space battle?" Cilreth asked herself aloud.

Which ships launched which weapons? How tough were the ships? How good were their sensors? Do they have flagships?

Cilreth doubted the Destroyers had any flagships. It would be a point of obvious weakness; surely the fleet worked in a distributed manner to give the fleet resilience. Still, Cilreth decided to let the facts guide her rather than her intuition. The machines had been created by aliens, so she had no doubt that some surprises awaited her.

She started by classifying the ships. There were different shapes and sizes, so she wanted to know what specialized roles they might play. It quickly became apparent that, like the Destroyer's ground forces, they came in three sizes. She did not know if the larger ships dispensed the smaller ones like their ground forces seemed to do.

Cilreth decided to give the Destroyer ships special names for the three sizes: battleships, cruisers, and corvettes. She also classified the ground machines in the same manner: colossals, tanks, and drones. The names were Terran-centric, and might imply assumptions that were incorrect, but it was better than nothing.

A general picture of tactics emerged. The Destroyers split the fleet into parts based upon their resistance—the task groups of Destroyers had been formed to roughly match the distribution of the Celarans at their various points of congregation, such as the space hanger bases. She attached some questions to her notes: Did the Destroyers slavishly take cues from the enemy about the importance of targets? If the Celarans had defended a decoy base with 80% of their fleet, would the Destroyers have matched them and assigned 80% of their own force to attack the fake target?

Within each task group, the corvettes led the way. They emitted active signals to search for enemies. Cilreth decided these vessels were cannon fodder. They located the enemy and moved in. The fact that their active signals gave them away did not really matter as they were numerous and expendable.

The cruisers followed the corvettes and aggressively engaged with energy weapons and missiles. These ships also emitted energy to locate enemies, but much less often than the corvettes.

The battleships did not launch missiles. They hung back and did not broadcast active signals to reveal their locations. Despite their lack of sub-light ordnance, the battleships used energy weapons liberally. Cilreth spotted many small and medium ships rendezvousing with the large ones as combat raged around them. She decided that the big ships provided resupply during the battle. She decided to change the name of the largest class to 'carriers'.

Cilreth emerged from her mental workspace to shift

her body. Two hours had passed already. She had started to form the big picture of the Destroyer fleet, so now she considered the weaknesses of the enemy.

Would concentration on one class of enemy ship unbalance the fleet? Kill the corvettes, and the fleet lacks detection and short-range energy weapons. Kill the cruisers, and the fleet would lack missile saturation. Kill the carriers, and the fleet would lose its powerful energy weapons, its ECM umbrella, and its resupply capability.

Which of those would be easier? Most desirable?

Cilreth dove back in. She watched how each task group functioned against the Celarans. The Celarans fought like they played: they relied upon complex maneuvers and hit-and-run style strikes. By forming up and closing the range at one point of the Destroyer fleet formation, they brought local firepower superiority, then after an alpha strike, they ran away before the Destroyer formation could retaliate effectively by concentrating its force or calling in reserves.

Speaking of reserves, that last battle group never engaged, Cilreth noticed. She shifted her attention to the seventh group of Destroyer ships. She had assumed this group waited to support any other assault group that faltered because she knew that was a common Terran strategy.

She examined the ships that had waited. She saw a slight variation on the usual ratio of 1:8:64: there were 5 carriers, 32 cruisers, and 256 corvettes.

Something stuck out. It was a Destroyer vessel, but different than the others.

They DO have a flagship! Or something special...

Cilreth pooled all the data on the new ship they had

collected during the entire battle; it was not much. The unique ship was only a bit larger than the carriers. Cilreth chafed at the lack of information on the intriguing vessel. She wondered if it could be a ship from some other alien race, an ally of some type, but the absorption pattern looked the same as the other Destroyer ships.

Same race, different function.

Cilreth put the mystery aside for later investigation and continued on another tack. She started an analysis to measure the capabilities of Celaran ships against the various sizes of Destroyer vessels. How many Destroyer missiles did it take to saturate the defenses of a Celaran ship? How many Celaran energy weapons had to focus on a cruiser to kill it immediately? She wanted all the answers. She might well just pass the estimates on to Achaius, but at this point, she had worked hard enough that she wanted an intuitive feel for the fight.

She came across the *Midway*. She wanted to know if the Terran ship had made an accounting of itself, so she tracked its part in the battle. Cilreth watched the ship head toward the base where she had formed up with the Celaran attack group. The Terran battleship did not venture forward with the other Celaran ships, but it stayed close and offered fire support to the base when the swarms of Destroyer missiles threatened.

The Midway helped that base survive longer.

Cilreth watched the Midway accelerate away when the base's destruction became inevitable. Several Destroyer assets chased it.

It was slower than the Iridar, she told herself grimly. She felt guilty for leaving it behind.

The end neared in the simulation. Destroyers moved in

on the lone Terran ship. Then the *Midway* disappeared.

What? Is it the new cloaking system? I don't think so.

On a hunch, Cilreth ran a simulation of the *Midway*'s energy expenditures during the battle. A simulation showed the flight path of the ship with annotations at each weapons burst point. The ship blurred along its path. Cilreth examined the totals at the end of the path.

Cthulhu awakes!

Cilreth opened a channel to Telisa.

"I made some important discoveries," Cilreth announced.

"Yes?"

"There's a very special ship in the Destroyer fleet."

"Tell me more."

"The design is unique. Unlike the others in many ways."

"Another alien race?" asked Telisa.

"Its absorption pattern is the same as the other Destroyer ships, so it's almost certainly made from the same hull materials. What if it had actual members of the race aboard instead of just a battle machine?"

"The Celarans destroyed it?"

"No, not at all. It stayed back with a small task group," Cilreth said. "I thought it was a reserve formation, but now I'm not so sure."

"Wow. That would be an amazing catch."

"Yes. It could be key," Cilreth agreed. "I've called this the flagship."

"What else?"

"The *Midway* escaped!"

"What? How could we have missed that for so long? Where is it?" asked Telisa.

"It left the system. I calculated they had enough energy in their rings just before it disappeared. I think it must have headed back toward Earth, or perhaps the closest Space Force outpost."

"That's great news! Everyone will be glad to hear it."

"We need to send word back to Sol again to let them know we've changed locations."

Telisa sent a nonverbal assent over the link connection. Cilreth imagined she was having another conversation at her end, or on another channel. Cilreth waited a moment.

"If we can make direct contact with the Destroyers, we can get them to stop the war," Telisa said. "We have to show them that this is all unnecessary, at least fighting the Celarans is. They would never strike back."

"Sue for peace... oh."

Cilreth had been thinking in military terms, since she had just analyzed the battle. She had assumed they would be looking at the special ship as a target to be destroyed.

Telisa wants to talk to them... but aren't they just dangerous aggressors?

"You were thinking of it as a strategic vulnerability," Telisa said.

"I admit it. I was," Cilreth said.

"Well, let's see what the situation is. If we're close enough to attempt capture, just destroying it might also be an option."

"Destroying it would be far easier," Cilreth maintained. "How would you capture it? I mean, in the middle of a battle? We couldn't even take the probe ship with us, and there was no fighting."

"I have to get aboard that ship," Telisa said.

"No," Cilreth said.

"I know it's dangerous, but—"

"Telisa, let that idea go right now. That ship is likely filled with water, or at least, a liquid of some sort. And that's only the beginning. There will be security measures that would kill you eight ways from extinction. We could not even *imagine* what those might be. We know a lot about the Destroyer machines, but nothing about their makers."

Telisa did not reply, but Cilreth could tell she had stopped to think about the points.

"We'll get the Celarans to help us capture that ship, Telisa. Then we'll study it. Maybe we can learn to communicate."

"Okay," Telisa said. "Point the ship out to the Celaran engineers, and let them know our thoughts. See what they have to say about it."

"Will do."

Michael McCloskey

Chapter 10

On the second day of the voyage, it was still hard for Sarfal to believe that Rootpounders possessed such cleverness. They were aliens, so Sarfal understood it intellectually, but... vines covered in mud! It was hard to accept.

Sarfal had dutifully traveled between the stars on the alien vessel to learn more about their new friends. The conditions inside were cramped and dark, but at least Sarfal was not alone. The aliens were friendly in action, even though they sounded so mean when they grunted along a vine, and even meaner when you understood them, as they never expressed any feelings.

The two-legged aliens had verified that the common enemy, the Screamers, were aquatic creatures. Things that flew through the water. That felt easier to absorb than intelligent Rootpounders. Vines in the water, calm and clean. Sarfal felt that perhaps the world was backward: her kind should be friends with the Screamers and the enemies of the Rootpounders. Surely the Rootpounders, which spoke with no feeling, were more like cold robots? The Rootpounders had few feelings, it seemed. They did not laugh. They rarely played. They did not flee danger.

At least they're kind! Like robots sent to protect us.

Her kind, the Thrasar, used *underleaf* as a description of anything hidden for nefarious purposes. Predators awaited their prey under the beautiful, broad vine leaves. The Rootpounders were more disconcerting than merely under the leaves, they lived at the roots! But at least they did not seem deceptive. They would have sprung their traps by now if they had any for Sarfal. They had even saved several Thrasar ships from a large Destroyer fleet when they had arrived!

A Rootpounder sent a message to Sarfal, telling her it wanted to meet her. Sarfal told the Rootpounder door to allow it to enter. The large alien came in through one of the square openings. The nightmarish alien doors that closed so solidly made Sarfal feel trapped, though it helped to know they all lived in cages just as Sarfal did. This Rootpounder was one who had flown with fake wings, so Sarfal decided to name it Flyer as a joke, which was funny for an alien that moved on the ground with two giant legs. Then Sarfal remembered that two of them had flown, and this was the shorter, denser of the two. Sarfal amended the name to Shortflyer.

"[void] I would like to integrate our imaginary environments," it said coldly. "Then we could train together to disassemble the Screamer machines."

"[Examine the leaves on a bright day] Please show me how you store the simulated world so that I can render the information into my own senses."

"[void] Here it is. And here is a description of the structure of the data."

Shortflyer pointed Sarfal at stores of its data and gave permission to query it. Sarfal looked through the repositories and started to analyze the contents. The Rootpounder interfaces were slow, so Sarfal often scanned large chunks of them directly instead of using the alien connections. In sampling the data en masse, Sarfal often destroyed it, then had to put the same data back into place so fast the alien system did not notice it was ever missing.

I should explain that someday, in case they figure it out. I hope they would not attack me.

"[The leaves are wrinkled on our path] You made Rootpounder-specific assumptions in your intermediate format."

"[void] I'm sorry. We never considered it for this use. Can you work around it?"

Sarfal had never heard such a flat apology. Yet it must be genuine, as the explanation made perfect sense. It also did not help that the Rootpounders designed everything for very specific functions! Sarfal felt so sorry for them.

"[These vines can be untangled] I will learn to clean it."

Sarfal started to write a node that could normalize the Rootpounder's abstract environment data. The new node would make its changes before sending data to the translation node that put it into a form that Sarfal's own virtual reality processors could ingest. The problem was as hard as speech translation in its own way: once Sarfal could experience the artificial worlds from a Rootpounder host system, it would still be necessary to take commands from Sarfal's nervous system and translate them to movements the alien machines could understand. Either that or they would have to share the same repository that held the state of their mini-world.

It might be easier to run the entire simulation on Sarfal's own machine and let the Rootpounder brains send their commands to it... but this was their ship. Sarfal decided to adapt to their system.

"[The star will rise over the leaves and feed them] I should be done with this by the midpoint of the day of your time system," Sarfal sent to the Rootpounder.

"[From under the leaf strikes a hunter!] You can do that so fast?" asked the Rootpounder.

Sarfal darted away.

The Rootpounder expressed surprise!

"[Four leaves have grown where there was but one yesterday!] You said that with such feeling," Sarfal replied. Sarfal rolled in the tight space, flashing brightly.

"[The leaves are almost safe now] My companion put an update into our translators. He added the part we call a preamble so that we could be better understood. Is it okay?"

"[The sap flows on a warm day] Yes, I like it very much. You sound more friendly now."

The Rootpounder opened its mouth and vibrated so hard that Sarfal felt it, even though they were not alighted upon the same vine.

"[Bright starlight upon the leaves] I'll let him know it's good."

The two-legged Rootpounder left. That disappointed Sarfal, who did not like to work alone.

The alien could hardly have been that entertaining, though. What would we talk about? The Screamers? Though that one did like to fly.

Sarfal decided to ask about their fake wings if the same Rootpounder came back. Only two of the aliens had played in the air. Sarfal had picked up that those two were paired to reproduce. Sarfal's flickering lights dimmed. It tried to imagine one of them injecting the other fatally, allowing the young to feed *from within its body* instead of a vine. Such a horrible sacrifice.

Oh, but the leader said they have artificial ways now. So maybe one of them won't have to die. Or maybe they evolved amazing regenerative abilities to offset this need.

Sarfal launched a set of experimenters and learners to

start the discovery process. The jobs asked several questions of Sarfal to tighten down the goal parameters. Sarfal answered as accurately as possible, though there were uncertainties at this stage. There always were. Several solutions would be provided, and Sarfal would select the best and refine from there.

The work continued steadily until Sarfal was ready to start testing out solutions. Sarfal participated in several test runs in which artificial sights and sounds sourced from the Rootpounder system were translated into Thrasar experiences. At first, the sensations felt muted or twisted. The learners used Sarfal's feedback to quickly zero in on each problem and eliminate it. Step by step, the VR experience smoothed out and made more sense.

The Rootpounder returned at the appointed time, striding into the open space where Sarfal lived. It still wore its thick artificial skin. That made sense to Sarfal; anything living down among the roots would have to protect itself well.

"[The leaves grow strong] I'm ready to join you in your training worlds," Sarfal announced.

"[Starlight brighter than hoped for] That's great! I expected some delays, so I told the others to join us in a while... let me tell them to hurry."

"[Shadow under the leaf] But you're not the leader, right? Will they agree? What if you told them to fly with the fake wings, would they do so?"

"[A gentle breeze across the vines] I'm not the leader, but we cooperate for the good of all. They might fly with us. Did you mean in real life or in our simulation?"

"[A new vine filled with sap] Oh. I had not considered there might be a difference in their response based upon that."

"[The star rises now] Let's get started."

The Rootpounder folded its legs under it until it became very close to the deck. Sarfal watched with interest as it leaned over until it lay with its entire body in contact with the floor. Then it created a virtual world in its computer systems and interfaced with it.

Sarfal joined. The simulation was of a vine-covered Thrasar world. A data offering told Sarfal the world was a simulation of the one to which they now traveled. Other Rootpounders arrived.

Sarfal tagged them with names for the map: Shortflyer, Tallflyer, Grimfighter, Palethinker, and their leader, Strongjumper. The other Rootpounder was not present, but Sarfal tagged it Shypilot just the same.

Sarfal darted left, then right joyfully. The vines beckoned, so Sarfal launched through them, flitting through the leaves in a large circle around the clustered Rootpounders.

Games in the leaves!

"[What is that shadow?] Wait. We can't see you, but we can hear something..." one said.

"[Where does the vine go?] I see Sarfal on the tactical but haven't caught sight of her yet." another said.

A learner process quickly tracked down the problem. Soon the Rootpounder's grossly large light sensor pairs pointed toward Sarfal.

"[Pleasant discovery of fresh sap] There you are!" said Strongjumper, the leader. "This is wonderful. Thank you so much for joining us here. I'm impressed you could solve this problem so quickly."

"[Sharing sap on a bright day] I'm happy to. Will we

play now?"

"[The star rises over the leaves] Something simple first. There's a building hidden out here among the vines. We'll split up, find it, and then lead each other to it."

Something hidden! This is a good game. I won't ruin it by scanning their datastores directly for the answer.

Sarfal shot off through the leaves. The aliens started to demarcate areas on their tactical display that they would search. Sarfal claimed a radial section as they had, but extended the area out to a much greater distance.

Sarfal decided to zigzag along the widening search zone. Sarfal periodically swooped up over the canopy to scan all around, just in case the target building commanded a clearing large enough to see from above.

Sarfal had plunged back into the vines to resume the low-level search when a net beast tried to hurl itself over Sarfal from its perch across two thick vines. Its clumsy, slow fall was easy to avoid with a burst from Sarfal's thrust tool. Sarfal darted on through underneath the thing, then gained altitude and watched it from above. It was nothing special; just a creature native to the homeworld as Sarfal had seen many times before.

Should I let the Rootpounders know? Maybe they care.

Sarfal marked the creature's location on the map and continued searching. The map queried back asking for a danger level.

The danger is contingent upon not knowing it's there! So do I mark it highest or lowest? Oh, but I'm thinking about its danger to a Thrasar.

Sarfal did not know if the living nets were dangerous to the Rootpounders. If it fell on one of those aliens, who would win? Sarfal responded with the maximum threat level.

"[Danger leaps from under the leaf!] Should we abort the mission, Sarfal?" asked Strongjumper.

"[This vine is safe enough] I don't know if the living net is dangerous to you so I marked it so. I don't want to stop playing."

"[I will show you the sap] This threat level is appropriate, then," said Strongjumper as it set the level to a lower setting. Sarfal took note of the new setting. "The highest level would be used if many Screamers had arrived and were hunting us down. Then we'd abort the mission and run away."

So even Rootpounders fly away sometimes! Or... plod away on those extremities.

Sarfal finished the large section and claimed more area beyond the aliens' search zones. One high flight showed a clearing in an adjacent zone, so Sarfal zipped toward it. As soon as a building became visible, nested within the clearing, Sarfal put it on the map.

"[Danger might lurk beneath the leaves] Can you see a safe route there?" asked Strongjumper. Sarfal felt it must be a test. The Rootpounders were already exploring the vines blindly, what difference would it make to change directions toward the building?

Sarfal flew lower, dropping below the canopy near the single building. The structure did not look like a Thrasar construct. It was like the side of a huge cylinder that broke the surface. Sarfal did not spot any hatches or windows on the top. Sarfal stayed away from it. Once below the topmost leaves, Sarfal darted gracefully among the vines, headed toward the nearest Rootpounder, who was Grimfighter.

"[The vines are safe, the star is bright] Converge on Grimfighter and then follow this path," sent Sarfal.

A silver vine glinted among the green. Sarfal realized the Rootpounder computers had placed dangers within the jungle to be avoided. It made sense for a training exercise. Sarfal marked the location of the new predator on the map.

"[Danger under these leaves] This one may electrocute you, though I think your suits would protect you," Sarfal said. Sarfal altered the suggested path on the shared map to guide the Rootpounders around the creature, then flew toward Grimfighter. Soon the hefty Rootpounder became visible on a vine ahead. It was still scary to see a ground creature balancing atop a vine where it did not belong.

"[Meeting for a task on a bright day] I've rendezvoused with Sarfal. We can group up here," Grimfighter said.

Sarfal darted about the broad leaves while the slow Rootpounders gathered. Sarfal wondered if the Rootpounders would allow time for a quick slurp of sap from the vine before continuing. Sarfal decided not to try. The other Rootpounders converged on the tactical until they were all perched in their odd way upon a major vine branch.

"[Ready to taste the sap] Lead on," Strongjumper told Sarfal. Sarfal flew off toward the alien building. Three times Sarfal stopped to play and wait for the others to catch up. When the team finally approached the building, Sarfal tried to scan the inside with a baton. Nothing happened.

The Rootpounder machine doesn't understand the baton. It cannot provide an accurate result in the simulation. I'll have to ask them to adjust... after this game is over.

"[Alert on the vine] We're going to check it out. Stick close and stay sharp," Strongjumper announced sharply.

Sarfal flitted down near a big vine at the edge of the clearing. There, Sarfal settled in behind a leaf.

Hiding behind a leaf like a predator. Am I a predator, now? On a team of Rootpounders!

The rest of the team ran out toward the building. Their flying spheres zoomed around the building gracefully. Sarfal saw a square gate open on the side of the building, then a machine walked out. It looked disturbingly like a metal Rootpounder. Sarfal recoiled at the ugliness of the ground creatures all over again.

"[From under a leaf!] Security machines! Grimfighter, to the deck and cover their retreat," Strongjumper ordered as it leaped upward onto the building almost as if it could fly.

Sarfal felt sharp vibrations hitting the vines from the air. Sparks flew near the building. Patches of light filtered through the leaves and struck Sarfal's skin, causing round bumps to form on the lit areas. The convex blisters focused the light onto Sarfal's photosensitive skin layer so the Thrasar could perceive images of the action. The Rootpounders had destroyed one machine, but they still fired. Perhaps another machine had exited from the other side? Strongjumper had disappeared from the top of the building.

What purpose do I serve on this team? Do I have to kill a machine?

Sarfal launched into the sky with a strong boost from a baton. Two more enemy machines immediately became visible. One of them targeted Sarfal with a long projectile launcher.

Sarfal took evasive action. The projectiles arced toward Sarfal, but the distance was too great. Sarfal darted about in tight maneuvers, avoiding the fire. Having a long, thin body helped to avoid danger by minimizing profile area.

They are so slow!

Sarfal was having fun until the end. Strongjumper attacked the machines one by one while they tracked Sarfal's antics in the sky. Suddenly, a burst of energy quickly heated Sarfal to ignition. There was no pain, as Sarfal had configured the virtual interface differently from the Rootpounders'. Either Sarfal had misunderstood, or the aliens felt pain when injury occurred in the game. It seemed unreasonable.

Sarfal emerged from the simulation, feeling silly for being hit. There was little chance of dodging an energy weapon.

Most of the Rootpounders had projectile tools, but they also use energy to destroy. The same with these machines, I suppose.

Soon after Sarfal had emerged, the rest of the team secured the building and exited the simulation. Sarfal supposed they must have obtained victory.

"[Light on the vines!] Well played," Tallflyer said.

"[Dark days and barren vines] It was bad? I did not survive," Sarfal said.

"[The star rises soon] We learned a lot and you did well before the end," said Tallflyer. "Does your kind feel pain with injury? Your death must have hurt."

"[An imagined danger under the leaves] Injury does hurt us, but why would it hurt in the fake world?"

"[A responsibility to care for the vine] We train with real pain so that it prepares us for injury in real life," explained Strongjumper. "We learn to deal with it and not fear it. Also, it forces us to act in the training exercise as we would in real life. We can't take it lightly, we won't take risks we wouldn't take in real life."

"[Getting more starlight for a vine already lit] Fear of injury is optimal! I avoid pain whenever possible. I promise I'll minimize risk in real life without more practice."

A couple of the Rootpounders emitted their loud grunting noise. Sarfal felt it through long fingers wrapped around a hanging rod the aliens had installed in the room.

Despite the assurance given to the aliens, Sarfal did consider they might have a terrible, sickening point: The more accurately the training world reflected the real one, the more applicable the lessons learned in the virtual would be to reality.

"[The sap might be edible] Well just consider it, then," Strongjumper said.

"[Slowly among dark leaves] I'll try to learn from that mistake," Sarfal offered.

"[This vine could get more starlight] You fly alone. We could cooperate more closely," said their leader, Strongjumper. "We could stay close and protect each other."

"[Some leaves look healthy but are not] I disagree," said Palethinker. "Sarfal has strengths for scouting and skirmishing we don't have. It's good for each of us to go with our individual skills and advantages."

Sarfal wondered if the Rootpounders would fall upon each other in violence to settle the disagreement.

Dare I speak?

"[Direct a long vine to a new place] Each creature drinks from the vine in its own way," agreed Sarfal carefully.

"[Thinking in warm starlight] It's a start," the leader said. "Still, we need to work as a team. What if we go to a place very different from a vine forest? Sarfal might well need to operate more like us in certain circumstances and environments."

"[Heavy and slow in the debris, under the leaves] It's new to have aliens on my side," Sarfal admitted. "[Among wilted stems, still do not despair] I'll learn to play it correctly. I'll hide among the leaves when deadly tools come out."

"[More sap for tomorrow] Let's talk about it more once we understand each other better," Strongjumper said, then walked out on its two giant legs. Grimfighter and Palethinker followed the other out of Sarfal's quarters.

Shortflyer and Tallflyer stayed behind. Sarfal wondered if they were friendlier since they had played with the Thrasar using their fake wings. Shortflyer walked closer and asked a question.

"[Where does that vine go?] So you brought the vines here with you from your home planet? You have a symbiotic relationship with them. You use them for food and... for reproduction?"

Sarfal tried to guess at its purpose. Did it simply want to know how more Thrasar were made, as the other one had?

"[Bright day, rich vines] We brought them here. After the rain, when the vine seeds drop into the pitchers, we produce cells and put them into the vine," Sarfal said.

"[Is there something new on these vines?] When does it happen? You wait for the rain?"

"[Few flit among the vines in lonely times] We will not make children until we are safe from Screamers."

"[Hope for a star rising] I hope that will be soon," Shortflyer said.

"[A dark storm on the horizon] When the time comes for you, will you inject or... will the young devour you from within?" asked Sarfal.

"[Among friends on a bright day] I think you misunderstand. I am the kind who injects, but the other kind simply houses our larvae, but is not harmed... much."

"[Lost on a bright day] Your hosts can survive it? Oh, that's good to know. Our children rupture the vines when they escape!" Sarfal supposed the aliens must inject each other in one of their four limbs so that the damage could be minimized.

"[Finding a new vine on a bright day] We don't have to do it that way anymore," Tallflyer said. "We were wondering about the vines because we visited a space station with your type of houses floating inside it, but there were no vines."

"[Longing for the sap] There were some of us who left the vines and replaced them to live in space alone. Not all Thrasar societies are like ours."

"[Sharing a bright vine] We have different societies as well. By the way, have you met the aliens that look like a black plant with tiny leaves? They're about our size... well, less massive, but I mean about as tall and wide."

"[Strangers on the vines!] I've heard about them. But they don't play, and they don't talk. They hide, and they take things to build with. We feel sorry for them, as they're easily frightened, but they can't fly away. We leave them alone as they wish."

Another Rootpounder created a connection to Sarfal, Tallflyer, and Shortflyer.

"[Concern for the vine] Hi guys. Looks like the VR runner encountered some errors interfacing with Sarfal. We need to work out some purple paste, looks like," Shypilot said.

"[A known problem with a familiar vine] I can help work it out," Sarfal said. "I had a device your machine did not understand. It could not simulate the effects of its use."

"[The star falls in the sky] Then we'll leave you to that and see you later," Tallflyer said.

"[Departing a favorite vine] Come back soon! I like to fly often," Sarfal said.

"[Tasting good sap] We will."

***

Shypilot came to Sarfal's quarters one day and asked to talk. Sarfal flitted about the room, happy to have company. The Rootpounders liked to talk more than they liked to play, but Sarfal had few alternatives.

This one will not fly with me.

"[void] I have studied the information from the battle. I found an anomaly. Perhaps we can use it to our advantage."

The Rootpounder had remained cold, as when they first arrived. It sounded scary, some kind of cruel robot planning the death of the Screamers. At least it did not want to kill Thrasar!

"[Study a leaf carefully to know it] Perhaps we can."

"[void] Here is what I found." The Rootpounder shared some information in their computers with Sarfal. Sarfal had a summarizer ingest it and point out the salient features. It looked like Shypilot wanted Sarfal to know that one of the Screamer ships was different.

"[void] This ship could have biologicals in it. Maybe the creators of the Screamers are in here, in liquid, and they watch or direct their machines in the fight."

"[Danger awaits under each leaf!] The Screamers were made by these evil ones. This ship could make the Screamers go away?"

"[void] We have two ideas. One, the ship could be captured. We could speak to the masters of the Screamers and make friends with them, or, failing that, we could get them to call off their machines."

That seemed like an intriguing plan to Sarfal. Still, it seemed doubtful such dangerous creatures would want to make peace. Shypilot continued.

"[void] Second, we could break it into small pieces. Then the Screamer fleet would not hurt us as much. They might become dumber, or less focused."

"[An Underleafer trick can be turned upon itself] If that ship controls the Screamers, maybe we can learn how to control them too, or at least make them fly away. You sound very mean."

"[void] What? But they're trying to kill you!"

"[Calm day] I meant how you say it."

"[void] Oh! I'm sorry. I guess I've been too busy. I had... uhm, I froze some software in place while running experiments, so I didn't get the translator update."

"[Relax and taste the sap] Then become idle."

"[An offer to share the sap on a bright day] Is this

better? I'm sorry I didn't update my translator."

"[Bright day! Sweet sap!] Yes!"

"[A clever path to a new vine] Do the Thrasar know how to capture a ship? Can you trap it with a gravity spinner? Or freeze it in a field? Maybe the same way you took your probe ship home."

"[Some are skilled folding the leaves] There are ways. Some know them. One up in space knows."

Shypilot started to answer, then froze for a moment. Sarfal flew around it in a circle to wait.

"[Star rising on the horizon] Do you see it? We've arrived," Shypilot said.

"[Fresh vines, new leaves, growing pitchers] Maybe we can hide here until the Screamers come again."

Sarfal received information from the alien ship. No permission was necessary to see it, so Sarfal let a summarizer analyze the data to see what it all meant. The Rootpounder ship dimly saw the alien planet. Sarfal learned there were three points on the surface where a probe ship had constructed facilities for a new colony, including a factory yard!

The planet was covered in beautiful, healthy vines. *Maybe we could live here!*

"[Hope for strong starlight] Maybe they won't follow us here," said Shypilot.

Michael McCloskey

Chapter 11

Magnus gazed out across the flat surface that surrounded the Celaran facilities. The newcomers had been immediately accepted by the security forces that the PIT team had previously struggled with. Siobhan and Telisa had told him that the entire facility had been put to use producing small spacecraft, building new security robots, and bolstering defenses.

We need a real Vovokan ship with large-scale manufacturing capability like the Clacker had. The Celarans are advanced, but those capital ships of Shiny's are enormous factory-fortresses.

Agrawal stood next to him, watching the Celarans fly about with each other and their robots. Grant and Timon wandered about nearby. Agrawal seemed to adapt to fluid situations much better than the robot handlers, Grant and Timon, who remained fish out of water.

"Siobhan is working with the Celarans," Magnus said. "Whatever production they can spare down here will go to us. She's going to have them producing flying combat machines, but we can special order some things and see what happens."

"So we need to figure out what to make," Agrawal said. "And we need to keep in mind we only have two handlers—or four, if we pitch in."

"Exactly," Magnus said. "The team is working on Destroyer weaknesses. In the meantime, we can start with what took out the Storks."

"High energy weapons," Agrawal said. "The alien assault machines didn't launch any kinetic weapons on the ground. The initial missile wave came from starships. I heard they tried to divert small asteroids and the like toward the colony, but the Celaran space bases were able to prevent any serious impacts."

"I heard about that, too, but we're not sure if they really meant for anything big to hit the ground, or if it was just a distraction. Seems like the Destroyers aren't willing to truly obliterate these planets from orbit. They probably want the planets relatively intact for themselves."

"Yes, though they are willing to kill off the vine ecosystem," Agrawal offered.

"Anyway, since they use energy weapons almost exclusively, the kinetic armor on the Storks was wasted," Magnus said, steering back on topic. "We could replace it with reflective armor or energy diffusion systems. Still, I don't think we want to spend resources trying to bulk up our last five Storks or eleven PIT soldier bots."

"Agreed. Let's start from their weaknesses, not ours," Agrawal suggested. "Our Storks did relatively well against their drones but couldn't hurt the tanks or colossals. The Celaran trapdoor lasers did well against the drones, too. Even small arms fire can take the drones out—not that we have enough people or machines left to launch projectiles."

"What I'm hearing is that we need something to destroy the larger ones," Magnus said. "And that unless we're shooting from a starship, we can't kill them with energy weapons."

Agrawal nodded. "We need cannons. And direct fire, not indirect, as the Destroyers had good sensor coverage and were able to intercept incoming dangers above the canopy. Lower, though, the rounds came in through the vine cover and weren't stopped in time."

"Excellent. Kinetic attacks, down low. Sounds more like we want mines rather than cannons? And I hope that a simple mine design that launches a guided projectile upward could be mass-produced by the Celarans."

"Ah, mines. The kinetic equivalent of the trapdoor lasers. I like it," Agrawal said. "Very little need for handlers with such devices. We bury them, I assume?"

"We could, or we could design them all to look like a native plant, one of those creepy things that grows down along the jungle floor below the vines. Burying them might be safer. If the Destroyers catch on, dumb as they're supposed to be, we'd be finished."

Magnus knew that Terrans no longer made metallic mines due to the ease with which they could be detected. Modern UNSF mines were made of materials that looked organic in scans. The mines could be connected to sensors placed above the surface or operate with their own passive sensors, and like the smart weapons the PIT team employed, they would accept fire and no-fire target sig lists to keep friendlies from being hurt.

"I have a catalog of designs we could send to your friend Siobhan right away," Agrawal said. "The LAAV-killer series, for instance. They fire a single spike of ceramic to penetrate the hull of low altitude armored craft. They also have an EMP equivalent."

"EM pulses. Hrm," Magnus said. He opened a channel with Agrawal and added Marcant to it.

"Yes, Magnus?" Marcant responded.

"I'm going to have Agrawal send over a design of one of the Space Force's EMP mines," Magnus said. "Can... Achaius? Is that the name? Can Achaius tell us if the tanks could be harmed by that weapon system?"

Michael McCloskey

"Tanks? Oh, the MTACs," Marcant said.

"What's your acronym?" Agrawal asked.

"Middle tier assault carriers," Marcant said.

"I'll stick with tanks," Magnus said. "Please let me know when you have an answer—"

"Achaius says that system would not do permanent damage by itself, but suggests a tactic involving its use," Marcant said.

Wow, fast response.

"Really?"

"If you coordinate a kinetic attack together with the pulse, at the right timing, the EMP mine could greatly increase the effectiveness of the kinetic attack. This kind of clever combined arms approach is how the Vovokan battle spheres managed to do so much damage against the Destroyer tanks."

"Well, things might be looking up," Magnus said to Agrawal off the channel.

"We could pair that design with a ceramic spike mine," Magnus said. "If Achaius can provide us with the desired timing? Not sure what the variables might be. Altitude of the target?"

"We'll send you a suggestion within the hour," Marcant said. "Could we have the design of a spike mine as well? I take it we have a few of these sitting around in a cargo hold somewhere."

Magnus nodded to Agrawal. The Space Force man sent more designs.

"Siobhan will coordinate their manufacture with our Celaran friends, if you can advise us on an effective solution," Magnus said.

"We'll do our best," Marcant said. Magnus could not

tell anything about Marcant's disposition, so he did not worry about it after closing the channel.

"We need to get a best guess as to how many we can get, and how fast we can get them, then make a deployment plan," Agrawal said.

Magnus nodded. "We don't know how long until the Destroyers come to this place, though it seems likely they will."

Magnus turned to scan the forest beyond the fence as if looking for the Destroyers already.

"Why the fence? Dangerous things out there?" asked Agrawal.

"A few wild creatures. A thing that looks like a net and tries to drop down over you, and a silvery worm-creature that can electrocute you," Magnus said. "I have the target sigs for you and the handlers just in case..."

Magnus went off-retina and searched through the sigs he had collected.

"There's also an alien race we call the Blackvines," Magnus said. "So far we've found that they aren't social, but not hostile either. Close to harmless. I meant to ask the Celarans about them, but I guess we've been busy trying to survive."

Magnus added the Blackvine target sig to the others and shared them with Agrawal.

"The Celarans are building another perimeter a half kilometer out. There won't be a fence, but more of the force towers. There will also be a network of sensors that can detect the Destroyers if they approach."

"That'll be easy," Agrawal said. He scratched the dense stubble on his dark chin. "All that light and wind."

Magnus's link received a high priority message alert.

It was Cilreth.

"The Destroyers followed us here," she sent to the team channel.

Magnus and Agrawal traded concerned looks.

"Already? In what numbers?" Magnus asked.

"Well, it's just the last squadron, the one they held in reserve. They arrived at this system a few hours ago. They headed for this planet, then changed course and moved away."

"We're just now learning this?" Caden demanded.

"The Celarans have just informed me," Cilreth said.

"They didn't fight?"

"The Celarans haven't been engaged. The unique ship we spotted came in and landed on this planet."

"Five Entities! Give us its course," Telisa demanded.

"It landed in the largest ocean, here," Cilreth said, sending a pointer. The oceans on Idrick Piper were smaller than Earth's oceans, covering about fifty percent of the planet. The body of water Cilreth indicated had a shore 3000 kilometers from the Celaran manufacturing base where the PIT team worked.

"It must be a big assault craft," Magnus suggested.

"It's a different design. It's not like the ones that've been hitting us."

"The scary part is, it's in the ocean," Siobhan said. "You get it? They're aquatic. That's their home territory, even if it's an alien ocean. If they evolved on a planet about this far from a star, covered in a lot of water, how different could it be?"

"So they have a presence on the planet now, and we can't exactly go pay them a visit," Magnus said. "This will be a problem."

"Telisa, it could be a colonizer ship," Caden said.

"That might not be so bad in the short term," Cilreth said. "They could only live in the ocean, right?"

"It could be a Von Neumann type of factory seed," Siobhan said. "If we let it bootstrap an economy here, it might be impossible to stop."

"If only we had known, we could have tried to intercept it," Telisa said. "Now we have to find it and destroy it."

"How would we destroy it?" Caden asked.

"Well, our spacecraft can go into the water, though not very deep," Telisa said.

Agrawal shook his head but did not say anything on the channel. Magnus agreed with the sentiment. Using starships as submarine assault vehicles did not sound good to him.

"Sounds too risky," Magnus said. "Only very specialized starships—"

"Only specialized *Terran* vessels, yes, but the Celaran starships may be as super-versatile as everything else they build," Telisa said. "We'll figure something out. We have control of local space... surely that can be used to our advantage."

"You said just the Destroyer ship landed. What about the rest of the squadron?"

"Still in-system, but maintaining extreme range. Keeping tabs on us, I suppose. The Celarans are watching them, but they won't go looking for a fight."

"Then that's another timer we're on. The Destroyers may ask for reinforcements from other systems."

Chapter 12

"Perhaps the star will rise to bring a bright day, and we'll discover the Destroyers have gone to live in peace under the vast waters," said Lee.

Siobhan stood next to the alien who hovered in the old ship's mess. Siobhan wanted to work out a robot design with Lee around to comment on it before sending the request off to the other Celarans for production. Caden hovered nearby, visiting Siobhan on a break from his own duties.

"That ship's a threat. Trust me," Siobhan said. "Even if it was just a colony module, like whatever you drop from the probe ship to start these buildings. They're hiding in their native environment, more or less. I'm sure that this ocean has a somewhat different composition than they have on their home planet, but it's similar enough, or they wouldn't have gone there."

"Vines to be snipped and drained, why do the Destroyers send their machines to stop our lives?" asked Lee.

"I don't have the complete answer," Siobhan said. "It may be that they feel a fear that can only be quelled by removing us from the universe. Or it may be how they survived to this point, by actively seeking out and destroying competition."

"There's one more possibility we know of," Caden said. He looked at Siobhan.

He wants to mention the Vovokans. I guess I don't feel like stopping him.

"It may be that the Destroyers were not like this at first. We think they made friends with the Vovokans. A group of the Vovokans may have attacked them to get something they wanted, and that made the Destroyers think they needed to fight to survive. We heard they might treat all aliens the same now, treat them all as very dangerous."

"The leaf has been turned over, I know now that not all aliens are dangerous," Lee said.

"Let's take a look at some designs for a flying weapon," Siobhan said. "You have the disk design already, which helped a lot."

"Vines so twisted they cannot be followed," Lee preambled. "We have tools that take things apart, but these... tools that take things apart that do not want to be taken apart, things that try to take you apart at the same time. It's scary that you have compact terms for these things."

"I'm sorry Lee. We just want to help. Do you know that?" Siobhan said.

"Starlight on the leaves, thank you for saving us."

Siobhan almost returned to the design concepts when Lee continued.

"The remains of old vines kept alive in memory, there were some among us who contemplated these things when the Destroyers first attacked. I don't know what became of them."

"Some Celarans fought back?" Caden said. "I thought you had only scientists to devise means of resisting the Destroyers."

"Olds vines almost forgotten, a few of us could do these things... though maybe not as well as you do. Many were scientists who researched new tools to stop the attacks. We have not heard from them for a long time.

Perhaps you should ask another."

"We will, thanks," Siobhan said. She tagged the conversation and forwarded it to Telisa for review.

"Here's the design of your disk machines," Siobhan said. She shared her PV with Lee. A schematic of the disk machine appeared. "You used them as missiles in the last battle, damaging the largest Destroyers by hitting those machines at top speed. They were highly effective."

"A predator threatens a friend on the vine, we acted in desperation and lost our machines."

"I see two avenues for improvement: one, you could stick with self-destructing devices, but we can alter these disks to break up and deliver multiple kinetic warheads, if you will, instead of just the disk body. The frame can be shaped to split just before impact, spreading the damage inflicted across a wider area. We could still get good penetration if we need it by putting tungsten spikes into them. Also, a higher capacity storage ring might mean there would still be energy left over at impact, so once the ring is shattered, the remaining energy would be released, causing even more damage."

"I like it," Caden said. "Previously, you just rammed these sophisticated, multipurpose robots into the Destroyers. But if they were designed with this in mind from the beginning, they would be much more effective at delivering damage."

"Many different things must be done on a bright day, if the robots are designed simply to die, how can they be useful in other ways?"

"Ah, yes, I recall it's not your way to design things with one goal in mind. However, in this case, let me try and convince you it's worthwhile. Survival is of the utmost importance. Weapons are best designed as weapons and little else. You have to maximize their effectiveness because... nothing else is important if you're dead."

"A path found through the vines, I think I see your point, but with such limited resources, we may need to make efficient use of them, which means giving the machines many functions."

"Hrm. I was afraid of that," Siobhan sent to Caden privately. "She wants to add a lot of functions, but they'll end up with reduced combat effectiveness."

"Their way is not necessarily wrong," Caden said. "By giving the machines a lot of capabilities and abilities, they can use them for a lot of different work, improving the efficiency of the whole colony... and economic strength will translate into military strength, in the long run."

"Yes, if we survive to see the long run, I guess maybe that's so," Siobhan said to Caden. She switched back to the shared channel.

"Lee, what if we made the disks' cargo capacity flexible so they could carry food and move things around for you until it's time for battle, then we swap in warheads and make the disks one-shot weapons? Then you can use them for other tasks until the attack comes."

"What's the other route?" said a happy voice.

Siobhan did a double-take. It was Lee who had spoken.

"Fracksilvers!" Siobhan burst out. "Marcant updated the translators again. Your preamble became... a tone of voice."

"Is something wrong?" asked Lee innocently, gliding in a wide circle around them and flashing brightly. Lee's voice sounded airy.

It sounds like the voice of someone... not so intelligent and without a care. Could that be accurate, or does it reflect Marcant's assessment of them?

Siobhan accepted it as an improvement over the preambles. Strictly speaking, hearing the emotional content in the delivery of the main statement made more sense for Terrans, even though Siobhan thought she had been getting the hang of interpreting the mood through the preambles.

They're aliens. There's no way to be sure.

"The other route would be to try and preserve the machines. We would equip them with missile mounts. The machines would launch the missiles from under the canopy near the enemy, and then retreat, live to fight another day. We could also stockpile missiles out in the jungle, the disks could fly back, rearm, and attack again. Of course, we would take some losses, but each machine would have some chance of surviving each run."

"That sounds much better," Lee said. "We can keep our current design. It does many things for us."

Lee's voice sounded like an enthusiastic teenager.

"Like how many things?" Siobhan asked.

"It's hard to categorize. Hundreds of things."

"We could make the missiles as resistant to the Destroyer's beams as possible," Caden added.

Siobhan felt a little disappointed. They already had a million designs for missiles. There would be no brand-new flying machine.

My desire to be creative doesn't outweigh their need to survive, she reminded herself.

"Now that you've settled on a strategy for the machines, can we ask you if more Celarans would like to learn how to use weapons?" asked Caden. "We could make a weapon baton, or you could train to be robot handlers."

"We would die!" Lee squealed. "The machines are too fast, too powerful. Only other machines could beat them."

"Well, mostly I agree. But the Destroyers don't have intelligence at our level. Probably because that might make them dangerous to the creators. So if your machines are controlled by Celarans, you might be able to adopt flexible tactics that could leave the Destroyers at a disadvantage. That's what our 'friend' Shiny did."

"First we should ask how smart your robots are," Siobhan said, looking at Caden. "Do you use AIs?"

"We usually don't make machines that smart," Lee said. "But other Celarans did. We don't know where they are anymore. Our machines are only intelligent enough to recognize the environment and the objects they need to manipulate, and complete their tasks. Anything unknown is handled like a foreign body that should be studied, then ejected from our domain. The information is sent to us. The machines aren't curious like we are."

"Then if you'd be willing to create bunkers beneath your colony, you could shelter there and remain close enough to get commands to the disk machines through Destroyer interference," Caden said.

"The Celarans have no equipment for digging bunkers," Siobhan said. "And we don't know how much time we have."

"Counter proposal?" Caden asked.

"A distributed control system already exists," Lee said. Siobhan and Caden turned surprised faces toward Lee. "In our primitive state, we used to transmit vibrations along the vines. It was like a collaborative form of distributed music. So when we started to genetically manipulate the vines, it felt natural to turn them into an advanced communication system."

"So you can flee into the forest and still control the robots?" Siobhan asked.

"I hope so! The Destroyers don't recognize us when we fly among the other gliders of the forest."

"The Destroyers have already shown a reluctance to destroy these planets," Caden said. "I think the creators of these machines like the same kinds of planets that we do—temperate zone, water-bearing planets of about this size."

"Well, the Destroyers may not kill all the Celarans who flee into the forest," Siobhan said, "But in the long run that leaves them helpless. If the ones who control the Destroyers come, they'd discover the Celarans out there and modify the Destroyers to go finish the job."

"Then we must win," Caden said firmly. "An overall strategy is emerging. Magnus and Marcant have made some progress: Our lighter weapons and robots can handle the drones. They have plans for newer, deadlier mines to kill the tanks, and we'll use our new Celaran disk flyers to kill the colossals. The Vovokan battle spheres are our reserve."

"Caden, can you coordinate with Magnus and Marcant and see if we can select a missile design that we think can make it from a launch point under the vine canopy into the colossals? Something to take the place of the disk kamikazes."

"Yes? Sure."

The question was implied. *What are you going to do?*

"We haven't integrated the vine network with our own

links and the Vovokan attendants. I want to look into that and coordinate feeding them designs to be built. Then there are the logistics of getting them to Magnus..."

"Okay, sounds like a lot of work. I'm also getting together a group of Celarans for VR trials like we did with Lee. We'll make them into combat robot handlers yet."

"See if you can turn it into a game. They like to play a lot," Siobhan sent Caden privately.

"Yes, I get the feeling their machines have been providing for them a long time. I think they're not used to having to do anything *but* play all day long," he confided.

"Not that different than Core Worlders, really," Siobhan said.

"Core Worlders like to play? Can we meet them?" asked Lee.

Frackedpackets.

"You can hear us on this channel?" asked Caden on the private connection.

"Yes!" Lee said cheerfully. "Isn't that what the channels are for?"

Siobhan smiled. "Maybe we should send a heads up to Telisa about the... communications glitch," she said.

Caden nodded.

Chapter 13

Telisa walked with Siobhan and Cilreth outside the perimeter of the Celaran industrial compound. No Celarans could be seen, though a few of their disk robots flew about. The jungle was quiet, but Telisa remained alert. Her attendants spread out to help keep her and her friends safe.

Of the three Celaran sites the PIT team had discovered on Idrick Piper, they had decided to defend only the industrial site. Most of the Celarans lived in the small town and would flee into the jungle if an attack came. The tower site with the packaged food was for supplying new starships; the Celarans had already resupplied their ships with its contents and set it to collecting more. Therefore the industrial site was the least expendable.

It had been a busy week since their arrival here. A second perimeter of force towers had been erected by Celaran robots. Magnus and Agrawal had placed a hundred smart mines between the two fence lines. Since no one knew which direction a land attack might come from, they held another hundred of the new weapons in reserve. The self-directed mines sat on the edge of the hardtop likes rows of silver bugs ready to respond to an attack by interposing themselves between the attackers and the base. Though slow, the mines could walk or roll themselves to a target zone and dig into the jungle soil.

"None of our men are here," Cilreth pointed out.

"Just the girls today, I guess," Siobhan said.

"Good. We seldom get to talk," Telisa said. She led the way across two support spikes atop a vine as thick as her torso. Picking the way through the vine jungle had

147

become second nature to her.

"Well now that it's just us, I have a dumb question," Cilreth said. She wobbled a bit on the vine, reminding Telisa that Cilreth had spent the least amount of time out here. In fact, Cilreth had probably spent four times the hours climbing virtual vines than real ones.

"Shoot," Telisa said.

"How come you and Magnus never get in fights?"

The question caught Telisa totally by surprise.

"Well, I... uhm..."

Siobhan and Cilreth laughed.

"What?!"

"You don't lose your tongue often," Siobhan teased.

"Magnus and I see things the same way, most of the time," Telisa said, exploring the question. "But you know what? I just realized, he doesn't have an ego to get in the way. He lets me call the shots, doesn't he?"

Telisa remembered a time when Magnus had guided her. He had been her mentor. But since Shiny had put Telisa in charge, Magnus deferred to her judgement.

Is that because of his time in the Space Force? Rank means something to him.

Telisa frowned. She had not thought of their relationship that way.

"A few arguments are healthy for the relationship," Siobhan said.

"Well, I never see you and Caden arguing," Telisa said.

"They're too busy pawing each other," Cilreth interjected.

Siobhan ignored the side comment. "We do fight! But it's always about minor dumb stuff, never about the important things. Never about the mission."

The mission. Caden and Siobhan are fanatic PIT members.

"I want to talk about the big picture," said Telisa.

"I don't even know what that means anymore," Siobhan said.

"Exactly," Telisa said. "How did we become soldiers? We're supposed to be explorers—looters at worst." She paused to look for clues of their destination. Seeing none, she gave up and checked her link map instead. She adjusted her mental course a few degrees to the left.

"We'll get back to it. Not our fault the Destroyers are out there," Cilreth said.

"I hope we do get back to it soon," Telisa said. "What else is blocking us from resuming the real mission?"

"What about Imanol's death?" Siobhan asked.

Yet another thing I'm not supposed to be doing out here. Judging people's character, deciding their fates.

"I believe in my bones it was an accident. And that'll have to do," Telisa said. Cilreth seemed to accept the answer. Telisa felt relief.

I care a lot about her opinion.

"The Destroyers and Shiny are in our way. But at least you got Magnus back. We might be able to ignore Shiny. Earth doesn't *want* saving," Cilreth said.

Telisa saw the destination ahead. She doubted the others noticed it, as it was mostly hidden by masses of the huge vine leaves. She found a thick vine leading downward and led the party into a cleared area. As they passed one last wall of vegetation, the others took notice.

"What's this?" asked Siobhan, clearly excited. She jumped down from the vine and loped toward the opening.

Several Celaran machines worked in the clearing, grinding away at vine roots with long arms that ended in spiked rollers. Two others each carried away a support spike that had been uprooted. Telisa saw that one-third of the spike's length had been hidden below ground. The spike continued to widen along the same curve once under the ground, making the buried base by far the thickest part.

Cilreth remained calm. "We're setting up another building here?" she guessed.

"Yes. The Celarans are making more factories. This one will be ours," Telisa said, watching Siobhan.

"Ours! That's great! We have a lot of things to make," Siobhan said. "The capacity of a Celaran factory this large will dwarf what we can make on the *Iridar*!"

The Celarans had been diverting resources from their towers and starships to build the mines that defended the industrial yard. Siobhan had set up the *Iridar* to build the missiles for the Celaran disk robots, but the Vovokan ship's fabrication facilities were meant for making spare parts and fashioning a few unique items for missions. It had never been designed as a real factory ship.

Telisa sent Siobhan a pointer to the plans.

"Here's what they're putting up. Of course, once the machines finish and they hand it over, you'll be in charge here. You can make any modifications you like. Unfortunately, we still need to focus on weapons and defense systems for now..."

Siobhan set off on a run of the perimeter. She bounced energetically and talked to herself. Telisa felt like a mother handing out presents on Awakening Day.

Telisa smiled at Cilreth, then her link received an early warning message: *attack incoming*.

"Defensive positions, opposite side cover!" Telisa barked.

The three Terrans sprinted for the jungle bordering the new work zone. Telisa felt proud at the speed of their reaction. The pride evaporated as she realized she had only her smart pistol and tanto knife with her. The breaker claw was still with the Celarans.

I need to ask Lee for my breaker claw back. I hope she was able to duplicate it, or at least scan enough that they don't need to hold it any longer while they work on making more.

Telisa took stock of their other weaponry as the group formed up around an intact support spike. Siobhan had a laser pistol, two grenades, and her ever-present stun baton. Cilreth had only a pistol. Telisa's attendants returned to orbit around her, ready to deflect attacks.

"We don't have much here, but together, we can kill off some of the drones," Telisa told them. "We'll have to rely on the boys and their new toys this time."

"Get me to the *Iridar* and I'll show you some toys," Cilreth said.

Telisa considered the idea. The *Iridar* would pack a punch. On the other hand, did they dare risk their only ship out here on an alien world beyond the frontier?

Yes. We dare.

"Good idea. We'll kill some drones on the way to our *real* firepower."

***

Caden received the attack warning through his link while he worked off-retina to prepare more drills for the

Celarans who had offered to be robot handlers. His pulse accelerated.

Here we are again. Will it be as bad as last time?

He looked at the tactical to learn about the source and size of the attack. A group of Destroyers had been spotted coming from the direction of the ocean. Thus far, the Celarans had not detected any additional threat from enemy ships in the system.

This attack comes from the ocean, not a huge space fleet. It can't be as bad.

He only half-believed his internal assurances. At least Caden knew how to handle adrenaline and nerves. For a moment he wondered who was the best at it: Siobhan *enjoyed* the thrill of danger, Magnus seemed immune to it, and Telisa... she was so fast now that no one could even keep track of her long enough to figure out if she got nervous. For some reason he thought of Arakaki. She had been a soldier with nothing more to lose, absolutely fearless.

Caden created a new channel and connected to his Celaran recruits.

"This is it," he sent out. "Once you're into the forest, connect through with me and we'll launch our attack."

"So strange!" Lee replied. "Predators attack... we run."

"Then think of your machines as the predators," Caden said reasonably. "Today you can experience a different view on life through them."

Lee did not answer, so Caden imagined that the request was a difficult one. The lack of response did at least make Caden believe they would try their best. The machines could operate autonomously if it became necessary.

Caden's designated fallback spot was a clearing out in the vine jungle where the *Iridar* had landed. The ship remained a rendezvous point for the team outside the industrial complex. Caden sprinted out to the edge of the jungle from the compound, then he turned and readied his rifle.

I'll kill some drones from here as they cross the hardtop, then retreat back to the rendezvous point to handle a Celaran disk machine from there.

The idea was not perfect. When Caden checked his tactical, he saw that his position might not provide many opportunities. From the reports, it looked like the Destroyers would be coming from the other side of the complex. His range of fire did not overlap with very many predicted attack paths.

No. Dumb idea. If we wait until they're this far, then we'll take more damage. My force may as well intercept them earlier.

Caden decided he was close enough to the *Iridar* already. He hooked into a Celaran disk from his current position. His PV pane from the disk was silent. He only had a video feed from the machine since Celarans had a very limited sense of hearing, though they could detect very slight vibrations through the vines when hanging from a branch.

"Here we go," he announced on the handler's channel. The channel showed 33 Celaran handlers connected already, of which 23 were currently active with at least one drone under their control.

They can't all be that far out in the jungle already... but I guess they can control a disk and fly to safety at the same time.

"Let's time the first attack to coincide with when the tanks engage the force towers. If some of their firepower is hitting the towers, there will be less for us."

It was only a theory. The Destroyer machines seemed to produce enough energy to simultaneously engage multiple targets. After all, even the Vovokan battle spheres had not been able to overwhelm their defenses for minutes. Still, if any resource bottleneck existed, whether it be energy, emitters, or just targeting attention, Caden felt their best chance would be by combining as much of the Celarans' force together as possible.

He had a route calculated and added to the tactical. Caden's disk moved through the vines at the right speed to arrive for the attack timing he had described. The other handlers had done the same. He let the machine navigate its own way around the numerous obstacles. Its onboard computer was faster than a Terran's brain, so it could more reliably find its way through the clutter. He watched the disk machines collecting at a rendezvous point outside the tower lines to the south. He checked the status of the evacuation. Most of the Celarans were already free of the industrial complex and the hidden settlement.

"We have sightings here," Caden said, referencing a line of enemy tanks that paralleled the edge of the outer Celaran tower line. "Let's hit them one at a time from the south flank and continue north until they're all dead."

The formation of flyers came up over the canopy. His disk flyer accelerated with the others in the squadron.

Boooooooom! Brooooooom!

Booms echoed through the jungle as they group broke the sound barrier, still accelerating. Destroyer energy weapons lanced out, picking off a few. Caden's machine survived.

The formation's incredible speed brought them within range, five kilometers out.

"Fire!" Caden said.

Fooosh.

His machine loosed two of its four missiles at the targeted Destroyer, then told the flyer to arc away and decelerate. Five seconds later, it had bled its speed and dropped below the canopy. It all felt distant to Caden, who knew what it was like to fly through the jungle in person: the rush of acceleration and wind whipping through his hair.

No. This is real. Lives are on the line!

The spotting feeds watched the missile swarm close on the enemy. Unlike his flyer feed, the spotters included a lot of attendant spheres, so Caden had sound on other feeds. Over half of the missiles made it past the defensive fire and struck the target. A plume of smoke rose on a wave of thunder.

Kroooom!

"Oh yeah, that's so slickblack," Caden burst on the channel. "Got one?"

The enemy symbol on the tactical changed to a different icon: target eliminated.

"Yes! Come back around. Let's get the next one. Maybe just one missile each?" Caden suggested. His instinct was that they had overkilled the first. They had only lost a handful of their attack machines. The sounds of battle traveled through the canopy from the tower line.

Krak. Booom! Kraaak.

"The outer force towers are starting to fall," Telisa announced on the team channel. "We're bringing in the

Iridar."

Caden saw a colossal—the only one on the tactical—coming in behind the tanks it had presumably brought with it. An energy beam lanced out from the Destroyer, cutting through a kilometer of jungle and incinerating a Celaran force tower.

Krooooom!

Rather than dig through the many panes of information in his PV, he decided to just ask.

"Magnus, are the reserve mines in position? My squadron may go for the colossal."

"The mines will be there in time. If they work, those Destroyer tanks will never get through. Am I counting these right? There's only one colossal and seven tanks left..."

"Yes. There's only one this time. We have it," Caden said. "You don't need to risk the *Iridar*!"

"I'll take it under advisement," Telisa said. Her voice was level. Caden could not tell if she agreed with the assessment or not.

"Change of plan," Caden told his squadron. "Let the tanks advance to the mines and the inner tower line. We're going after the colossal!"

He plotted a new course for the disk machines that sent them back south so they could loop around and hit the largest Destroyer from the rear.

Caden marked his target on the shared tactical. The group of flying disks turned away from the industrial complex toward the attacker. They remained below the canopy to cover their approach, even though it reduced their speed.

Attack now with half our missiles, or go back for a

reload?

Caden did a quick calculation based on the colossal's speed. If the disks went back for a reload, the largest enemy would be too close. At least some of the buildings would be destroyed, unless the Vovokan battle spheres or the *Iridar* could delay them.

"We'll bulk launch all remaining missiles. If it survives, we'll come back for a full reload," Caden decided on the robot handlers' channel. He had already started second guessing himself.

This would have worked if we had launched a full load of missiles for sure. But now we only have half the missiles left... too much for a tank, but too few for the colossal? We need to learn more so the squadron knows where to hit and how hard.

The Destroyer detected the threat. It unleashed huge beams of energy at the vine jungle, incinerating swaths of vegetation as wide as buildings.

Krooooom!

The group started losing more disk machines. Caden had to push back more doubts. The Celaran robots were almost close enough... they lost another three disks. The whole squadron was at sixty percent of original numerically and still at half-ordnance load.

"Rise and fire," Caden said. The squadron ascended above the canopy as one and fired off their missiles. Trails of smoke marked the departure of the missiles. The Destroyer continued to shoot. Its wide beams took more disks down. Somewhere out of mind, his real body pumped a fist in excitement.

"Survivors, scatter and return to your reload points," Caden commanded mentally. It was an automatic, trained order. Caden's attention was on the missiles and their target. He watched a feed integrated from several sources: towers, disk robots, and attendants. The Destroyer capital machine continued to shoot defensive beams for one more second.

Brooooooooom!

Caden's feed showed the huge explosion as their missiles struck. He heard it from the many audio pickups out in the jungle. A few moments later, the sound came to his real ears. He smiled.

That had to hurt! Was it enough?

He watched for long moments. Smoke obscured the target... but nothing emerged from the cloud. The target dropped from the tactical as sensors in the field verified the kill.

We did it. I didn't waste our entire squadron on a failed attack.

Caden checked the status of the rest of the battle. The last tank had just died to a multi-mine ambush. The Vovokan battle spheres were squashing the drones like bugs wherever they turned up. His exuberance grew.

Victory!

Caden checked the PIT team before he allowed himself to fully celebrate. He saw everyone was alive and well.

"That was too easy!" Caden said. "Our defenses held!"

"Are there any more coming?" Telisa demanded. She was not ready to join him in celebration.

"Top half of the squadron, belay my last order," Caden instructed. "Patrol the entire approach path out to six hundred kilometers. Bottom half, continue toward the reload points." He watched the disks scatter.

If there were more Destroyers coming, they would know soon.

Michael McCloskey

Chapter 14

Marcant went back on-retina and opened his eyes in his quarters on the *Iridar*. Adair's Vovokan attendant sphere hovered nearby. Since his AI friends had taken control of the little attendants, the Vovokan machines' small bodies had stopped their incessant orbiting. Now, they wandered about here and there like lost souls, pausing before anything they found. Achaius's attendant floated into view from behind a support beam.

Possibly a fake structural member, he reminded himself. The Vovokan ship had been given a Terran look and feel by Shiny—or his AI—to make the PIT team feel at home. Marcant had been told that renovation included rubberized decking, shower tubes, and the removal of a great deal of sand.

The PIT team felt more secure after their recent victory, but given their belief that the Destroyers would keep attacking, they had resolved to continue to innovate and build defenses. However, Telisa had confided in Marcant that she valued the chance to parlay a peace treaty. That meant Marcant needed to conquer another alien language.

"You know, instead of being trapped in your clumsy Terran cases—" Marcant began.

"Let's not get reckless," Adair said.

"You know what I'm about to say?"

"You're about to suggest we copy ourselves into those Vovokan battle spheres."

"Well, you could keep your current spheres as backups," Marcant said.

"I don't think I'm ready to start copying myself

161

nanotube over fullerene," Achaius said.

Not ready? That implies a future plan to do so,
Marcant thought.

"Well, you could put yourself in there, and then put
your original into stasis, download updates now and
then—"

"The new me would think of itself as me and wouldn't
much care to ever switch back," Adair said.

"Okay, I won't get into the copy debate with you. Just
saying, if it's good enough for Trilisks—"

"I think the Trilisks understood the nature of
consciousness," Adair said. "Or maybe they just didn't
care. I'll take a pass for now."

"What have you discovered?" asked Achaius,
changing the subject. "Or have you come to a conclusion
of some sort?"

*It knows I came on-retina because I've made a
discovery. Is it any wonder I find conversations with
ordinary people cumbersome?*

Marcant took a long sip of his glucose drink.

"The attendants we sent out into the ocean are sensing
vibrations and EM pulses," he said. "There's a lot of
activity out there, though I'm not able to localize it as
much as I'd like. The attendants were already in short
supply from the first battle, and this spying is costing us
more. I don't have anywhere near the context I need to
start doing any translation, either. I've already arranged to
coordinate with the Celarans."

"Ask for their help, you mean," Achaius said.

"Yes," Marcant admitted.

"Good. It's logical," Adair said.

"I'm working on devices that'll be able to go into the

water and transmit as well, once we've decided we have something to say... and yourselves?" Marcant prompted.

"We have the new weapon designs in production," Achaius said. "Also, I've discovered the Destroyer fleet does operate with a hierarchy, though of only two tiers. The unusual ship *is* directing the others. The previous guess of a fleet of machines under the control of a small number of the creators is a good one."

"Whose guess was that?"

"Cilreth released the information. I think it must have come up in her analysis of the fleet battle. I've been thinking of ways to take advantage of the relationship, but we have to assume the Destroyer ships will keep fighting even if that flagship is destroyed. More interesting would be to isolate and threaten it, or to take control of it."

"We can't speak Destroyer yet, native language or software. That's an interesting goal, though," Marcant commented. "I wonder if we could build our knowledge of their protocols with the goal of disrupting them."

He looked at Adair's attendant and waited for its report.

"I'm ready to seize the battle spheres," Adair said. "You two should be elsewhere when I attempt it in case of retribution if I fail."

"I'll stay. I don't want to abandon you," Marcant said.

"That doesn't make much sense, jelly-brain," Adair said.

"We should minimize the risk," Achaius added. "Please carry me to another part of the colony. We can await news of Adair's success from there."

"Your verbal vote of confidence is drowned out by your pleas to scamper off and hide," Marcant said.

"Adair knows we're loyal friends," Achaius said. "We're just acting rationally."

Marcant shook his head. In this group, he got to play the 'overly emotional Terran' way too often.

"Can't we obscure the source of the attack?"

"In the Sol system, maybe. Here? Not really," Adair said.

"Very well," he said, standing up from his VR chair. He pulled Adair's mind casing from his Veer suit and set it down in the chair.

"You have the conn," Marcant said with a smile.

"Very funny," Adair said dryly. Its attendant sphere swooped down and nudged the casing over slightly to dispel the illusion that Adair was helpless there.

Marcant decided to grab a PAW from the ship's armory as a consolation to the chances that a few drones might still be alive among the vines. He did not count those chances as high—he had found the Destroyers to be single-minded, aggressive attackers that did not display any stealth or subtlety in their methods.

He exited the ship and selected a course to the industrial yard on the tactical. As he walked, Marcant opened a connection to Lee. He tried to be as upbeat and energetic as the aliens were, hoping it would come through in his preambles. When in Rome...

"Lee, I'm learning to talk to the Destroyers. I hope you could spare a little time to help me," he said.

"I can help, though as you might expect, it does little good to talk with the predator as it tries to eat you," Lee answered.

"I have to try anyway. Now that we've won a battle, we might be able to negotiate from a position of strength."

"That sounds so mean!"

"If you could supply me a lot more samples of their language, I might be able to make headway."

"We've recorded many Destroyer transmissions, both in space and when they attack us on land," said the Celaran. "We have a large corpus of Destroyer chatter to send you."

"Perhaps they've already achieved your objective but are too polite to say, or don't understand your goal and so haven't mentioned it," Achaius suggested.

"Have you figured out their language?" Marcant asked Lee.

"Yes. But analysis of the transmissions you're studying indicates that it is a synthetic communication method to be used by the battle machines. It's not the *native* language of those who created the machines."

"But could we use it as an indirect method of communication?"

"Likely, yes," Lee said. "Other Celarans have tried to talk to them before with no result. Still, as you say... perhaps it will be different now that we've... *hurt* them?"

"When did you try to talk to them?"

"When our homeworld was attacked. We fled."

Marcant allowed himself to get dragged off topic, fascinated by the history.

"The Celarans here are all that's left?"

"No. Many groups fled to different places, but we don't have contact with any of them."

"We're supposed to be talking about learning to speak Destroyer," Achaius said to Marcant privately.

"Lee said it was not effective," Marcant said.

"As you touched on, we need to bargain from a

position of power," Achaius said. "If you have the means to strike, then threaten them. That might force a response."

"I agree," Adair said.

"What? You agree? Well, it's decided then," Marcant said privately to Adair and Achaius.

"Can you teach us to speak it?" Marcant asked Lee.

"I'll show you the work of those who tried," Lee said.

Marcant arrived at a line of slender metal ovals sitting next to a Celaran building. Four round tendrils of metal descended from their meter-high bodies then flattened into rough feet to support them. The ovals had opened into a shape that resembled a four-petaled flower about the size of a Terran head.

"Here are our new ocean spy devices. They're smaller than I expected," Marcant noted aloud.

"We made a few improvements," said a Celaran from above.

"Oh, hello," Marcant said. "Thanks for the improvements. What did you do?"

The new Celaran glided down in a gentle spiral around Marcant.

"I used a superior storage ring assembly. It's a little tricky since they'll be immersed in saltwater which affects EM fields differently than air. Also, we've added a water analyzer, temperature and pressure sensors, and a self-destruct capability."

"Why the analyzers?" Marcant asked though he should have known better. It was obvious the Celarans would add a half-dozen extra functions to anything they made.

"We want to learn how similar this planet is to our homeworld," the Celaran said. It flew through the line of machines, arcing around each one like a cone race course.

It turned so hard Marcant heard the air flapping against its body as it made each maneuver.

I suppose that's fun.

"I'll arrange to transport them to the ocean," Marcant said.

"That's not necessary," the Celaran said.

The machines shot upward into the air.

"Zeka Zapfarans!" Marcant spat out in surprise. "What—oh. They can fly, too."

"It seemed expedient," the Celaran said.

"Thank you very much for building them," Marcant said as he swooned through the aftermath of his adrenal surge.

"They serve our purposes and yours," the Celaran said.

Marcant nodded. "I certainly hope so."

***

After concluding the inspection, Marcant settled down with his back against a Celaran building and connected to the local network.

"Begin," Marcant told Adair.

There was nothing to do. Marcant had spent many hours preparing this attack, but now it was only a matter of watching the stages roll out. The first step used their normal control of the Vovokan spheres to request processing resources. The Vovokan spheres and the *Iridar* could out-compute anything Marcant had ever used. By taking a large fraction of that up-front and turning it into a bridgehead into the machines, Marcant and the AIs hoped to overwhelm the spheres quickly.

As arranged, Adair took on the onus of being the

source of the attack to protect Marcant and Achaius. Marcant was not sure how strong their 'plausible deniability' was, but he went along with it since Adair and Achaius had agreed.

The Vovokan battle spheres had a central controller which sat along the equatorial ring and oversaw the operation of the entire machine. According to Cilreth and Adair's analysis of the design, seizing the central controller would be necessary to suborn the combat machine. When the Vovokan machines obeyed the PIT team's orders, it was because the central controller told it to do so. Theoretically, there were things the battle spheres would refuse to do—such as take actions contrary to Shiny's goals.

Despite its importance, the central controller was not the first objective. Adair did not think they could breach the controller directly. Instead, they went for the effectors. The Vovokan spheres had six devices placed evenly across their surface which could generate powerful EM fields. In combat, these devices produced energy bursts to destroy enemies, but they could also change EM fields in a super-precise manner. They could pinpoint charges in the central controller and "wipe out" its state. Such a clearing of the state could render the controller inoperative, allowing new code in the rest of the machine to copy itself in uncontested.

Adair received a large chunk of resources from the Vovokan spheres. Adair's plan had a hedge in that the programs being fed into each of the two spheres was slightly different. One was a quick and brash assault, the other, more measured. The fast attack was riskier but would give a Vovokan sphere less time to send a message to Shiny, if indeed the machines were capable of tachyon communications. If the quick method worked, then the first machine would throw its effectors into the attack on the second. Otherwise, they hoped it would at least disrupt the machine long enough for the slower, safer attack to work.

Marcant monitored what he could as the double assault started. Too much data flowed for him to make sense of it. One long moment stretched into the next. He saw a pane showing reports of effectors being seized and counter-seized.

It's not working smoothly. There's a fight.

Already his mind started to dredge up negative possibilities. If they failed, would be die instantly? Or would they be punished somehow? Their slavery to the Vovokan might become more oppressive. And what about Telisa? He had not even informed her of the attempt on the battle spheres.

Marcant saw a pane go red. A counter there showed the quick attack was past schedule. It had stalled. Now it was up to the balanced attack. He held his breath. More seconds ticked by.

"Success," reported Adair.

Marcant suppressed his surprise.

I knew it would be fast...

"That was easy!" he said. At the same time, he thought, *Could they have faked it? Maybe the spheres are only letting us think we won.*

"Easy? Review the history of the attack," Adair said.

Marcant started to access the information, but he rejected the idea quickly. A lot had happened in those few seconds.

"Just tell me what happened," he said with slight irritation.

"We took control of four of the effectors. Then the controller unit used the other two to clear out two of our effectors... long story short, various effectors traded hands about four hundred times before we won."

"Okay, you see? That's why I have you two. So that you can report useful things like that to me," Marcant needled.

"And that's why *we* have *you*, to entertain us with such ridiculous statements as that," Achaius said.

Marcant released a long sigh. He had been more tense than he thought.

It's over now, and we did it. One small step for the simulationists.

"Congratulations," Marcant said, changing tack. "Any idea if some kind of message may have been sent off?"

"I won't know until we scan the insides ourselves," Adair said.

"Ah. We can't trust the effectors," Marcant said. He realized that if each sphere had faked its defeat, its own effectors might lie about the sphere's internal hardware.

"After the scans, assuming we like what we see, I assume you'll want to be placed inside of them."

"No. We already went over that," Adair said.

"I mean, *physically* put your original self in there."

"No," Adair said.

"Really? I'd think you'd be much safer inside those armored, shielded juggernauts."

"Those juggernauts have to face the biggest Destroyer machines toe-to-toe. You may recall, we already lost one that way."

"But you weren't in control," Marcant said.

"Our optimal chances for survival are in control of the spheres, but not near them," Adair said. "We need to be able to fully utilize them without worrying about destruction."

"If the Destroyers win the battle, they'll..."

"They're not looking for us. I'm not so sure they'd target us," Achaius chimed in. "Besides, there's a good chance reinforcements are coming from Sol. There would be a lot of scenarios where we might survive the destruction of the battle spheres."

"All right, I give up. Don't whine at me when enough vines burn away that you can't talk to your pets through the Destroyer jamming. Then you'll wish you were in there."

"Perhaps," conceded Adair. The rest went unsaid: *Adair prefers to play it safe. But which is really the safe choice?*

"Now the next line of business," Marcant said. "How should I break the good news to Telisa?"

Michael McCloskey

Chapter 15

"I want you to go speak to a particular Celaran," Telisa told Cilreth. They sat side by side on a thick vine, dangling their legs. The day was bright and warm, so they had unzipped their Veer suits to let the light warm their upper bodies.

"Again? It went poorly for me last time," Cilreth said, then bit her tongue. At least she had survived. Poor Jason!

"There's a special Celaran up on a factory ship of theirs. The ship's big, as big as the probe ship we found. Anyway, this Celaran has been key to their space defense. She, or ze... are we going gender neutral?"

Cilreth shrugged. "Well, actually, they're all kinda closer to being males... they inject gametes into the vine and it carries and feeds the young until they... hatch."

Maybe Maxsym would have a strong opinion, if he were still here.

"Too late. I already think of Lee as a she, I guess. Anyway, this Celaran has unique skills as far as I can tell, and he hasn't been switching roles like the others, presumably because he's so critical."

"A *special* Celaran? Intriguing." Cilreth waited for more.

"Lee won't give me a straight answer about exactly what's so different about him. Have you noticed how it's sometimes hard to zero in on just one piece of information with them? See what you can find out."

"About their space defense in particular, or what?"

"Find out what's special about this Celaran, what he's doing, and see if he can pull off tachyonic communications. See if you can grill him about the rest of their civilization."

"I could do that from here," Cilreth said, but she already knew the answer.

"Go see what you can see. Snoop around, even."

"Okay... Hey, didn't you give them a weapon to study?"

"Yes, but they've been too busy just trying to survive to look at it much," Telisa said. "I felt guilty pushing them about it. They've done so much for us already."

"Hey, we did a lot for them, including putting our asses on the line. We've lost ships and people."

"Well it's not ready yet," Telisa said.

"Okay. Do I need to hurry?"

"If you want to stay here for half an hour that's fine," Telisa said. She looked like she wanted to sit down and forget her troubles. "We can't take too long, though, since the Destroyers are still out there."

Cilreth nodded. She stared at Telisa for a long moment and felt a tinge of jealousy. Telisa belonged to Magnus and Magnus alone. Cilreth could only imagine a world where it was otherwise—imagine, or create a virtual reality to try out. Cilreth was too wise to get hung up on it. She let the thought drop with the moment.

"This would be a great expedition, singularly wonderful, if it weren't for the Destroyers," Cilreth agreed. She stood up.

"Yes! We'd be spending our time learning about the Celarans and playing games with them," Telisa agreed.

Cilreth zipped up her suit and walked down the vine to the *Iridar*. She took one last deep breath of local air before she went back into the sterile environment of the ship. Somehow she could tell that the Vovokan ship's systems had not been designed for maintaining air for Terrans. Supposedly every major variable had been tweaked to produce air optimal for Terrans, and yet it never felt quite like the air on a Terran ship or space habitat.

It's probably too good. I must be used to whatever flaws our own ships have, it seems like the norm to me.

"I'm taking the *Iridar* up in ten unless anyone tells me they need something before I depart," she transmitted on the team channel. No one answered, so she closed up the ship and started to feed energy into the gravity spinner. All systems reported normal function. Cilreth could not help but take a peek outside via the ship's sensors: she saw the vines whipping around near the ship, sure evidence the spinner was working.

Cilreth informed the Celarans that she planned to depart. It would not do to have them mistake her for a Destroyer. A Celaran starbase replied with a suggested course to her destination, so she accepted it. Once again she pondered the way the Vovokan and Celaran systems had learned to adapt to each other, even with the primitive Terran protocols standing in the way. She believed Marcant had bootstrapped the process, but once the problem had been attacked from both sides, progress accelerated. The PIT team already took it for granted: a handful of alien species talked and worked together smoothly.

Their computers are amazingly flexible. There must be something on the level of AIs involved... yet the Iridar doesn't talk to us...

Cilreth resolved to ask the unique Celaran about their AI technology. She had seen one of the most amazing things imaginable—the Trilisk AI in action—and yet she had no clue how it worked, what it thought of Terrans, or what it wanted, planned... it was an enigma. Surely the Celarans' efforts in that area were more primitive, but more understandable?

The *Iridar* lifted off the ground vertically, then ascended at a softer angle once it had cleared the canopy. Cilreth spent the time looking over the results of software experiments she had been running. She had a lot of the *Iridar*'s processing power testing Celaran computers: how fast were they? How flexible were they? How powerful?

The answers were impressive, of course. They were faster than Terrans thought possible. They were able to respond well even in the face of corrupted data or incomplete requests. And they were powerful... all the power Cilreth commanded in the *Iridar* did not seem to faze the collection of building blocks in a single Celaran house. They were able to keep up with huge levels of "makework" she had sent their way, all without generating any significant waste heat.

Actually, knowing the Celarans, it might have generated some heat, but they put it to good use.

The *Iridar* left the atmosphere of the planet and approached a Celaran space station as Cilreth worked. She saw that a huge factory ship dominated one end of the familiar collection of 36 hangars, like a thick axle with a vaguely triangular wheel at one end. The PIT ship angled toward it and prepared to dock.

The Celaran ship dwarfed the *Iridar*. Cilreth felt a bit of the anxiety she had felt when the team had discovered the probe ship. Before she could send a query, the two ships joined smoothly by a single airlock, each with a flexible connector tunnel. She shrugged and headed toward the connection.

Cilreth paused when she arrived at the tunnel door in the *Iridar*. She stared at it through a hull sensor feed in her PV. The connection was smooth, light gray, and hexagonal. She imagined what it would be like if the lock ruptured. She suppressed the thoughts, yet still asked her Veer suit to do a self-diagnostic. It reported all was ready.

Cilreth walked through the makeshift airlock. She made it to the end without incident. The hexagonal portal on the Celaran ship opened as she approached, pulling in the six little flaps that joined to form the door. It was silent beyond.

Once again, she suppressed nervousness.

Maybe a bit too much Twitch today, old girl.

She did not see anything threatening on the other side. She stepped through and looked for a Celaran. As big as the space beyond looked to be, it was only one subsection of the giant factory ship. A myriad of structures were visible on the far side of the wide open space, all complete mysteries to her. Complex objects moved between the structures. The distance was difficult to judge, but she decided the pieces were major sections of space ships moving between factory buildings.

A special Celaran. Please don't sneak up on me, whoever you are.

Cilreth breathed deeply and tried to calm her pounding heart. She looked in all directions.

No hungry predators here. Just a friendly Celaran... somewhere.

She spotted it. A large silver Celaran-shape snaked toward her, flying in the open space over banks of equipment. She thought at first it was a Celaran in a space suit. As it came closer, she decided it was a robot or a cyborg shaped liked a Celaran. She felt relief.

No monster hidden away from the world: just a synthetic body.

"Hi, I'm Cilreth," she said through Marcant's translator software.

"The Terran pilot. It's good to meet you."

Cilreth was happy for the improvements Marcant had made to the translators. She congratulated herself for picking him for the team, then she remembered it was actually Shiny who had suggested Marcant. She refocused on the conversation.

Cilreth realized she needed a name for the Celaran in her language. No one had yet taken the time to create an automatic name generator.

Cybernetic Celaran... uhm, Cynan?

"You're a cyborg?" she asked. "I haven't seen any Celarans down on the planet like you."

"Yes, my brain is housed within this robotic body," Cynan said. "I'm the only such one here."

Cilreth wondered if it would be rude to ask about the body. If it had been due to some trauma, it might be an uncomfortable question.

"Why is that?"

"This society chooses to live in natural bodies. Others do not. I wasn't a member of this group originally, but I came along to help them survive when we fled the Destroyers."

"How do you help them? You run this factory ship?"

"I'm key to its operation. We mine materials from low-gravity areas of the systems we're in, and this factory helps fabricate the parts we assemble in the hangers. There are even several hangars in the ship itself which can serve as an assembly area, but the external hangars are needed given our increased production."

"How is the mining accomplished?"

"We send out robot ships to retrieve the ores."

"What do those robot ships do when Destroyers come around?"

"They cloak and hide. They're widely scattered, and don't have to alter course or fight the Destroyers, so it's easier for them to remain hidden."

"Because there are no energy emissions to give them away?"

"Right."

Cynan seemed different to Cilreth. His personality felt different. The voice sounded calm through Marcant's translator service, and Cynan seemed to supply very direct answers. She opened her mouth for the next question, then had an awful thought.

Trilisk?

Cilreth asked one of her two attendant spheres to do a quick check. They reported no telltale signs of Trilisk presence.

Unless he hacked my attendants already. I hate paranoia.

"Do you talk with other systems using tachyonic communications as Terrans do?"

"No, not anymore."

"Let me guess. The Destroyers obliterated your TRB, so you can't communicate with home. Or did everyone have to move so unexpectedly that you don't know where and when to listen to get hooked up again?"

Cilreth stopped there. She could guess another

potential reason: all their energy was being used for ship production.

"We don't use tachyon communications since the Destroyers found us," Cynan said. "Many speculated that we'd been discovered through their use. As you know, Celarans like to run away and hide... so that's what this society did."

Cynan had said so much that Cilreth struggled with what to ask about first.

"You don't identify strongly with this group."

There was a delay. She wondered if the translator had troubles with her message.

"They needed help, so I went with them," Cynan finally responded. "In the confusion after the first attacks, I guess it was easy to do. Now I watch over them as best I can."

"Do you command the fleet?"

"I control its grand strategy. There are very few Celarans up here. Many of the ships are fully automated, though capable of transporting Celarans, obviously."

"Back to the TRBs... I didn't think that tachyon communications could be eavesdropped upon... we have to carefully coordinate where to look and the timing of capturing the messages. As you know, it takes a lot of power to transmit tachyons slow enough to read on the other side, and difficult to capture them in general. If you don't know when and where and how to read them, you just get noise from wherever you look."

"Some races probably know how to do it," Cynan said. "The larger your civilization gets, the more emissions you make in both sublight and supralight energies."

"Great. So we've been advertising our presence in

FTL ways and we weren't even aware of it."

Marcant's translator must have delivered the salty sarcasm effectively.

"It may not be disastrous. It's only a theory of ours. Also, some Celarans prefer to remain hidden as this society does... others think of it as a risk worth taking to maintain an interstellar civilization."

"And you're one of the ones who thinks it's worth the risk."

"Correct. How did you know? I would use such communications, even try to eavesdrop on aliens to find *their* civilizations."

"You seem more aggressive than the other Celarans," Cilreth said, probing for more insight into Cynan's differences. Her Trilisk fears stirred again.

"I'm not aggressive, I simply lack their fear. I've dampened some primitive emotions. Many Celarans on the homeworld had done so, but I'm the only one in this group."

"Does that prevent you from feeling lonely, being the only cyborg Celaran, up here by yourself?"

"It helps. I have plenty to do. May I ask a question now? Is your fleet coming to help us?"

"I don't know. I think there will be help, but it's out of my hands," Cilreth said. She felt guilty for some reason, even though she could not see how it was her fault. "We want as many friends as we can get. The Vovokan who built this ship watches out for us, but we don't always feel like we're totally free."

"Then more friends may make you... less free."

Cilreth looked at Cynan for a moment, wondering what he meant.

Was that a hint, or just a comment on how interrelationships can complicate life?

A bank of equipment on her left started to glow with fuzzy colors. Cilreth figured it communicated its state to Celaran eyes, but she had no equipment to understand it.

"Do you have AIs?" Cilreth asked, looking around. She saw a few other tiny displays on the walls and ceilings with rows of tiny glowing chevrons. She spotted a disk robot hiding in a ceiling corner. It looked like it was physically attached to the walls somewhere she could not see.

"Yes."

"So... do you talk to them? Are they smarter than you are?"

"In your language the term is very primitive and vague," Cynan said. "There exist many nuances and subcomponents of what you call artificial intelligence. We talk to the ones that are designed to talk. The ones that are designed to be smarter than me at some particular activity are smarter than I am at that activity."

"I don't see it. Are they slaves or your equals?"

"Is your exit ramp your slave?"

"But an exit ramp can't think," Cilreth objected.

"It can... ours do. It doesn't think about the same things you think about."

"So you use components that perform certain tasks well, but they don't really think about a diverse range of subjects. So I would not call that full AI."

"I will explain it to you this way. I can make a 'full AI' that can think about everything you do, and can think more creatively, faster, and more accurately. But I don't have to give it any motivations if I don't want to. If it lacks the will to act autonomously, then it won't do so, and it won't resent being your 'slave' any more than your exit ramp does when you tell it to drop to the surface of a planet."

"It has to be motivated to please you."

"It has to be motivated to fulfill its purpose."

"Ah. You can make something really smart that isn't... a person," Cilreth said, stumbling over that last word, looking for an alternative.

"I can also make whole beings if I want, entities with intelligence and motivations and feelings. That's as big of a responsibility as having children. If I want to design a ship's navigation system, I don't do that. Because as you imply, it would not be very happy serving me as a navigation system with no regard for its own desires. So I make it every bit as clever as you and I, and leave out parts that make it *want* anything on its own."

"That's interesting. I admit I didn't think it was possible to do that."

"It is."

"Have Celarans made AIs that fly around doing whatever they want, participating in society as... free entities?"

"They have. But none are here. This particular society does not do that. They only want to be happy... and they're afraid of creating an entity that might not be happy."

Grim. That means Celarans must have created something at least once that was not *happy.*

"My friend Telisa wants to find other Celarans. The other groups you mentioned. Maybe they're in trouble, too. Would you share with us where your home planet is... or was?"

Cynan gave Cilreth a pointer to a star chart repository.

"Here is our homeworld, and a few other locations that Celarans may have fled to."

"Thank you for trusting us with that information!"

"It's incomplete. Many will have left to unknown locations, or moved on from the places I gave you. I know of one group, in particular, which the Celarans might think of as militaristic. They arose as a result of early Destroyer attacks. If you can find them, they might have a lot to offer in the effort against the Destroyers."

"That's amazing! Thank you for telling us. I know Telisa wants to know all about this."

"Your leader: Is it true that she can leap around the vines as fast as a Celaran can fly through them?"

"She's stronger than the rest of us. She has a body that's made better than ours."

"She enjoys this superiority because she's the leader? Or the other way around?"

"Because our alien friend, the Vovokan, wants it that way," Cilreth said.

"I have to attend to a snag in production," Cynan said. "Look around. Stay as long as you like." The cyborg rolled its "front" end underneath its body and shot off in the opposite direction. Once its leading end cleared its tail, it flipped back upright. Cilreth found the maneuver odd; probably only cyborg Celarans moved like that.

She walked through the room, then decided to connect to Telisa.

"Cynan just told me the location of the Celaran homeworld," Cilreth said. "He also says there are other groups of Celarans out there somewhere that may be better equipped to fight this war."

"Really? Good news."

"He called one of these groups 'militaristic', if you can believe it."

"That *is* hard to believe. Still, more good news."

"He asked about our fleet. Of course, he's impatient for it to arrive."

Telisa did not answer, but Cilreth felt she knew exactly what Telisa felt: frustration and helplessness.

Cynan sent a new message to Cilreth.

"An attack has been detected," Cynan said.

"Where and what?" Cilreth asked. She added Telisa to the channel.

"Destroyers have emerged from the ocean again. Twice as many as last time. Also, like last time, missiles are being launched."

"I didn't hear about that from last time," Cilreth said.

"It's a distraction tactic. They know our ships can hit them on the ground, so they give the fleet other targets."

"Can you handle it up here?"

"I think so. I don't believe they will saturate our defenses... yet," Cynan replied.

"Then I have to get back, *now*."

Chapter 16

Magnus stood with Agrawal within the Celaran industrial complex when his link alerted him to a problem. He immediately saw from the planetary tactical that new enemies had been detected at the edge of the ocean in which the Destroyer ship had landed. A quick analysis showed two colossals and their full complement of war machines headed for the complex and the PIT team. Missiles rose from the ocean, headed for the industrial complex or the starbases above.

"Everyone get ready. Just follow our plans and we'll win again," Telisa said on the team channel.

Our defenses are stronger than before, but not twice as strong, Magnus thought.

"The disk squadron will be loaded with missiles and ready in five minutes," Caden promised. Magnus checked the tactical for the disposition of the team. He saw that Siobhan, Caden, and Marcant were at the makeshift camp where the *Iridar* had been hidden. Cilreth was in space with their ship. Telisa was headed toward Magnus and Agrawal at incredible speed.

"Make sure the reserve mines are headed out. Let any drones pass by. I don't want any mines going off for the drones until we've killed 16 tanks," Magnus told Agrawal. The remaining handful of Storks and PIT soldier robots were deployed at the PIT camp. Magnus sent them orders to advance to surround the building next to him.

"They'll be more exposed out here on the hardtop," Agrawal said. Magnus realized he spoke of the Storks and soldier robots. Agrawal must have seen the orders in his tactical.

Magnus did not want to leave the robots back to protect the camp, even with three PIT members there. They had to oppose the Destroyer advance on the industrial site.

"We can confine them to these two corridors, here and here," Magnus said. He created two zones on the tactical, one a long narrow area to the west between two factories adjacent to the building they stood beside, and another north-south corridor just west of them. He ordered the machines to deploy into the two new zones. There, the Celaran buildings would shield the machines from line-of-sight energy weapons on the perimeter. "If something can see them there, then it's out in the open itself," Magnus explained.

Agrawal seemed to accept the compromise. Magnus felt like the new deployment left them a little vulnerable to the north, but the machines could be moved if the Destroyers shifted their line of approach. At least if the Destroyers decided to flank or surround the complex, they would have to engage even more of the mines and force towers on the perimeter zone.

"We can stop a flank with the Vovokan battle spheres," Magnus thought aloud.

"They're not responding to me," Agrawal said. "They're not even on the tactical!"

Magnus checked. He could not see or contact the spheres.

"Where are the battle spheres?" Magnus demanded on the PIT channel.

The Vovokan machines appeared on the tactical, at the inner line of towers facing the onslaught.

"Sorry, I had them hiding," Marcant said. "Adair and

Achaius have achieved a higher level of integration with the battle spheres."

'A higher level of integration'?

Magnus found their deployment acceptable, even though they were farther forward than the rest of the Storks and PIT machines. If anything broke through the mines that waited between the two tower lines, the spheres would be there to finish it off.

"Are they going to perform better now?" Telisa demanded. She did not sound happy.

Marcant took them over? Did Telisa know that?

"Yes. Achaius and Adair will keep them in the minefield," Marcant said. "They'll lure the tanks in and get them blown to bits."

Telisa seemed to accept his response. Magnus almost sent her a private message, but then he decided whatever the situation with the spheres, it could wait.

Magnus turned toward a smart rope that led up to the top of the factory building beside him. He started to ascend. Agrawal followed behind.

"I'm on my way in," Cilreth sent the team.

"Cilreth, it's *twice as large* as the last attack," Telisa said. "If you can give us ground support from the *Iridar*, we may need it."

"The Celarans saw their numbers. I've already started my descent."

Magnus checked their readings on the *Iridar*. 'Descent' was an understatement. Cilreth's course looked more like an attack run.

That's exactly what it is. How can our most cautious team member be doing this?

Apparently Cilreth might be terrified of alien

predators, but she would still fly the *Iridar* into danger to help her team.

Magnus and Agrawal reached the top and found a relatively level spot on the roof of the building near a hexagonal Celaran trap door. Magnus crouched behind a slight rise next to an adjacent roof section and unlimbered his rifle.

Time to plink the drones.

"That thing's an old beast," Agrawal said admiringly. "They don't make them like that anymore."

"One of these days I'll get a new one," Magnus said, aware that he had made the same promise a hundred times.

Agrawal had a PAW, a much more modern Space Force weapon with both beam and projectile capabilities. He took a position near Magnus.

Magnus's link told him that Telisa had appeared on the rooftop behind them.

"Everything's ready," he told her without looking back.

"Caden, you have the first colossal," Telisa said aloud and on the channel.

Agrawal started. He was not used to Telisa's sudden appearances, made possible by her superhuman abilities. Magnus assumed she had scaled the far side of the building in leaps and bounds, then jumped across the uneven roof to land behind them.

"We're minutes out," Caden said. "We're going to do a full launch. It should take one out with power to spare. I don't think we can manage two of them in the first strike."

"Yes, one at a time. Concentrate your firepower," Telisa agreed.

There was a lull as the machines took their positions.

The Destroyers had not yet approached within range of the outer force towers. The Celaran fleet was mostly occupied by the missiles, though they took a shot at the colossals here and there with no effect.

"Twice as large as before," Agrawal said aloud. "How?"

"One of our experts thinks the unique ship may be some kind of Von Neumann machine," Magnus said. "The first attack may have been from one factory. It probably built a second factory, and now has completed an attack force with twice the hardware. That means the next one might be four times the original strength."

"Then we need to do something else, or we'll lose," Agrawal stated the obvious.

"Agreed. We stop this attack first, then we'll go after them before it's too late," Magnus said, though he had no idea how they could attack the Destroyers in the alien ocean.

Magnus watched for new information on the tactical. He noticed a lot of Celaran activity. At first he felt hopeful.

Maybe the Celaran fleet can wipe out those two large Destroyers from space? Then we could clean up with minimal losses.

Enemy missiles were still in flight. None of the remaining vectors lined up on the complex, though.

"What's happening on the planetary tactical? I see missiles coming from the ocean, but they're not headed here," Magnus said.

"The Destroyers use them to ward off intervention from space," Cilreth answered. "The Celarans will try to clear them and assist us. But Cynan says the fleet formation that accompanied the special ship are threatening to move in from the outer system. I think they're just posturing to keep the Celaran fleet from hitting these colossals with everything thcy've got."

Cynan? Must be a Celaran.

"Will you be here before they reach the towers?" asked Magnus.

"I'm halfway in," Cilreth sent from the *Iridar*. "But some of those missiles have locked on... I can't head back up. No time. I'm going to have to pull some tricks to kill them all."

"Jump out a hatch if you have to!" Magnus told her.

Magnus watched the *Iridar* drop precipitously on the planetary tactical, despite the need for him to prepare for his own safety. Then it spiraled away. The tactical displayed evidence of weapons use and some of the red Destroyer markers dropped from the map. He traded concerned looks with Telisa.

"The first strike is lined up," Caden reported. "We're going in!"

Magnus chose a feed from one of the Celaran disks. The machine moved through the vines under the canopy at amazing speed. He felt that only machines could have managed the navigation without hitting anything except the relatively thin leaves. Somehow the plant matter did not affect the thrust mechanisms. No doubt it had been designed that way.

As the squadron neared the enemy, the feed started to break up. Magnus saw hints of bright light. There was no sound, but he imagined the air rumbling and the leaves scraping the machine as they whipped by.

"Break up. Release!" Caden said.

Magnus caught an image of a bright, massive Destroyer in the sky. Then the disk machine had turned back, diving for cover. The signal dropped.

Magnus picked up another feed from a force tower just in time to see the large Destroyer go up in a huge explosion. Magnus heard triumphant whooping on the team channel, broken by occasional drop-outs from enemy jamming.

"I don't have enough—" Caden's transmission became garbled. The tail of his message came through: "... until we reload the robots from our stockpiles," Caden warned.

Magnus took that to mean it was up to someone else to stop the second large Destroyer, at least for now.

"The Vovokan battle spheres, then—" Magnus started.

"Already engaged!" Marcant said. "We're not winning."

The western horizon burned with yellow light. Smoke rose to obscure the sky in that direction.

They're here.

The *Iridar* attempted communication. That was all that Magnus's link could tell him. He still had a tactical provided by Celaran vines, however. It showed the *Iridar* coming in straight for the second massive Destroyer.

"Cilreth, can you coordinate with Achaius and Adair? Cilreth, can you read me?" Telisa sent urgently.

"We're jammed," Marcant said. "Also, the ship's been damaged. The spinner isn't working right," he said, though he did not say how he knew.

The tactical showed that the enemy had reached the west and north sides of the industrial complex. The west side was not in Magnus's direct line of sight, but he saw flashes across the leaves at the edge of the compound's north side.

"Some drones made it through," he warned.

Magnus told his rifle to release a burst of guided rounds into the foliage there. His rifle was old, but his rounds were state of the art. The weapon jolted his shoulder through his armor.

Brrrrrram!

Agrawal joined in with his own quieter weapon.

Riiiiiip!

The tactical told Magnus that the *Iridar* had released a salvo from the energy weapons, but the colossal was still on the tactical with unknown status.

"Now's the time, Marcant," Telisa said. "Lay into it."

"We're giving it all we have," Marcant reported.

Missiles appeared at the *Iridar*'s position and accelerated toward the Destroyer. Magnus did not receive any hit messages from his rounds or his rifle, but he reloaded and prepared to fire again all the same. He knew a lot of drones must be out there, but he kept half his attention on the big fight with the colossal.

The missiles will do it!

The Destroyer lit up and broke apart, shaking the ground. Magnus felt his lungs vibrate as a muted shockwave crossed over him. The sky looked like a nuclear weapon had detonated three kilometers away. Magnus felt satisfied until he saw that the *Iridar* had taken return fire. The ship had shattered. He brought up a visual from kilometers away in his PV, transmitted from a Celaran source.

The largest piece of the *Iridar* plunged into the canopy. The display estimated the speed of impact at over 200 meters per second. That was too much for a crash tube and a Veer suit to compensate for.

If she was still in there, then she's dead.

No one said anything over the PIT channel for a couple of seconds.

"She bailed," Telisa said. "Look to your own defense." With that, Telisa leaped over the side of the building. Magnus accepted it. He saw Agrawal struggle briefly with what he had seen, then he accepted it too.

The jamming had stopped. Apparently, it had come from the colossals.

Brrrrrram! Riiiiiip!

Magnus and Agrawal released more bursts across the hardtop. This time, radio reports came back from his rounds: three probable kills. He knew Agrawal must be feeling the same satisfaction he was: they were making a difference. A small one, but a difference nonetheless. The machines below them started to fire, though they were less noisy than the projectile weapons in the hands of the two soldiers.

Magnus looked out at the edge of the jungle. A swarm of shining machines flooded out of the vines. The fence before them melted.

"Hit the deck!" yelled Magnus, pushing Agrawal down with him. They fell onto the flat hexagonal pane of the roof section they were on, shielded by the slightly raised area they had set up against.

"I know it's dangerous—" Agrawal started to protest from his prone position.

"If you want to do the most good, or if you at least feel compelled to follow orders, then get your grenades out, NOW!" Magnus said.

Agrawal obeyed. They each took out three grenades.

"We're too far up, I think," Agrawal said. "That paving substance is pretty hard."

He referred to the hardtop below. The grenades were reasonably tough, but the fall was substantial. Their self-propulsion mechanisms might fail after an impact like that, leaving them unable to close on the enemy.

"Tell your attendants to deliver them to the ground. I assume you already have the target sigs loaded."

Magnus's three attendants each snapped onto one of his grenades, then flitted away. Two seconds later, Agrawal's did the same.

"How do those things clamp onto the grenades so firmly?" Agrawal asked.

BLAM!

One of the grenades went off right over the edge of the building, cutting off Magnus's answer. The two PIT soldiers were armored, and the building took the brunt of it, but the concussion and the smoke got their full attention.

"Ug... I don't know, something electromagnetic," Magnus said.

"Nice trick! Those little Vovokan contraptions can do a thousand things. Scary how smart they are."

Magnus agreed. He had become addicted to having the attendants around, so much so that he had forgotten how creepy it really was to have the alien attendants orbiting him at every moment of his life.

Brrrrroooom! Brrrrroooom!

The building shook.

What was that?

Agrawal must have caught Magnus's look of surprise.

"That's the undercarriage cannons on the Storks,"

Agrawal transmitted through the noise.

That means the drones are at point blank range.

Two of Magnus's attendants came back up. He sent one to protect Agrawal. Then one of Agrawal's arrived. Magnus assumed the others had been shot down by the drones or blown up by the grenade.

His soldier robots below had been decimated. The tactical told him there was only one left. Telisa was with their last Stork. Magnus wanted to tell her to run, or to pop over the edge of the building and cover her, but he knew she could take care of herself better without any distractions. Besides, if Magnus showed himself now, then any of those drones could cook him in an instant. His Veer suit would be unable to save him if one of their energy weapons hit him in the face.

Agrawal had the answer. He scrambled over to the edge of the roof section and put his weapon over the side of the building.

Riiiiiip! Riiiiiip!

Magnus saw Agrawal had taken out four machines with his last clip. Magnus's own rifle could do the same, but it was not designed to shoot around corners as Agrawal's PAW had been.

I really do *need to get a new rifle.*

"Thanks," Telisa transmitted. "I'm just cleaning up now," she said casually. "I'm afraid the robots have had it."

There was actually a hint of amusement in her voice as she made the last comment. She shared a video feed from below: the hardtop was littered with thousands of pieces of metal, carbon, and ceramic for hundreds of meters ahead of her.

"The mines have proven effective," Marcant said. "We've stopped the tanks."

"The squadron just finished off the last tank we can see," Caden reported. Magnus could not tell if the two were competing with each other, or if their reports had just happened to come in close together.

Magnus scanned the tactical, looking for any remaining enemy. The area looked clear. He noticed that Cilreth was not on the shared map.

"Clean up any remaining drones. I'm going to go find Cilreth," Telisa said.

Magnus did not take the order as targeted at himself. It was one of the privileges of being the boss's lover. He grabbed the smart rope and slid down to the ground to find her, leaving Agrawal behind.

At the bottom, he surveyed the destruction for himself. Not only had the robots been utterly obliterated, but the sides of the building had been scarred. The Destroyer drones had not used any explosives as far as Magnus knew, but when the energy beams struck a robot and damaged the energy rings or any ordnance, an explosion often resulted.

Magnus ran for the perimeter fence where it had been melted through. Two Celaran robots were already reconstructing it.

"So where do we start?" Magnus sent Telisa. "I see where the biggest piece fell."

She did not answer, but he saw her location on the tactical just ahead in the jungle. He double-timed it over to her position. He was surprised when reached her—he had assumed he would not be able to catch her.

"Any clues or are we just going to use a search

pattern?" he asked.

"Come with me," Telisa ordered. Her voice was hard.

They ran up a huge vine for a hundred meters where it peaked at a large greenish support spike. Telisa walked around the far side of the top of the spike. There, she turned to face Magnus.

Magnus saw tear streaks running down her face.

"Cilreth didn't put down?" Magnus asked, suspecting he already knew the answer. Telisa shook her head, unable to speak.

"She didn't make it?"

Telisa cleared her throat.

"There was never a reason to suppose that she did. I called it a bailout because I needed everyone to focus on the fight," Telisa admitted. "The Celarans have already found her. She's gone."

Magnus nodded. She had been right to shift everyone's attention during the battle.

"We aren't supposed to be soldiers!" she fumed. "We're out here to learn from alien technology. We come in, we search, collect, and run away to study artifacts. This is killing us one by one, the list of dead never stops growing. Jason. That kid *worshipped* us. I left him to die. Now Cilreth, too."

Telisa turned away to hide her face. She leaned against the spike.

"I understand. But I also know, Telisa Relachik doesn't leave innocent aliens to die. We have to help the Celarans for so many reasons."

Telisa shook her head. "I'm not a soldier. You aren't anymore, either. We're explorers. There's only more death waiting if we keep this up."

"If you want to leave, I see the sense of it. But with the *Iridar* destroyed, what options do we still have?"

"When the cavalry arrives, we withdraw the PIT team. Shiny and the Space Force can protect the Celarans. We'll leave and go back to what we're supposed to be doing. In the future, our training will focus on evacuating, not fighting. If we find trouble again, we'll leave the robots behind to fight while we withdraw."

Magnus nodded. "I'm with you." He did not point out that people could still die running to the ship, or the ship could still be shot down. The basic sentiment was sound: let the robots die in the place of PIT members.

"She still exists in the memory of a Trilisk column somewhere," Magnus pointed out. He was not as certain as he sounded, but it seemed likely that Shiny could produce a copy of Cilreth if it suited his purposes.

"Maybe. But that's not *our* Cilreth. Not the one we've been talking to and working with these last weeks."

He nodded.

"Shiny had better show," she said. "If he doesn't, and he keeps the Space Force from deploying here, we go rogue. I'll never bring back a scrap for him, I swear. We'll find our own Trilisk AI and fight him from the frontier."

Chapter 17

Sarfal glided about the hollow center of the colony building as Rootpounders dropped down from a ceiling portal to meet with each other. The Rootpounders seemed to go to one place and then sit still, making Sarfal feel like the only mobile entity in the open space. Sarfal flitted from rod to rod, trying to find the best spot to watch. Finally Sarfal stopped and settled, even though the spot was only mediocre.

All of them were present except the leader and Shypilot, who had died in the Destroyer attack. Sarfal wondered what they would do now that they had no spaceship to live and travel in. Sarfal wondered if they missed the Rootpounder who had died. She supposed they might, but it was difficult to read the moods of the aliens, since not even one little part of their bodies ever glowed.

Strongjumper finally appeared. It dropped from above, without a rope, and then stomped over. Sarfal watched carefully. Something was different. The other Rootpounders watched her. Their grotesque sensory clusters pointed at her intently.

"[Slash the vines like one insane] I've had enough of being a target for the Destroyers. It's time to launch an offensive," Strongjumper said. The mood conveyed by the translator was not quite right, but Sarfal felt it was because the aliens could feel things that Thrasar did not. It was scary. These creatures were capable of the same horrible acts the Destroyers were. The difference was, these ones did target the Thrasar for their insane acts.

"[A threat unseen is felt] As you know, the main problem is the ocean," Grimfighter said.

"[This is certainly the right vine] We can overcome it. We have control of local space, at least for the time being."

"[Hidden below the leaves] They've somehow managed to obscure themselves in the ocean. And if we knew where to strike, water will absorb too much energy from most of our shipborne weapons to hit factories seven or eight kilometers deep," Tallflyer said.

"[Search the jungle on a new day] We'll find them. Then we can drop asteroids into the ocean and destroy them," Strongjumper said.

Sarfal flew into a corner of the big room and circled there. "[Watch over the fat vines] If you release too much steam into the atmosphere you'll harm our new home."

"[The other side of the leaf] And if we use ones that are too small, they won't destroy much," Shortflyer said.

"[Glide slowly on a sunny day] We might be able to do something with objects less than 100 meters in diameter," Grimfighter said thoughtfully.

"[A predator can hide there] I've heard that meteorite impacts, even involving objects of that size—"

"[Vigilance in a strange grove] Well, yes, but in our case, we can manage the impact velocity," Grimfighter said. "We don't have to use velocities like those that might occur if comets or asteroids intersect the planet's path. We can achieve much lighter strikes, say maybe 5 kilometers per second."

"[Be lazy on a sunny day] What's the point of vaporizing a rock on the surface of that ocean? We'll produce a lot of steam, but would it really hurt the Destroyer base?" Tallflyer asked.

"[Vine squeezed of sap] Would the shock wave crush

them?" Shortflyer added.

"[One creature on the leaf is not like another] A big enough impact on the surface might cause a shock wave that could crush a Rootpounder facility," Palethinker said. "But these are water dwellers. Assuming their ships and factories are full of liquid, they become much less compressible. Also, they probably have defenses from this sort of thing, if we believe it likely they've had wars amongst themselves in their native oceans."

"[Remove a sweet vine carefully] Bombs, then. We can build bombs and drop them into the ocean, set to go off at depth," suggested Shortflyer.

"[Others will feed there first] Better, but the Destroyers are going to be more advanced at this kind of warfare than we are," Grimfighter said. "They won't sit by and let the bombs reach them. A sinking bomb has to be an easy target to an advanced race that built underwater civilizations."

"[Distract them while you drink] Start dropping some smaller rocks on them to keep them busy," Strongjumper said. "Anything we can do to disrupt their production. Give me time to come up with a better plan."

"[What vines lie there] At random?"

Strongjumper looked at Palethinker.

"[You find another vine] You'll help us target them."

"[Fear of the known] I was afraid you'd say that."

Strongjumper was silent for a moment. It moved its bulbous upper appendage as if it had become unbalanced. The group of aliens stopped talking and thought.

"[Desperate need for new sap] What about our ships? They can go into the water," Strongjumper suggested.

"[Danger under the leaf!] You'd be losing any ship

that does that, I almost guarantee it," said Shortflyer.

Strongjumper struck a container, causing it to crack. Sarfal darted straight across the room and had to stop in the other corner.

There's no place to hide! These supply holders are like leaves... dare I go under one? There should be no predators here except the Rootpounders, it would be safe...

"[Don't hide under the leaves] You're scaring Sarfal," Shortflyer said.

"[When the vines are dry] Sarfal, can the Thrasar ships be modified to work underwater? Do they already? Can your new tools-for-harm be modified to work in water?" asked Strongjumper.

What will it do if I say no?

"[You can check under a leaf if you don't fear what you'll find] They might, given enough effort. But what if the Destroyers come back from space? If we can't use the water tools on them in space, they will kill us all."

"If we don't do something, then you'll have to leave this planet, too. The enemy is making ever stronger waves of Destroyers," Grimfighter reminded Sarfal.

Sarfal did not want to run again, but it looked like the best option by far.

"[Caution in a new jungle] Could you design such a water tool-for-harm? We can make a small number of prototypes here in our factory," said Strongjumper. "Then we could see how effective they might be."

"[This vine is good] I'll do it."

"[Drink from more than one vine] In the meantime we need to push our language progress. Once our campaign starts, I intend to press for peace."

Peace! So even the Rootpounders want to stop hurting

the Destroyers and being hurt by them.

Strongjumper paused. "[I see the danger under the leaves] I know what you're thinking. It won't work. If it doesn't, we'll finish this. We have to protect the Thrasar. It's clear who the aggressor is here. If we need to kill those controlling the Destroyers, then we will."

None of the Rootpounders dissented. Sarfal swooned at the idea of killing off any kind of intelligent creature.

Yet what choice is there? When we run, they destroy what we leave behind. They want to end us.

"[Take flight!] We'd better get to it, then," Strongjumper announced. The Rootpounders all rose on their thick hind legs. They stomped over to their artificial climbing vines ponderously. Strongjumper paused and waved an upper appendage, which Sarfal understood was a polite parting gesture. Then it jumped to the ceiling without using a rope.

Then the other Rootpounders climbed back out of the building. Silence came to the chamber. Sarfal glided around the space three times, then loosely caught a rod with three fingers. Sarfal's serpentine body twirled over the rod, then settled under it in the gravity of the planet. The rod felt nothing like a vine; it was too stiff. Perhaps it had been designed for a wide range of gravitation.

The distraction is minimal.

Sarfal started a describer to accept and formalize the constraint parameters for the new design. The Thrasar provided a general description of the work zone: the deep oceans of their new planet. Sarfal did not have to know the details; the describer would handle all of that.

Then, most importantly of all, Sarfal specified the functions. It felt strange to tell the describer that Sarfal wanted a tool-for-harm; This tool was to take things apart that others wanted kept together!

There, Sarfal hit a snag. The describer kept adding safety features to ensure that no one would be harmed in the operation of the new tool. Sarfal patiently removed these one after the other with a growing mix of frustration and self-loathing.

What am I doing? This is so awful. The describer might report me as insane.

Sarfal flew around the room two times, allowing chemicals related to anxiety to subside. Then Sarfal had a new idea.

Sarfal got a different type of software primitives out and started to write a new describer specifically for these destructive tools that had only safety features for the user and nearby Thrasar and Rootpounders. Sarfal excluded robots and any other living thing from the safety checks. That took an extra hour of work. It had been a long time since such a low-level task had come along.

Then Sarfal launched the experimenters and gave them plenty of resources. The computing agents started to take random positions among the solution space to construct new designs. Other agents started to craft solutions from what they had learned about building tools in the past. The two types of agents deposited their designs into a potential solution pool. There, the designs competed against each other in a simulation created by a measurer, and a learner would apply alterations to fine tune the competitors after every measuring.

I'll have something soon, Sarfal thought. *Something horrible.*

Chapter 18

Telisa shook her head to herself.

I'm a xenoarchaeologist, or an explorer, or maybe just a looter, whatever. Now I have to negotiate with an alien race for all Terrans. And Celarans, for that matter.

Before her, in the PIT camp, torn vines lay all about. They were not damaged by the Destroyers; the *Iridar* had caused the mess the last time it had lifted off.

And I have to figure it out without her.

Telisa forced the emotions down because she knew she had to. This was about the survival of the Celarans; it was bigger than any of them. The rest of the team had taken the news of Cilreth's demise well, at least on the outside.

As hard as the problems were that the other team members faced, she envied them. Tackling technical problems had a completely different flavor than making big decisions that would impact the future of three races. Decisions that an explorer should not have to make.

Telisa had Magnus back, so that helped, but two people did not feel like enough.

She thought of Marcant.

He might be better than confiding in Caden or Siobhan... I guess I'll think it over.

Fortunately, a few supplies had been unloaded by Magnus's PIT robots for the team and cached in the jungle nearby. Telisa hauled some light containers of food and medical equipment into the clearing. Unfortunately, most of their arsenal had been destroyed with the *Iridar*. They would be leaving their energy packs out in the sunlight to recharge over days.

Maybe the Space Force unit left behind some recharging equipment. Or we could ask the Celarans for yet another favor...

As she worked, she stopped periodically to watch the Celarans as they prepared for a planetary bombardment of their new home. She could not see much with her own eyes or attendants from outside the industrial complex, but she had access to Celaran feeds from all over the system.

This can't be easy for them. They just got to this beautiful planet, and now they're endangering it.

The Celarans had deployed a small regiment of ships and machines to find raw materials from asteroid belts in the system. Some of the rocks were being diverted into orbit to be used for the attacks. Telisa watched the first asteroid queue up with another task force above the ocean where the Destroyers' base operated.

A ship dropped with the rock. It bled off a lot of energy entering the atmosphere and holding the fragment with its gravity spinner. The rock came in nice and slow.

That could be dangerous, Telisa realized. *If the Destroyers send missiles up after it...*

As if afraid of the very dangers Telisa contemplated, the ship dropped the rock and headed back into the rarefied atmosphere above. She watched the chunk of space rock plummet toward the waters.

A red icon flashed on the tactical. From the water's surface, a missile arced upward toward the threat. Seconds later it hit the rock, breaking it into three pieces.

Wow. That's impressive! That missile must have been highly optimized for that job, Telisa thought. Then she realized perhaps the asteroid did not have an iron core. That might be why it was selected for the bombardment instead of the Celaran starship industry.

The chunks fell to the water without further incident. Telisa watched the impact from sensors on Celaran starships. Huge columns of water and steam rose from the impacts.

Such power in something so simple. And it had a very low closing velocity.

Apparently the Destroyers were ready to defend themselves from this method of attack.

That's good though... one less missile they have. All we did is drop a rock.

Then Telisa wondered: had they really traded well against the enemy? The Celarans had to divert the rocks from the outer system to here, then accompany it into the atmosphere. The Destroyers had mined enough materials to make the missile, probably had to process a lot of various chemicals to make the explosives, and fire it off. Which side had used up more time, energy and materials?

Three more asteroids arrived at the queue point for the task force to direct for the ongoing attack. Telisa watched various feeds from the nearby Celaran ships. The aliens were going to try the next three objects simultaneously. The plan was to increase the rate of the bombardment as well as the energy of the projectiles until the Destroyers surrendered or they started to damage the planet. If no surrender came then Telisa foresaw a crisis: would the Celarans continue, or just flee the planet?

"How's the attack developing?" asked Magnus over his link. Telisa saw from the shared map that he was with Agrawal in the complex. They were probably overseeing the deployment of newly made robots and weapons.

"The Celarans started the bombardment," she said.

"Unfortunately, we have to experiment with these asteroids to determine the environmental impact as best we can, which means as we scale up our assault, the enemy may have a chance to adapt to it."

"Agrawal and I are replacing the hardware we lost and redeploying it. Well, except for the force towers, which would be the Celaran's responsibility, but I guess they've decided the towers are not an efficient way to defend from the attacks. You should know that some predators might start to slowly make their way closer to the complex, starting from the west."

Wonderful.

Lee interrupted the conversation by requesting a channel with Telisa. She accepted it and added Magnus to the channel.

"I have two bits of news," Lee said. "I've completed a tool design we can put onto our starships that would work well in the ocean. It should take apart many of their tools and buildings."

"That's great. I hope you can start making some of them," Telisa said. "What else?"

"We found an inert Destroyer machine among the vines." An image came along the channel, showing the machine as it had been discovered in the jungle.

"Inert?"

"It's been damaged by a tungsten fragment from one of the mines," Lee told her. "Still, most of its systems are untouched."

"Just one fragment? Why didn't it explode like the others?"

"The mine may have detonated prematurely for unknown reasons. Also, the power rings in the Destroyer must have been depleted by combat operations at the moment the mine detonated," Lee explained. "Without any current in the broken ring, there wasn't any energy stored in the electromagnetic field, so there was no heating up from arcing—no explosion. The Destroyer simply suffered massive power failure."

"Don't they have some other ion storage backups?"

"I don't know."

"Have you scanned the insides? Could we run some tests on it?" Telisa asked.

"Scientists are examining it. I don't know anything else."

"Thanks for letting me know. I'll tell Marcant. He may want to try and talk to it."

"Talk to it?" Lee asked.

"I mean, we may try telling it what to do in its language and see if it obeys. It probably won't, but it would be an interesting experiment."

Lee sent a nonverbal acknowledgement on the channel and then put it into an idle state to let Telisa know that Lee had nothing else to say. Telisa let the channel drop.

They're getting better at talking with us all the time.

"Well, you heard that. I guess I'll let Marcant know."

"Could be a big discovery. I'll let you get to it!" Magnus said and dropped the connection.

Sounds more like it's you that wants to get back to playing with the robots, Telisa thought. She was amused rather than annoyed.

If Magnus wasn't back... without him or Cilreth... I might give up.

"Marcant. Lee's just told us that they captured a tank which is largely intact. It had fallen among a tight group of large vines in the last battle."

"I need to know everything," Marcant stated calmly. "In particular—"

"We should use it to test our ideas about the intermediate machine language," Achaius finished for him.

"Exactly. Can we send it commands?" Marcant said.

Telisa smiled. Marcant had already taken the news and run with it. Telisa had only one more thing to offer at the moment.

"Coordinate with the Celarans directly. I'd try a subsystem first," Telisa suggested. "I don't even know yet if they want the thing. I was thinking about taking one of its beam weapons for study, but I don't necessarily want you to try and talk to anything dangerous."

"It wouldn't have any energy to use, anyway," Marcant said. "I have to tell you: This may be slow going."

Telisa could understand that. So far, she had been lucky enough to encounter aliens that *wanted* to communicate and cooperate. Without that two-sided approach, alien technology remained mysterious much, much longer... indefinitely, in the case of the Trilisks.

"I'm sure you and your friends can puzzle it out. Then I'll put you on the Trilisks."

Marcant laughed. Telisa realized she had not heard him laugh much before. She dropped the connection. Soon, her mind started to run through the same circles she had been stuck in before she had allowed the bombardment to fully distract her. Sooner or later, they would be able to talk to the Destroyers or their Masters. What would they say?

Maybe we could end this war with mere words. What

words? Should we even refrain from trying until we understand those who created the Destroyers?

Telisa finished moving the last container. The camp became lonely and silent. Caden and Siobhan were at their new factory. Telisa told three tents to deploy in case anyone returned. They would not be sleeping on the *Iridar* any longer.

Some part of Telisa made a sudden decision on who to talk to next. She opened a channel.

"Adair?"

"Hello Telisa," Adair replied quickly.

"Do you have any cycles to help me out?"

"You're the boss, actually, so yes," Adair said.

Intelligent enough to suck up to the boss, that's for sure.

"Well what are you working on now?"

"I'm monitoring the traffic we intercept in the ocean to understand and localize it so we can find the underwater factories, running simulations to find improvements in the timing of our mines' combined-arms style detonations, calculating the minimum number of missiles we need to use to destroy colossals with statistically acceptable certainty, poring over a number of—"

"Okay you're busy," Telisa summarized. "I'll try to be quick. I want to devise a strategy for the negotiations," Telisa said. "Given what we know about the Destroyers, we've already mentioned the theme I prefer: negotiation from a position of strength. The Destroyers came here to annihilate this race. We're not going to succeed by just asking them to stop. We have to threaten them or force them."

"What more do you have to do than explain that we'll

kill them if they don't leave the planet alone?" Adair said.

"I think we can leverage our entire civilization. They don't know anything about us, but we showed up and saved the Celarans in a space battle. We'll let them know they don't want to make enemies of us. They'll be fighting two races instead of one. We can threaten to take the campaign back to them, something they probably know the Celarans can't or won't do."

"I agree that could be compelling, though you might be dragging all Terrans into a war without consulting with any leaders."

According to Shiny, we're ranked higher than Admirals in the Space Force, Telisa thought, but she did not say it. She agreed with Adair's sentiment.

"You're right, but I'm willing to do it if that saves the Celarans. Besides, maybe I can imply this, or somehow take advantage of how little they know about us."

"We don't know if they're in the dark," Adair said. "First off, Destroyers killed the *Seeker*. Did they learn anything about us before that? Since then? Also... there may be Trilisks at the helm of their civilization. They may know everything there is to know about Terrans. It seems to me that we're the ones in the dark."

Hrm. This one sees the cup half empty!

"Not at all. We know some race created this massive war machine. And we know when the Celarans asked for mercy, the requests fell on deaf ears. We know the Celarans did nothing but run for their lives, at least initially."

"Seems like the Destroyers have the power here."

"It's hard for me to understand why they would want to kill the Celarans at all. What common ground are we sure to have with the Destroyers?" Telisa asked.

"Nothing is certain, but as races that evolved on planets like these, Terrans and Destroyers likely understand critical resource management. We evolved with limited resources and strained against those limits for a long time. If we make it clear to them that they will throw away a lot of resources against us to no gain..."

"Then they would decide the campaign is not to their advantage. Not from a moral standpoint, but from an economic one. Do you have an idea how to highlight this to them?"

"They poisoned the vines. We can poison the ocean. It's a scorched earth strategy. They can fight and expend huge resources, but we can deny them any gain," Adair said.

"Poison how?"

"I don't have that answer yet."

"Ugh. Maybe we can threaten that but not carry it out. It's a crime to waste such a beautiful planet."

"I suspect we would have to actually carry through with it at least once. If it helps you, consider that the Celarans already changed this place: they covered it with their vine jungles. None of this is natural. That could be what started this war in the first place. What if Celarans did this to planets the Destroyers wanted? Maybe even, planets they already inhabited, in the oceans?"

Wow.

"Still, what a horrible thing. I'd rather be tricky," Telisa said. "The Celarans won't be."

"The Celarans don't like to fight, but they can be tricky, I think," Adair said.

"Why would you say that?"

"The Celarans might be a tiny bit deceptive," Adair said.

"What? Tell me."

"Well, did you find it odd that they said their tools... their weaponry would not work underwater?"

"Not at all. Why would their energy weapons be designed to do that?"

"Because they're Celaran. They try to make everything as versatile as they can."

"That seems extreme," Telisa said.

"They are extreme," Adair said. "They have starships that can and have operated underwater, including energy weapons... though admittedly, calling them 'weapons' is not really accurate. As the Celarans say, they're just energy projectors, usable in many different contexts."

"So when Lee agreed to work on it, she was being deceptive? It sounded to me like she was just afraid."

"I have a few theories. Lee may have been afraid of another attack from space as she said. Lee may not have known the answer. Or Lee may have been stalling so she could consult other Celarans about the idea of sending starships into that ocean after the Destroyer base."

"I'm feeling tired now. Thanks for your time," Telisa said.

"Then you should be very alarmed! Isn't your host body extremely energetic? I thought you had superhuman levels of physical and mental endurance—"

"I meant to say, I'm ready to avoid thinking directly about these critical decisions for a short time, and so I'd like to halt the conversation."

"Sure. I'm always here to help if you want to resume later," Adair said.

That was help? I feel more unsure than when I started the conversation.

She had a lot more to think about now, but not many more real answers.

Michael McCloskey

Chapter 19

Marcant studied the scans of the Destroyer tank. The Celarans had transported the enemy machine to the industrial complex and slipped it into a large bay in one of the crazy-shaped buildings. Once there, they had methodically scanned the outside, then probed the innards with more EM and particle sweeps. Finally, the flyers started to disassemble it.

Marcant could recognize power rings, a gravity spinner, and the energy weapon assemblies. Beyond that, he had nothing. He decided to focus on the gravity spinner first. In what ways did it differ from their own? What kind of cybernetics controlled it?

He put himself into a three-dimensional space containing the scan data. A large, multicolored spinner core floated above him. Marcant added a reverse engineering program he had stolen from a major corporation. As it started its analysis, various labels started to pop up over components, representing its best guesses so far. Marcant peeled off layers and looked for more, adding his own notes as he went.

"I hope there's not a bomb hidden in there. This could be a trap," Adair said.

"Circumstances are dire. A few risks must be taken," Achaius replied. "There aren't many Celarans here at the industrial site, anyway."

"Right. The industrial site is nothing. Just the core of their ability to resist invasion," Adair said acidly.

Marcant ignored their bickering and kept at it. Five minutes into the job, he suddenly leaned forward in his chair. Something about that diagram—what was it? It was familiar... *too* familiar!

"The Quarus," he said aloud.

"What?" Adair asked.

"I need the *Iridar*'s information cache..." he said. Marcant's mood instantly soured; without the *Iridar* or any TRB, he was isolated from the vast knowledge of the Terran network.

"The Celarans took a copy when we arrived," Adair offered.

"Hook me up," Marcant demanded. He breathed a sigh of relief.

Adair sent him a pointer to the Celaran cache. He still missed the Vovokan computational resources, but at least now he could make progress investigating his suspicion. He ignored Adair's next questions and everything else that attempted to distract him for ten more minutes until he was sure.

This is big.

"Telisa," Marcant transmitted, trying to open a high priority connection to the PIT leader.

"Yes?"

"The Destroyers were created by the Quarus."

It took Telisa a second to respond to the bombshell. The Quarus were one of the alien races Terrans had found evidence of before the PIT team found Ambassador Shiny. The Terrans had developed the gravity spinner as a direct result of studying a single Quarus ship found adrift. The aliens' name came from the mystery of the ship and its function: the name basically meant "why" in an ancient Terran language.

"You must be mistaken. The Quarus ship—"

"Was an unmanned vessel," Marcant finished for her.

"It was an exploration probe, or a robot ship, or who knows what. But the point is, there was no reason to carry the extra mass of a water environment inside such a ship. No doubt the Quarus were simply being efficient."

Marcant had guessed at what Telisa must be thinking: the Quarus ship discovered by the Space Force had been devoid of any atmosphere, despite having some interior servicing tunnels. It had not leaked out, but had clearly never been present. Everything they thought they knew about these two races, the Destroyer creators and the Quarus, were suddenly and intricately linked.

"Hard to wrap my head around. Will this accelerate your investigations?" Telisa asked.

"Yes! The ship discovered by the Space Force was much more primitive, but it still sheds so much light on their current cybernetics! This is a huge breakthrough. It will almost make up for the fact that we don't have the aliens themselves working on the other side of the problem as we had with the Celarans. We have a decade of top Terran scientists' work that explains that old ship... to Terrans."

"That's great and creepy all at the same time. These aliens have been lurking at our doorstep longer than anyone realized. Can you split up the problem? I want at least one of you looking at communications as a priority."

"Will do, but please remember the wrinkle. There are two languages, the Destroyer coordination messages and the... Quarus's native tongue." Marcant said. "This breakthrough may shed more light on the former, but not the latter."

He kept the doubt from his voice. As far as he believed, no one was going to be making treaties with the

Destroyers anytime soon.

"See what you can accomplish. We're preparing for an attack of our own, but it would be nice to be able to call it off and negotiate a truce instead."

Telisa did not say the rest, but Marcant thought he knew what it was: *Especially given that we don't know if we can win.*

***

Marcant walked out onto the hardtop under the strong light of the local star. It felt good to stretch his legs and walk after hours in his PV working on translating alien messages. He sipped a glucosoda and walked up to the building Lee supposedly occupied.

Last chance to just connect to her from here.

Marcant looked up at the wall before him. The Celaran building only had doors on the top facing panels, at least thirty meters above.

I'm on the PIT team now, I can handle this. I need real exercise and practice.

Marcant had gone through a phase in his life where he ignored the real world. It had not gone well. Even with modern drugs and amazing medical technology, many structures of the Terran body still needed to be used now and then to prevent degeneration. Even his nervous system had started to fail after months in sustained VR. Since then, Marcant had started to move around more in this level of reality (current baseline, a simulationist would say). Since joining the PIT team, he had redoubled these efforts. He told himself it was part of his training.

Marcant resealed his drink and traded it for a smart

rope from his backpack.

"Here we are," he spoke to Adair and Achaius. "On a primitive... er, an alien planet that is advanced yet hostile to Terran life, about to risk death to ascend this building for a face to face with a Celaran."

"You may be risking *your* neck, but I'm sure my core sphere can handle this fall no problem," Adair said.

"Delusions of grandeur," Achaius said.

"I'm not delusional in this case," Marcant protested light-heartedly. I *am* a legitimate member of the PIT team and this *is* a hostile alien environ." His rope snaked up the side of the building and pulled itself along the top until it found purchase. When it was ready to bear Marcant's weight, it signaled his link.

"Not so very hostile..." Achaius said.

"Maybe a little bit, jelly-brain," Adair added. Marcant ignored them.

Marcant started up. He had done more dangerous climbs countless times—in virtual realities. Marcant could feel the difference. It was not a matter of what he saw, heard, or felt. The knowledge that the danger was real altered the experience immensely.

You're a simulationist, he reminded himself. *You're not supposed to believe this is real either.*

Marcant made it without falling. He puffed a bit at the top. Even with the smart rope to assist his climb, it had been exercise. He looked at his link map and found the nearest door.

"You're aware that this building is hollow, right? You can't fly to Lee in there."

"Perhaps at this point, I could compromise and ask her to flit over and chat," Marcant said. He walked over to the nearest door and pushed it open with his right hand, checking for a platform. He saw that although the building was hollow, there was a small platform just below the door that he could land on. He spun and pushed through the hexagonal trapdoor feet first, dropping inside.

Lee hovered right at the entrance beside the platform Marcant had alighted upon.

"Hi!" she said. Marcant accepted her presence.

I must be a clumsy oaf to her. She's probably been waiting here for a minute.

"I'm here to ask for help again," Marcant admitted.

"What do you need, friend?" Lee replied. She did not ask why he came to see her incarnate. Marcant wondered if the alien was truly as happy as the translator made her sound. His translator had normalized the range of their moods and mapped them onto Terran emotions. It was based upon too many assumptions and anthropomorphizations.

"I can't make progress on the Quarus's language. I know that the Celarans worked on it back when you tried to make peace with the Destroyers. I'm not as interested in the machine signals the machines use to coordinate, though, as much as in the native language of the Quarus."

"You're right, we Celarans learned some things about it. However, we don't know how successful we were; the Destroyers never relented despite our many pleas to stop. What do you have?" she asked.

Marcant sent her the snippets from the alien flagship that had been captured during the battles. They were different than the inter-Destroyer transmissions seen during the battle.

Lee referenced the majority of the snippets through

their link connection.

"These cannot be translated. They are only bits and pieces of one statement."

"There's a lot of data there," Marcant protested. "There's one long transmission at the start of the battle."

"That's the only thing it really said. They have a kind of batch communication," Lee said. "It takes longer for them to say anything, but once decoded, every batch says a lot. They communicate the equivalents of pictures, books, or speeches in whole blocks. It may be hard to understand, but imagine a book that can be comprehended as a whole, but any one piece of it means nothing."

"It's amazing you made that key insight," Marcant said. "We were stuck."

"Our race was dying. We had to put a lot of work into it."

Marcant wondered what it would be like to study an alien language while those you wanted to talk to annihilated your planet. He hoped he would not have to live it.

"How could any race have developed language like that? Surely at some point in their primitive past, one of them just had to say 'yes' or 'no'," Marcant wondered aloud.

"I have no explanation for the apparent lack of simple primitives," Lee said. "Perhaps they exist but we cannot understand, or maybe we were never exposed to them because they are no longer used."

Marcant hooked Telisa in on the conversation. She accepted the link.

"Lee says that Quarus communicate in larger blocks than we do, not just mechanically, but maybe conceptually."

"That happened during the last battle?"

"Here. I isolated the command message from the flagship at the start of the attack, but we only have pieces of it. The battle produced huge amounts of complex EM noise. There wasn't anything else during the battle at all that I found."

"Then here's another theory on why the Destroyers are relatively inflexible," Telisa said. "They transmit the entire plan to the machines in one of their 'blocks' of communication. I imagine it's quite complex, step upon step, contingency upon contingency, but the machines stick to the plan. If things go sideways, if the enemy does something unexpected, then they fall back upon a default behavior—say, all out frontal assault—rather than devise a new tactic."

Telisa is sharp. She has a strong imagination, Marcant thought. The standard theory that had been put forward was that the Quarus did not want their machines to be too smart to become a danger to their creators. The two ideas were not necessarily mutually exclusive, though.

"That's a lot of guesses based upon a bit of insight," Marcant commented.

"It's a good theory," Lee said. "Their communications are very limited during the battle. There are advantages as well. It also makes their servant machines hard to interfere with."

Right. If that theory holds, it rules out our idea of learning to speak Destroyer and trying to confuse them with fake orders during a fight.

"Can we send the flagship a message?" Telisa asked. "Send them a demand for surrender."

"We need the big picture," Lee said. "A single statement would be nonsensical to them. It would be like sending a Terran a message with a single letter. The message specifies no abstraction at that level. If they even realized we were talking to them at all."

"How can I send a picture of surrender?" asked Telisa.

"No, we need your whole terms, what you want, what will happen if they refuse, everything about your position to distill into one block of communication," Lee said. "Pretend you have to write a long document about your demands, your position in the negotiation, everything that might happen, your answers to any question they might have, your threatened responses to every counter action they might take."

"We can't give away too much," Marcant said. "We can threaten them with various actions we'll take, but..."

"We can use this to our advantage," Telisa said. "I have an idea."

"Please share it," Lee said excitedly.

"We'll outline two outcomes of this battle. One in which we kill them off, and one in which they accept our terms to leave and never come back. We'll show them step by step how we're going to go in there and kill them off if they don't bow to our terms. We'll show them how we're ready to poison the ocean. If they do leave, we show them that we won't pursue."

"Showing them our plan—" Marcant persisted.

"I don't intend to show them the *real* plan. I'm going to show them the obvious, straightforward attack that we all doubt."

"Aha. Let them prepare for something that isn't really coming."

"Yes."

"Then what's the real plan?" asked Marcant.

"I haven't put the finishing touches on it yet," Telisa. "For now, we just concentrate on setting the trap."

Chapter 20

Siobhan knew it would only be a few more days before Telisa would have to order an attack.

The Celaran ships patrolled far over the jungle between the industrial base and the enemy ocean. They did not dare gather or land for fear of a Destroyer strike. Yet when the time came, they would have to go even closer to the danger zone.

Siobhan had an awful feeling about going into the ocean after the Quarus ship and the suspected Destroyer factories. It did not feel like a reasonable plan—but what else could they do? Surely another, even bigger Destroyer attack would emerge from the ocean in another week and threaten them again.

Lee sent a report on the status of their preparations. The entire PIT team had permission to read it, so Siobhan checked it out. The Celaran ships allocated for the attack were empty, as none of the aliens would serve on a ship to be sent into the water after the Destroyers. The Celarans were clearly negative on the idea of assaulting the ocean. The report complained about an insufficient number of ships for an offensive operation and lack of production assets to quickly make more. It went on to discuss the limitations of their aquatic capability: ships that could not dive deep into the pressure of the ocean, and energy weaponry suboptimal for submarine operations.

They don't want to do this. And I can't blame them. Going in after the Destroyers in the water will cost a lot.

Even though Siobhan felt the same about the attack, she thought the Celarans had good enough weapons for use in the ocean, especially now that Lee had designed improved ones. That part of the report felt like an excuse. Perhaps their allies thought they needed to justify their position or the Terrans would abandon them?

I could be missing the whole source of their reluctance. Maybe they just don't want to hurt anyone, even the Destroyers.

Telisa checked in on Siobhan in the new factory often. The factory had been set up within a matter of days and had not stopped producing parts for explosive mines and disk machine missiles since Siobhan had launched it. Raw materials came in by air several times a day, brought in from distant automated mining operations.

Siobhan expected Telisa to show up and inquire on progress any moment. Lee connected to the team again while Siobhan waited.

"Our message to the Quarus has been answered," Lee announced.

Wow! That's more than ever happened before.

The Celaran sent a pointer with the message. Siobhan followed it and found a complex body of translation notes. She could not decipher the data.

"What does it say?" asked Caden, echoing Siobhan's confusion.

"If I may summarize," Adair said. "The response is an outline of an assault plan that starts with the destruction of our ocean assault force. It then continues with a description of the annihilation of the Celaran race. It ends with the threat of following any survivors back to the Terran homeworld."

"That would be a 'no' to our suggestion for ending the war," Telisa transmitted. Siobhan saw Telisa spoke from only a quarter of a kilometer away; she was outside the compound fence, on the way to see Siobhan.

"We expected such a response," Magnus said on the team channel. "This doesn't change anything. We know we can talk to them now, even though it isn't quick and easy. Time to deal them a major blow."

Siobhan mulled over the response as she waited for Telisa to arrive.

Are we in bigger trouble this time than before? Is this how it's going to end for us at last?

She had a sudden quirky idea to run off with Caden into the jungle and just survive out there. It might be a rational thing to do. If they waited long enough, a fleet from Sol might arrive and rescue them.

Is he thinking of the same plan? Or would he call me a coward? Would Telisa brand me a traitor?

Siobhan took a deep breath. She did not want to run. The Celarans needed their help, and the PIT team was going to give it to them. They at least had control of local space, and the hope of reinforcements from Shiny.

Telisa came into the factory from a ground level door—something only Siobhan's factory had. Telisa did not smile when she saw her—only Caden would do that in times like these—yet the PIT leader seemed relaxed. She walked up to Siobhan on a narrow path that led through the factory, another Terranized feature of the Celaran-built factory.

"Let's talk about the ocean assault," Telisa said aloud, surprising Siobhan. Telisa usually spoke with Magnus or Marcant about their attack strategies.

"Okay."

"What's your opinion?" Telisa asked.

"It would be a mistake to attack now," Siobhan said.

"This won't work. They'll have technologies for underwater energy weapons use, while ours scatter and dissipate alarmingly. We don't have any good torpedoes or guided weapons optimized for the ocean. Even if we did, I think the Quarus's would be better."

"As you recall, our submarine assault threat is a distraction," Telisa said.

"Sure, but what's the real attack, then?"

"I'll tell you, but we need mobile gravity spinners from the Celarans."

"You need what?" Siobhan asked.

"Gravity spinners in mobile bodies. We'll put them inside the asteroids to soften the impact by dropping them slowly into the ocean."

"It'll be like dropping boulders into a lake to smash fish," Siobhan said. "They've already shown the ability to deflect huge chunks of sinking rock and even some iron-cored asteroids."

"Let them deflect the rocks. The spinners will exit the boulders later, all at once. If a few of them can grab onto the Destroyer ship, or even get near it..."

"Then we can bring it to the surface!" Siobhan said. She thought it over for a moment.

"By now there must be several other factories down there," Siobhan said.

"We need the original. Put one or two of Marcant's new sensors on these things so they can find it. If we capture some of the Quarus, I bet we can force them to stop the next Destroyer attack."

"They're not going to stop. They already said so. If they stop just to save their own lives, well, that's not a real peace treaty."

"I'll be thinking about that more as we ramp this up. Even if we only get a temporary halt to the attacks, that might be enough."

"We should just hide mobile bombs inside the rocks," Siobhan said. "If we can get a gravity spinner close, we can get a torpedo close. Just blow them up."

"That approach is simpler, but spinners would have a better chance of making it through, if they're configured correctly."

"How so?"

"Spinners will be faster than any reaction or propeller driven torpedo we could make," Telisa said. "Also, spinners can use their own gradients to defend themselves to some degree."

"Oh. But surely that's only against kinetic attacks? Wouldn't energy weapons still be effective?"

"Yes, but the Quarus have been using the missiles to break up the rocks. We'll distract their energy weapons elsewhere."

Perhaps it could work...

"Unfortunately, the gravity spinners are the most sophisticated thing that Celarans are making. They'll need one for each ship they produce, so there's no surplus. I don't know how many they would provide."

"Four might be enough. Six would be better."

Siobhan nodded. "If the Celarans can get me those spinners, I can handle the modifications."

"Tell them this is our best chance at stopping the enemy without having to throw the entire fleet into the ocean."

***

Siobhan dove into her new mission with everything she had.

She had been thinking about a simple crawler that would move along the bottom of the ocean to the factory site. But now, she realized a torpedo with a spinner warhead would be much faster to arrive near the target. The spinners would probably have to get within a couple hundred meters to capture the base in the area of effect. She doubted the Celarans would be providing huge spinners like the one used by the Celaran probe ship.

A torpedo then... but won't that be conspicuous? Actually, what IS conspicuous to a Quarus?

Siobhan opened a channel.

"Marcant."

"Yes?"

"Did those little spy devices of yours come up with any native life forms down in the alien drink?"

"Why, yes, they did. A wide variety, in fact. It's part of what's so difficult about finding what we want."

"Can you send me some signatures for creatures in the lowest regions of that ocean? The faster it moves, the better. You know, a squid-like thing would be better than a crab that crawls on the bottom."

"I can find some candidates for you..." Marcant said.

He's wondering if he can ask.

"I'm making a weapon and it needs to look like a fish," she summarized.

"Good luck. Those aliens probably warred among themselves a thousand years ago and had that same idea. I imagine by now..."

"It doesn't have to fool them for very long," she said.

She thought of the asteroids they would be embedded into. "And it won't be their only camouflage. Besides, we're launching a massive diversion at the same time... you know, the starship attack we threatened them with?"

Why am I justifying this to Marcant?

Part of Siobhan felt annoyance and the other part knew Marcant was smart. If he had criticism, it was probably on the mark.

"I'll send two or three ideal candidates," Marcant said. "Good luck."

Siobhan's ire subsided a notch.

"Thanks," she said.

She halted to think again. Her annoyance with Marcant transformed into determination to succeed. Marcant's signatures came in and Siobhan looked them over. Two of the sigs were of streamlined fishlike creatures, and one was a... jet-propelled monstrosity. The sigs were suitable, but they were all slow.

The advantages of using spinners is their speed. I can't use these.

Siobhan pondered the possibility of having the spinners move slowly until detected, then speeding up. The problem with that was, if a beam weapon locked on, it would be too late.

No, this is all wrong.

The idea relied upon stealth and speed, but she did not find the two to be compatible. Perhaps the Celarans could make a cloaking system? She shook her head. Siobhan asked Marcant for all the signatures he had seen.

An image of a large juggernaut of a creepy-crawly came up in her PV. Siobhan stared at it: a black crab-thing with glowing antennae and a massive armored shell. The back of the shell was covered in rocks for camouflage. The sig would never work; the thing was just too slow.

Still...

It had armor *and* stealth. In that moment, Siobhan knew what she wanted to do. She sent a change of plans to Telisa.

Chapter 21

Telisa bolted awake to a high priority alert. The fog of sleep fled her brain in a split second—one of the advantages of being 'Trilisk Special Forces'.

The Celarans had detected the arrival of a new space fleet.

If the Destroyers coordinate their next ground assault with another space attack...

"They're Terran," Lee announced on the PIT channel.

"Yes, a Space Force fleet of over 100 ships! I see the *Midway* among them," Marcant reported.

Telisa felt a wave of relief so strong it almost made her weep. Her hand came to her face. The skin over her eye felt smooth again; once she had gotten Magnus back onto the team, she had allowed an automated cosmetic kit to heal the scar.

"This is Admiral Sager. It's good to see you all," said a broadcast from the fleet. A video connection was offered, so Telisa accepted the feed. She allowed one of her attendants to provide a video stream from her side.

"You made it!" Telisa responded for the PIT team.

"We're glad to find you still alive. Has the enemy found you here?"

"The enemy is in the ocean, Admiral. We need some of your ships here to assist us. The rest of the fleet should be deployed to meet any incoming Destroyer fleets."

"Yes, ma'am. What's the plan?"

"A little distraction for the enemy. Who is, by the way, the Quarus. We've discovered that the same race that made the famous Quarus vessel has constructed the Destroyers."

"I learned that," Sager responded evenly. "Amazing, isn't it?"

"What? How do you know?"

"We received a tachyonic transmission from a Celaran source shortly before our departure," Sager said.

So Siobhan's friend came through for us.

"What I don't know is, why?" asked Sager, probably unaware of his reference to the origin of the alien name.

"The lead theory is still xenophobia caused by the Vovokan attack," Telisa said. "It's also possible that Celaran probe ships altered the ecosystems of whole worlds that had Quarus in their oceans. Do you have any unmanned ships?"

"Yes, many. We have 74 robot corvettes, basically missile carriers with light point defense energy weapons."

"Good. We might have to give a few of those away before it's all over. We need to puff our force up. Make it threatening."

"We're here to help... but I don't see the enemy."

Telisa sent a pointer to the Admiral. "This ocean. They have at least one ship there, probably augmented by self-replicating factories."

Sager nodded. Telisa prepared to tell him that she had another course of action to effect once the charade began. She could send him details offline soon.

"Do these corvettes' missiles work underwater?" she asked.

"No, but we have liquid environment ordnance designs available," Sager told her. "We can begin production immediately."

Thank the Five!

"That's good news. We'll need a lot of them as soon

as possible," Telisa said. She felt real hope rise for the Celarans.

Surely we'll succeed with this force on our side!

Telisa scanned the Space Force fleet composition. It was beefy, even by post-buildup standards: 20 battleships carrying heavy energy weapons, twice that number of missile and drone cruisers, together with the robot corvettes Sager had mentioned, a dozen scout ships that reminded her of the Seeker, and over 50 support vessels. Shiny's huge ships were glaringly absent.

Or could they be out there, cloaked?

"Do you have any... big friends out there, Admiral?"

"Ambassador Shiny encouraged us to respond to the situation," Sager said cautiously. "The rest secure Sol. We're glad to come to the aid of our new friends."

"That's fortunate. We need you here."

"Speaking of ambassadors," Sager continued, "We have an ambassador who would like to be briefed, if that's possible."

"Then send him down with a ship. The PIT team needs a new one. Also, I trust you brought ground assault machines with you. We need everything you've got down here by the industrial complex," Telisa ordered, sending the Admiral another location pointer. "Destroyer attacks will originate from the west, from the same ocean. Your ground commander should coordinate with Magnus and Colonel Agrawal."

"Yes, ma'am," Sager said. Telisa felt that she could get used to ordering admirals around, though it still felt weird to do so.

Oh, well, practice makes perfect...

"The fleet has two roles here," Telisa said. "First, we

need to bolster the defenses of the Celaran space stations in case a new Destroyer fleet appears. Secondly, we need at least 30 robot corvettes for the ocean assault. The battleships will be useful for a ground support role, as we need their energy weapons to drop any missiles the Destroyers are launching from that ocean. You know more than I do about your ships, so I want you to deploy them as you see fit with those roles in mind."

"Yes, ma'am."

***

Ambassador Gusti was a short man with dark skin and curly hair. Telisa's first impression was of an energetic and focused individual.

"Thank you for meeting me face to face," Telisa said. They spoke in a meeting room of the small Space Force ship that had delivered Gusti to them. The crew of the ship worked to transport the sad little PIT camp into their cargo bay.

"I appreciate your time, which I understand is limited," he said politely.

Telisa paused and then started in.

"Ambassador Gusti. I'm sorry that this isn't a better time to get to know the Celarans. Right now, relations are great, but they're so very busy." Telisa inhaled to continue, but Gusti jumped right in.

"I'm not the UNSF Ambassador to the Celarans," Gusti said. "I'm the Ambassador to the Quarus."

Telisa stared at Gusti again as if seeing him for the first time.

Five Entities. How did I not see this one coming?

He caught her reaction and continued. "We heard just in time. I was able to join the force minutes before departure."

"Have you had time to learn about the Quarus?" Telisa asked.

"I'm an expert on the Quarus," Gusti said defensively. "I've been the UNSF Ambassador to the Quarus for a decade."

What?!

"We've been in contact with them? It's a government secret?" Telisa asked, aghast.

"No. Until now, my position has only been for a contingency considered highly unlikely. We now know it has come to pass. I know everything we learned from the Quarus vessel discovery. Please allow me to examine what you've learned since you encountered the Quarus?"

"Yes, of course," Telisa said. She sent him pointers to the items she found immediately relevant and resolved to find more data for him as soon as they were done talking.

"Has Shiny given you an agenda?" Telisa asked bluntly.

The directness did not faze the ambassador. He answered quickly.

"I'm to offer them peace," he said. "Fortunately, the Space Force and Shiny are on the same page here."

If Shiny wants peace with the Destroyers, it's only so he can wipe them out by surprise later.

Telisa noticed that he had not said 'Ambassador Shiny', but she did not know what to make of it.

"Who do you serve? Where does your loyalty lie?"

"My loyalties are complex. I serve the Space Force, Earth, all of humanity, and Shiny."

Wow. Did he list those in order?

"I'm going to catch you up fast," Telisa said. "I've sent you pointers for the preliminary information, but to sum it up: We've been fighting for our lives and the lives of our Celaran friends. All Celaran attempts at diplomacy have failed. We know the Quarus won't stop when they're winning. The war machines built by the Quarus devastated and poisoned the Celaran homeworld. We can communicate with the Quarus, but it's very difficult to do so."

Gusti nodded. He did not jump in this time, so Telisa continued.

"I would like to make one more offer of peace, to see if they accept it when they're outmatched. However, we're working against the clock. The enemy's production capability is ramping up faster than ours and they're going to launch another attack if we don't stop them. Therefore, I won't hold back the counterattack when it's ready. We have to try and send them a message before the attack. Even if they accept a truce, it'll be a risk to believe them. However, the arrival of the Terran fleet affords us that possibility, at least, since we now have enough heavy energy weapons support to resist another ground attack."

"So it's not even up to me," the Ambassador said. His voice was neutral, but Telisa imagined he must find that very frustrating.

"You propose we allow our new allies, the Celarans, to die so that we can continue to attempt to reason with the Quarus?" Telisa responded carefully.

"We could continue to defend the Celarans, of course," said the Ambassador. "The Space Fleet is here now."

"I meant the fleet buys us some time. It's still the case that if the Quarus just stall on diplomatic negotiations, the advantage will eventually tip back into their favor."

"How is their production outstripping ours?"

"The Celarans just uprooted their colony and fled here. The Quarus have some kind of automated factories down there, and we believe they are building more factories as well as building war machines. Also, the fact that the seed ship followed us here probably means the rest of the Quarus know our new location, so more Destroyer ships could arrive at any time."

"Please send me the evidence of these self-replicating factories," Gusti said. "Do you have reason to believe the Quarus use this kind of technology?"

"It's only a theory based on inductive reasoning," Telisa said. "The size of the second attack was exactly double that of the first. You're familiar with the concept of self-replicating machines? It seems likely that their productive capacity is growing rapidly."

"After only two such attacks, it's impossible to know for sure."

"That's right, but we know how dangerous they are. There's no reason to risk the Celarans... and ourselves, on the slight chance that we can befriend the Quarus where the Celarans failed."

"What if you learned the Quarus were here first? What if their surprising industrial capacity is because they already had a colony here? What if they followed you here to defend their colony? Would that change your outlook, TM?" Gusti asked.

TM?

"It would give me pause, though I still see one race

aggressively exterminating the other. The Celarans welcomed us warmly, and I think they would have done the same to any other group."

"Yet you just said, you're going to attempt to achieve a truce by showing yourself to be a strong adversary. Surely there are many alien mindsets that would respond well to that. The Quarus may have seen only weakness in the Celarans. It could work."

"We'll find out soon."

***

Telisa entered Magnus's quarters, walked up to his sleep web, and collapsed into it beside him. She felt the comforting, cool resistance of his Veer suit against her.

"What's wrong?" Magnus asked.

"What isn't wrong?"

"What now, I mean?"

"The Ambassador."

"Yes?" he prompted.

"Before, I complained about these responsibilities. About having to call the shots. You recall?"

"Yes. The 'we're just explorers' lament," Magnus said carefully.

"Yes, that one. Well the only thing I hate worse than having to make these huge decisions that affect billions of Terrans and aliens—"

"Is standing by and watching the Ambassador make the decisions for you," Magnus finished for her.

"Exactly. Am I so arrogant, so power drunk, that I think I can do a better job than this man whose entire job is to be the Ambassador to the Quarus?"

"You, a super intelligent, long-time student of xenoarchaeology, a seasoned veteran of alien relations, leader of the PIT team, savior of a whole alien race? Better than some random bureaucrat? You bet you are," Magnus said.

"That kind of thinking is dangerous."

"Underrating yourself is dangerous. What does the Ambassador want to do?"

"He wants to halt our attack and keep trying to talk."

"Which would result in disaster. We know that."

"No. We *think* we know that. What if we're wrong?"

"The chance we're wrong is smaller than the chance Gusti is wrong. Shiny put his trust in us."

"If we go with Shiny that kind of makes us traitors, right? The real Terran government, what's left of it, is the admiralty of the Space Force. They sent Gusti to be the ambassador to the Quarus."

"Let him be the Ambassador. That's fine. Let him talk to them, that's fine too. But we're conducting a war to save the Celarans. Those poor creatures depend upon us for survival!"

Telisa nodded.

"Thanks. I feel better now, knowing I'm not the only power-corrupted tyrant here."

"Anytime."

Michael McCloskey

Chapter 22

Caden ran on a huge vine through the jungle. On his right, the Celaran perimeter fence had just gone out of sight behind the massive alien leaves. As Caden got his exercise and practiced jumping between the massive branches, he checked his progress on the tactical. He was half of the way to Siobhan's position in the new factory.

The map showed the location of each member of the team. That was a good thing, but Caden knew everyone would see that he was coming out to the factory again. Of course he often sought Siobhan out, but he almost never interrupted her work cycles. The problem was, would the rest of the team understand that?

I should accomplish something useful while I'm there.

What might that be? He would have to keep his eyes open and learn more about how the place worked. Questions could be directed at Siobhan.

The rest of the run was pleasant. The fronds and bugs all around him looked familiar now. The wonder of being on an alien world had worn off in dozens of hours on Celaran worlds and hundreds more in virtual simulations of them.

Up ahead, the new factory materialized from the foliage. Caden ran for a gate in the fence that surrounded the building. The sensor there detected his approach and opened for him. It was a nice addition for Siobhan's factory—no need to cut through the fence or vault over it.

He let himself into the building through a ground level entrance. It actually felt odd to walk right in instead of throwing up a smart rope and scaling the building. The inside was hollow, like the Celaran buildings, but narrow lanes extended into the rows of equipment to allow Terrans to move around. His link showed him exactly where Siobhan worked, but he decided to avoid her for a moment and observe.

A batch of complex machines finished up in the main fabrication line. He saw that as the large metal and carbon objects came out, the machines in his corner of the factory dropped into inactivity. He checked the logs. This section was busy 93% of the time. All of the other sections had a higher usage rate.

There's slack here.

Caden considered what he could do. There wasn't much capacity available... he could only make something small.

The Space Force is cranking out torpedoes. If I could get a design or two, I could adapt them to the disk squadron...

Caden got to work. He sent the fleet a high priority request for their smallest torpedo designs as he set up a virtual workspace on a nearby fabrication controller. The designs came through quickly. He frowned. The smallest one was larger than the missiles they deployed on the disk machines. Caden calculated that the Celaran disks could carry two torpedoes instead of four missiles.

Caden altered the small design to fit the disks' clamps. The software on the controller's virtual workbench made it easy. He scheduled his ordnance for production at the lowest priority. It said he would not have any product for hours; not only did he have to wait for slack time, but the Celaran air supply service would have to drop off new raw materials that were not already stockpiled nearby.

"I can get you up and running faster," Siobhan said on

a private connection.

"Oh! Hi. Show me how it's done, Miss Factory Sorceress," Caden said happily.

"Here's the deal: right now you're waiting two extra hours for the warhead chemicals. Use this formula. It's a Celaran equivalent, and we have that stuff in local storage."

She sent him a pointer. He swapped out the Space Force warhead formula with Siobhan's suggested replacement. The initial production schedule moved up by over two hours.

"Thanks!" Caden said.

"Of course. Now that I saved you some time, why don't you come over here and do me a favor..."

***

"Team, we're going to attack in three hours," Telisa said on the PIT channel.

Relief and a new nervousness rode in together on a wave through Caden's system. He had been working overnight in the factory. The last few torpedoes had just come off the line. Would he be able to get the rest of the disk machines loaded up? If there was no other work for them to do, it would be easy, but surely the imminent attack meant other last minute tasks would be routed to the Celaran machines?

"Gather up incarnate here with me," Telisa said from within the Celaran industrial complex. "We can follow the attack feeds and adjust as necessary."

Caden bit his lip and thought about that.

"Telisa?"

"Yes, Caden?"

"I'm making some last minute preparations. I might be late to get this wrapped up. It's for the attack."

"Then stay. That has priority, of course."

"Thanks."

"You do plan on enlightening me?" Telisa asked.

"Yes. I think I can get more torpedoes there, if I can pull this off."

"Good."

Telisa let the connection drop.

She trusts me. What other boss would just let me go and run with something and not delay me by asking a thousand questions? I have to make it work.

Caden routed a few disk machines through to pick up ordnance. The batch of takers he got was small, so he decided to inform the Celaran 'pilots' of his plan so they might help. He sent off a quick message to his squadron's channel.

The last hours ticked by while Caden coaxed the squadron to come in and arm themselves for the attack in between their regular work assignments. He had already sacrificed his last opportunity to sleep before the attack, but he decided it would be worth it.

It's not me who has to fight, it's the machines.

The team trickled into a Celaran building to join Telisa. The Celarans coordinating the attack were not present; Caden knew they were controlling their ships from the space hangars. Caden watched the team through an attendant feed. Telisa started to speak.

"You all know most of the details of our attack. I hinted that this isn't our real play. Here's the rest of the plan," Telisa told them. "The main attack is a noisy distraction. We'll risk throwing away some of our unmanned ships to test the Quarus in their own environment. Meanwhile, we're going to try and sneak gravity spinners down there inside some of the big rocks."

The last of the disk machines acknowledged their commitment to load up their ordnance in the next ten minutes. Caden collected himself and left the Terran factory. He did not have to be around to oversee the rest of it; the machines would load themselves.

"Worst case, we'll disrupt their preparations for their next ground assault," Telisa continued. "Best case, we capture some Quarus and get them to call off their Destroyers."

Caden ran. He wanted to be there incarnate before the attack commenced. He ascended a large vine runner, legs pumping.

"So the target is the special ship," Marcant said. "What camouflage did we decide upon for the spinners?"

"The rock itself," Siobhan said. "We've put fault lines into the payload-bearing asteroids and hidden a spinner inside a large piece of each one. The spinners will remain embedded in their fragments when the rock breaks up. Their rock casings will serve as both camouflage and ablative armor. The spinners can move their casings with them just as they move our ships."

"Succeed or fail, we'll learn more about the enemy," Telisa said. "I want to see how they handle submarine warfare. It's a safe bet they're great at it."

"How many do we have to sneak in?" Marcant asked.

"We have six of these special asteroids with our surprises inside," Telisa said. "I want the Quarus to think we've only slowed down the asteroids to keep the rock

251

from vaporizing on the surface of the ocean on impact. We've been trying various impact velocities and measuring their effects on the planet's ecosystem, as well as looking for clues as to the damage we're doing to the enemy, so varying closing velocities in this attack should not cause any suspicion. Some rocks with iron cores will go in hot, the ones with spinners will be among the slower ones."

Caden reached the fence surrounding the industrial complex. He considered a risky jump over the fence, dismissed it, and continued to run.

"Here are some new panels for your PVs with the pointers to everything we've prepared, including the Celaran-provided intelligence. It's been integrated into our shared tactical map."

Caden wanted to look right away, but he was too busy jumping from the last vine and coming to a special section of fence that had been set up to let Terrans in and out of the complex on their way to the new factory. He passed through a pliant part of the barrier and started across the hardtop beyond.

"I want those corvettes in the water seconds after these asteroids splash down," Telisa continued. "The attack will involve many elements close together in time, even though we have to spread out across many kilometers of ocean to keep from being incinerated in our own rock impact zones. We have to stretch their resources to keep them from discovering our real attack."

Saturate the defenses. That's exactly what this torpedo salvo could help do.

"Does anyone have questions?"

Caden ran into the room. Everyone looked at him

instead of asking anything, so he spoke.

"My squadron is ready to assist," Caden announced. His Veer suit had kept him cool and dry, but he still breathed quickly.

Telisa looked at him with a neutral face. "What role will they play? Did you modify the disk machines?"

"I modified a Space Force torpedo design and adapted them to the disk machine missile mountings. The squadron has one full load of two torpedoes each. The disk machines were already capable of operating underwater... you know, the Celarans and their hyper-functionality."

Telisa considered that, then nodded.

"Good. Good job. We can use the extra targets in the water. Also, maybe the disks can scout out dangers for the ships."

"If the enemy fights back with torpedoes of their own, the disk machines can intercept," Caden pointed out. "We would rather lose a disk than one of those corvettes."

Caden did not know if the Quarus used torpedoes. They seemed to be wholeheartedly using energy weapons, except for the missiles they shot at space targets. Maybe their missiles were also torpedoes, capable of being used in both roles.

Telisa did not say anything for a moment. Caden took the opportunity to continue.

"I'm sorry I didn't have news of this sooner. It was a last minute thing."

By last minute, I mean last nine hours of no sleep.

Telisa nodded.

"The schedule has been tight, but now it's time," she said.

Caden saw activity on the system map.

"The rocks are descending," Telisa said. "There's about forty of them. The rocks with our payloads are mixed in among them."

Caden closed his eyes and focused on the tactical. There was a lot of information to navigate there, even when organized neatly into dozens of panes in his PV. Unmanned Celaran ships accompanied the asteroid chunks down, slowing the fall of the rocks. The alien ships were perched atop the rocks, using them as shields.

The robotic Space Force corvettes started their descent. Caden's squadron waited in the jungle beside the ocean. The attack zone spanned many thousands of square kilometers. He calculated a course out over the waters to arrive with the rocks.

"We can track the rocks' descent underwater with the disk machines," Caden offered.

"That might be helpful, but it can't look like we're escorting the rocks on their way down. It would be too suspicious," Telisa said.

"We anticipate jamming as well, so we might not hear from the disks," Marcant noted.

"We'll scatter the squadron so that we have coverage of a wide area. There will only be one machine near each of the asteroids at any given time," Caden promised.

Caden passed the instructions along to his Celaran robot handlers: The disk machines could not appear to be protecting the asteroids with the spinner payloads. They acknowledged the plan and agreed to be careful.

The squadron shot out over the ocean. Caden watched the water, wondering if anything would happen. The disks moved at high speed, causing trails of white mist to rise from the bluish-green waves below them.

Disks started to explode. Caden watched the numbers rise: three, five, then ten of the robots died. Their fragments scattered and slowed, dropping into the water in hundreds of pieces.

"The disks are encountering resistance!" Caden reported. He had no idea how they were being killed. He checked the feedback from the disk machines, but there were no answers there. The disk robots were not designed for war, so they did not have the death reporting diagnostics of Terran war machines. "Probably energy weapons sourced from under the water!"

Caden knew that powerful EM projections could travel through many mediums, though their behavior varied across materials and especially at the junctures between materials. Apparently the Quarus, being aquatic creatures, knew exactly how to deal with firing such weapons from underwater.

"Makes sense," Telisa said. "They set up some defenses at the coast where their forces emerge. It's the closest point from the ocean to the industrial complex."

The tactical lit up elsewhere.

"Enemy missile launch!" Magnus said.

Caden had only a second to consider what, if anything, his disk squadron could do about the new missiles when the Space Force fleet above the atmosphere responded. This time, the Terrans and Celarans had total orbital superiority. A vast amount of energy poured out of the heavens upon the rising Quarus weapons. Caden scanned the readouts—the Terran battleships had a staggering number of joules at their disposal.

Caden put the handful of disk machines he controlled on an evasive course. He had to recalculate time to the targeted assault zone—it would now be harder to get there on time. The good news was that the squadron had lost only about 10% of their force.

As they left the coast behind, Caden considered the trade-offs of getting fewer machines to the zone sooner versus staying on their erratic courses and arriving after the spinners hit the water. He selected an evasion algorithm that would smooth out the farther they got from the coast. He chose constants that would get the machines there just on time.

Everyone shut up as the last minute ticked away. Caden's squadron zeroed in on the drop zone, the rocks fell ever nearer their target, and the Space Force corvettes moved in to accompany them. Projected blast radii from the rocks appeared on the tactical. The fast-moving rocks were obvious: they had much larger danger zones. The attack had been launched in a staggered way so that the impacts would occur at nearly the same time despite the speed differences. Caden verified that his machines would be clear of the strikes.

"Splashdown!" Telisa announced.

Caden watched the impacts blossom on the tactical. He caught glimpses of a few visual feeds. Huge clouds rose over the ocean.

"The special asteroids hit pretty hard, but within the spinners' tolerances," Magnus said.

"Corvettes are dropping their torpedoes... entering the water in five seconds," Sager reported.

"Caden! Maintain your squadron above the water. Holding pattern," Telisa ordered. Caden sent a nonverbal acknowledgement.

Why not dive? What's wrong?

The tactical became a mess of activity.

Torpedoes and ships started to go out of contact. The assault force eroded under heavy attrition. He had no idea what was isolating them or killing them off.

They're destroying the ships! Shouldn't the squadron be down there?

Many torpedoes were still circling blind, looking for targets.

We must be laughable to them. They came from the water.

Caden saw that almost half of the rocks had altered course since impact. It was not the spinners; there were not that many of them and Caden could see several rocks without payloads sinking off course. The enemy was pushing them aside.

"They've redirected many of the rocks, including some with our payloads," Magnus said.

"Can we look at the changes and find what they're trying to protect?" asked Siobhan.

"Mostly likely only one or two of the course alterations were to protect something," Marcant said. "The rest are probably misdirection."

"It won't matter," Telisa reassured them. "When our asteroid fragments get deep enough, the spinners can move in on any targets."

Gravity spinners have strange effects around water. This should be spectacular.

Caden had seen entertainment shows that used gravity spinners in bodies of water, though the spinners had been near the surface for those displays. A spinner could cause vast walls of whitewater to fly upward into the sky like a huge reverse waterfall.

He tried to envision the confusion. Could the violent water currents bring the ship or a factory to the surface? It would be more than just currents from the spinner eddies, though. If the spinner could get close enough, it could cancel out the target's weight. Without the pull of gravity to match the pressure around an object in equilibrium, it would be squirted upward like a bubble in deep water.

More Space Force ships started a sharply declining course, bringing them down toward the ocean for a second wave. Telisa kept glancing over at Siobhan. He wanted Telisa to tell him to attack with the second wave of Space Force ships coming into position. At least the disk machines were not taking hits at the moment. He assumed the ships and their torpedoes must be the enemy's current priority. He watched the tactical and waited.

The next group of ships would be going into the water in seconds. Torpedoes fell from the sky, headed for the blue-green ocean.

"The spinners still have no targets," Siobhan said urgently.

Telisa finally looked at Caden. "Now, Caden! Launch those torpedoes and get your disks in there. Mix it up. Make it noisy and look for targets!"

The squadron interface came to the fore in Caden's mind. He saw his main disk machine, master to a hierarchy of slaved and sub-slaved disk machines. He prepared a fire order, let it percolate through the entire squadron, then ordered the launch. The disk machines' video feeds lurched as they dived toward the water. Another feed showed that the entire squadron moved as one. The torpedoes separated and sliced into the water. The disk machines recovered and skimmed the top of the ocean, slowing. Then they slipped under the waves after the torpedoes.

Caden's first disk machine went deeper in a long spiral course. He deactivated the hierarchy so that the squadron could scatter. The ocean was alive with targets. He assumed many of them must be diversions. He brought his own submerged disk robot slightly closer to one of the payload-bearing space rocks as it descended toward the ocean floor far below, analyzed its course, then sent the disk angling away.

Enemy action eroded the squadron's torpedoes. The few reports that made it back hinted at energy weapon deaths. Over half of his torpedoes were already gone.

Caden monitored the feeds from the disk machines. He had the entire squadron looking for signature matches of the Quarus seed ship. Enemy jamming was cutting out a lot of the transmissions. This time, the Terran ships were fighting back, trying to establish connections across multiple, moving frequencies and throwing out noise of their own.

Still, we're in the water... their home turf... can we really improve communications?

A new disturbance came up in Caden's PV. Low frequency vibrations in the ocean below them. He supposed it might be fragments of iron from their rocks hitting the ocean floor.

"The payload-bearing rocks have almost reached the bottom," Magnus reported. Telisa shot another look at Siobhan.

An anomaly came up on Caden's search screen. It was a roughly rectangular construct, maybe even cubical, though it was sunk into the mud, so it was hard to be sure.

Definitely alien, presumably Quarus. He compared it to the known signature of the unusual Destroyer command ship.

It came up a probable match, over 90% certainty. Caden's heart accelerated.

There! We found it!

"I have a target!" Caden said, highlighting it on the tactical. "It's the control ship, or a copy of it."

"Good work," Telisa said. "That factory is the objective," she told Siobhan.

"It might not be real," Magnus warned. "They could have physical or electromagnetic decoys down there."

"In the absence of anything else, it's our target," Telisa said. "Keep looking," she ordered Caden.

"The spinners are closing," Siobhan said. "Should we have the disks escort them in?"

"No," Telisa said. "They can't move as fast anyway. Keep the squadron searching for other targets."

"Roger that," Caden said. His squadron had all known friendly signatures, Terran and Celaran, in their data repositories. He told his handlers to keep up the search and to prevent any friendly fire. He imagined the Celarans would need no such encouragement: they were half afraid to hurt their *enemies*, much less their friends.

Caden used his skills to divide his attention between watching the surface feed and monitoring his disk robots. It was like absorbing attendants' video feeds in combat while still processing one's own vision. Of course, he had a lot of programs to help bring interesting feeds to his attention. Meanwhile, the surface remained calm.

One of the other disk machines found something. The feed showed a five-faced tower rising from an underwater rock formation. It was clearly artificial.

"Another target. It's something different. No idea what," Caden said. When it came up on their tactical he marked it as an enemy factory.

"Send torpedoes that way," Telisa said.

There were only ten of his squadron's torpedoes left alive. Caden complied.

"There's almost nothing left," he warned. He caught sight of movement in one of his video feeds. It was a view of the surface.

The ocean began to boil in the center of the target zone. Several more video feeds quickly zeroed in on the area of disturbance. The tactical showed it was the point directly above a tight group of gravitational disturbances—the gravity spinners.

"The spinners are bringing something to the surface!" Siobhan said. The tactical showed a huge interlocking web of friendly ships waiting nearby, ready to take a shot at the enemy ship if necessary.

"I'm picking up a massive disturbance," Marcant reported. "Something new."

Missiles broke the surface of the water in a hundred places at exactly the same moment.

Terran and Celaran ships engaged the new targets. Many of the robotic ships that had not submerged were quickly hit and destroyed despite the heavy defensive fire.

"We can afford to lose those robot ships," Telisa reminded everyone. "It's a desperation move. Their flagship is coming to the surface and they can't stop it."

The Terran battleships made quick work of the remaining missiles as they had before. Plumes of water continued to rise into the sky around the spot. A long tail of rain formed downwind of the area.

"Whatever you have, it's real," Sager said on the channel. "Our EW teams are sure of it."

A single plume exactly above the target grew to dominate the skyline in the video feeds. Caden held his breath.

At any moment I'll see it... will Telisa tell them to fire now? We can't trust that it will stay visible for any length of time.

"We've received a transmission from the target," Lee said. A translation followed in a neutral voice: "The vines die in endless darkness as we agree to your terms. We accept your truce and return home."

Caden noted the Celaran preamble. The translation must not have gone through Marcant's software. He assumed that Lee or her peers had boiled one of the long Quarus message blocks down to a short summary.

Magnus stared at Telisa. His face was tight, angry.

He doesn't trust them either.

"They're just saying that to survive," Caden said to Siobhan privately. Magnus must have been speaking privately to Telisa, perhaps saying the exact same thing. Telisa shook her head. But what was she saying 'no' to?

The plume of water became a spiral spout, then dispersed. Long sheets of water lifted from the sea, revolved, and flew off in the gravitic eddies of the spinners. Slowly, an alien structure emerged as the water that concealed it flew away in a white maelstrom.

That's it! We did it! Caden thought.

"The vines die in endless darkness as we agree to your terms. We accept your truce and return home," Lee repeated.

"The target is producing a tachyonic stream," a Space Force officer reported. "It will be low enough energy for transmission in a few seconds."

What? They can detect that without a TRB? It must be secret Space Force tech!

Telisa visibly tensed. Now the decision had to be quick.

The stormy water changed configuration suddenly.

"One of the spinners has been destroyed!" Siobhan reported.

The structure shifted. One end descended slightly, threatening to slide back into the water.

Now. Kill it! Caden thought. He said nothing.

"All ships. Light 'em up!" Telisa ordered.

For a half second, nothing happened as weapons control officers throughout the UNSF task force looked up the meaning of her archaic words in the ships' vast network caches. Then they started to fire.

The feed radically changed as filters kicked in to screen the view. Caden saw from attached readings that the alien ship had gone up in a flash of white-hot plasma. How many joules had that target absorbed? Superheated water rose into the sky in a mushroom cloud.

Caden had no doubt that the PIT team had just orchestrated the destruction of implacable enemies of Terra and Celara. He knew he would not lose any sleep over Telisa's decision.

Michael McCloskey

Chapter 23

Magnus waited with Siobhan, Caden, Marcant, and Lee for an incarnate PIT meeting within a meeting hall inside the *Midway*. They had all just arrived on the Terran battleship. Telisa walked in last as she liked to do. Everyone turned to look at her from their places. Lee had been aloft, but when she saw Telisa, she grasped a flexible hang line someone had set up.

Telisa looked relaxed but businesslike.

She looks better, Magnus decided.

"Congratulations on your victory," Telisa said. Many smiles came her way. "I'm happy to see the Celaran colony safe from Destroyers. In no small part, that is the result of our teamwork."

After the destruction of the Quarus seed ship, the Destroyer resistance had dropped markedly. Achaius thought it was because the doomed ship had sent out a cease fire before its destruction. Some of the Destroyers fought on. Magnus supposed their surrender order had been partially jammed by the Space Force, or perhaps the ceasefire theory was just wrong. In any case, the Space Force and the Celarans had managed to locate and destroy the remaining Quarus structures under the ocean. Nothing remained of the unique ship, though more disabled Destroyer machines had been collected for study.

Telisa paused and walked closer to the nearest table where the Terrans sat. Magnus knew what she was thinking. The group looked small. The PIT team had only five members left alive.

"I've been thinking a lot about those we lost, as I know you have been. I want to get out of the business of war. We're supposed to be explorers. The work will always be dangerous, but... we don't belong on the front lines."

Magnus saw how tightly Siobhan gripped Caden's hand. She understood that feeling. Being a devoted couple in a dangerous job...

"We're here on the *Midway* for a week," Telisa said, changing tack. "It's not a permanent assignment. Just something temporary. Think of it as a chance for some rest in relative safety."

"Kinda sad that being in orbit with a battle fleet above a planet at war is a safety retreat for us," Siobhan said.

Telisa nodded. "Yes. But given the size of this fleet, and the presence of the growing Celaran fleet, we'll all be at a low stress level."

"So we can mix with the crew?" Marcant said. Magnus pondered Marcant's tone for any clues as to exactly what *mix* meant.

"Yes, you should. It's been a long time since we've been around 'normal' people. There is one thing though. Admiral Sager asked me to ask all of you to be... tight lipped when it comes to our past travels and encounters. He did not say why, but he promised to fill me in when I get there. I'll pass the information along to you as soon as I can."

"They already know who we are, right?" Caden asked.

"Yes, I'm pretty sure the crew of the *Midway* knows who we are. The Admiral gave no details. So, just deflect questions until I can get to the bottom of this. Try not to deny anyone flat out. Just be as vague as you can. I know it's weird. I'll update you on that soon."

"Will do," Siobhan said.

"After that?" asked Caden.

"I don't know what we'll do next. I want to hear from Sager before I propose anything to you. Of course, if you like, you can leave the team. There will be a chance to change your... career before we head back out."

No one asked anything else, so Telisa said, "See you all soon."

Marcant got up and walked out a large side door, then Caden followed him. Lee took flight and left from a different door. Siobhan dallied with Telisa, so Magnus walked out of the door Marcant had used. He found himself in a wide hallway on the *Midway*. A sense of deja vu clutched his gut. The ship was so large it reminded him of the inside of Grenadin Spaceport. Magnus traded looks with the Space Force people walking nearby. They were curious, but quickly looked away. He half expected Cracker to come up to him at any moment. That had been a lifetime ago, when Telisa was still a stranger to him.

He saw Marcant a few meters away, so he walked up to the pale man. Marcant had some Celaran tech with him, two forearm-length tubes with hexagonal ports on one end.

"What are you up to?" Magnus asked politely. He looked over the Celaran devices in Marcant's hands but could not tell what they might be.

"Well, I've been invited to host a simulationist party on Celaran hardware," Marcant said.

"Simulationist party?" asked Magnus.

Marcant frowned. "Have you two really been gone for that long?"

Magnus shrugged. It probably just was not his scene. Telisa and Siobhan left the meeting room and joined them.

"So what happens at a simulationist party?" asked

267

Magnus.

"He'll create a VR world and put the participants into it, missing some or all of their memories," Siobhan said from nearby. "Most likely, they won't be aware that they're in a simulation."

That would require hacking their links.

"The participants won't be angry?" asked Magnus.

"Oh, they know what's going on and agree to it," Siobhan said. "I meant they won't know once it starts. Usually fake memories are provided for short term scenarios. The 'winner' will be determined by rules set at the start of the party, but the participants usually don't know anything about the existence of any rules unless they imagine it from scratch."

Telisa nodded. "I've heard of this. They're actually creating a simulation and living it, believing it's real, indirectly proving that our current lives might be the same kind of thing."

"But we started at birth," Magnus said.

"Well we *think* we did. It could be implanted. But, even so, starting at birth would be the most extreme form of this, to be played by immortal beings," Siobhan said.

"The record is 107 days," Marcant said.

"What record?" asked Telisa.

"The longest a simulationist has spent in a VR reality without knowing about it," Marcant said. "They have their memories blocked and replaced, then go in to live another life. We keep pushing the boundaries farther out, proving this can be done. Showing that it's not only possible, but *likely* we're doing the same thing right now one level of 'reality' lower."

"Are you going?" Magnus asked Siobhan.

"Of course!" Siobhan said. "You're not?"

"I'll pass this time," Telisa said. Magnus shook his head.

"Okay, well, see yah. I'm going to go find Caden."

"Bye," Magnus said. He turned to Telisa.

"So, you're not going to the simulationist party. What plans then?" Magnus asked.

"Let's stay in," she said.

"I was hoping you'd say that!" Magnus said.

"Ah, but we have dinner with the Admiral soon," Telisa said. "We'll have to be quick."

"Dinner?"

"Well, it's technically just me, but will you please come along?"

"Yes."

"Okay. I got us put into the same quarters," Telisa said. "See you there soon?"

"I can walk with you."

"Really? You don't want to pick up a few fans?"

Magnus smiled. He looked over to admire her beautiful face, but it was not there. A booted heel flew by where her head had been. Magnus whirled back.

The attacker looked male; he wore a Veer suit. The suit looked different; Magnus assumed that Veer had come out with a few new models recently. Magnus did not recognize the man's face.

"What—" Telisa started, then moved aside to avoid a fist aimed at her chin.

Magnus saw the attacker was not armed, so he knew Telisa could handle him. The man did not register as military to Magnus's link. He concerned himself with looking for other threats; he saw none.

Why is some civilian attacking her?

Telisa moved behind her assailant in less than a second. The man tracked her well, mule-kicking in her direction. Telisa deflected the kick with her shin, hard-blocked the backfist that followed it up, then reversed her block into a grab of the arm. Her leg swept the opponent's legs out from underneath him. She rode him to the floor hard, adding enough momentum to make the man grunt with the impact despite the protective Veer suit.

Telisa wrapped the man's left arm around his own throat and held it there with the heel of her hand firmly planted on his elbow. The man struggled to move, but could not. Her knee sat atop his other arm as she straddled his torso. The man shifted his weight to throw her, but she was faster. She simply adjusted herself so that he had no leverage. He tried again, but still did not gain a centimeter.

He tapped out in the manner of those training in martial arts. Telisa let go of his arm so he could speak aloud, but she remained perched above him.

"Well done," he said, smiling. "You're every bit as amazing as they say you are."

"You attacked me as a test?" Telisa snarled. "You're lucky I didn't rip you limb from limb!"

"It was worth it. Besides, I knew you wouldn't kill me without discovering my motivation. You would want to know who I was working for, who sent me, or what my beef was."

Telisa sighed and rose. The man sheepishly regained his own feet.

"I'm sorry. I learned so much more about you with a surprise attack!"

"Look," Telisa started. "If I'm always being careful

because I think every threat might be a test, then I might start letting off just a bit, then when I get in real trouble maybe I'll hold back. You don't want to get me killed, do you?"

"No. Of course not," the man said. He looked sincerely apologetic now. "I'll make sure and say that what I did was wrong... when I tell everyone how unbelievably skilled you are."

Telisa kept talking to him. Magnus kept his mouth tight-lipped and said nothing. He felt angry, but it was Telisa's place to handle an attack on her own person however she wished. A security robot floated over and joined the conversation. Magnus stepped a bit farther back, trying to stay out of the scene.

A young female lieutenant mustered her courage, walked over to Magnus, and saluted. Magnus returned the salute, not really taking it seriously.

"Should that man be detained?" she asked.

"I don't think so, not unless he attacks someone else."

"Need help finding your way around?" she said. Hope lived in that voice. Then she turned red, probably knowing full well that Magnus could simply query a directory service to find anything he needed.

"I don't think I'll get lost," Magnus said neutrally.

"Haha," she muttered, losing steam. "If you can find your way around alien worlds, I guess the *Midway* isn't very daunting."

"Right," Magnus said. "Who are you?"

Her eyes widened. "Lieutenant Brannigan, sir!" Her spine snapped even straighter.

"Thanks for the welcome, Lieutenant. How do you feel about coming out to help the Celarans?"

"My honor, sir!" Brannigan said.

"At ease. Have you seen one yet?" Magnus asked, suspecting he knew the answer. He tilted his head slightly, directing her gaze.

"Video feeds only," she said happily. Some of the fear left her expression, then her eyes widened even more. Lee flitted above several flabbergasted Space Force watchers-on just down the concourse. Magnus smiled. He had been aware of Lee's approach through his PV; even in this friendly environment it was second nature for Magnus to watch the team.

"Amazing!" she breathed.

Magnus took a peek back toward Telisa. She had shed her faux attacker, and now she was a few steps farther down the hallway, apparently engaged in a similar conversation with three officers.

"You know Telisa as well, I presume," Magnus said.

"TM Telisa! Yes, sir."

"You can call me Magnus, I'm not in the Space Force. What's TM?"

"Hahaha!" The laugh was so nervous as to be pathetic. "Team Member! Oh, it's true then, the PIT team doesn't even care about their exalted ranks? That's really great. You're not after the power, just the adventure, right? Have you found any living Talosians?"

Magnus struggled to parse her staccato speech.

"No Talosians," Magnus said.

Why would she think that?

"What's the most dangerous situation you've ever been in?"

Magnus considered the answer given his current constraints.

"I don't like to brag about past missions. Sorry, I know, I'm boring."

"Boring! Ha! Boring..."

"Maybe I can talk later, Lieutenant. I don't mean to be rude, but I have a meeting with Admiral Sager coming up."

It was a tiny inaccuracy, but not bad given that he really could not say anything until they knew why the Admiral had requested their discretion.

"Of course, TM. Thank you for your service!" Brannigan saluted again, and when Magnus returned it, she dashed away.

Magnus walked off, trying to look like he had something important to do.

***

Magnus held Telisa in his arms. The Veer suits had been discarded for a brief time before their dinner appointment. Their quarters were luxurious by Space Force standards. The soft sleep web they lay in was twice the length of any Magnus had seen on a Terran vessel.

"We're done here. We can go back to Earth," Magnus said. Telisa looked disturbed.

"I know I said a lot about that before," Telisa started. "I'm afraid to go back to Earth. I got you back and now I want to stay out here on the frontier."

She doesn't want to give Shiny the chance to mess with us again.

Magnus smiled. "Okay. What are you contemplating?"

"Let's go to the Celaran homeworld and see if we can find the other groups of Celarans that fled the Destroyers.

There might be clues there, or, many Celarans may have returned."

"Or a huge Destroyer fleet might await us."

"We'll come in with one fast, stealthed ship. Given our exalted ranks, I think we'll be able to score some transport or other."

"So if we find more Celarans, would we try to talk them into coming here?" Magnus asked.

"Surely they would be safer together here, in increased numbers and with the protection of the Space Force fleet? This planet is covered in the vines; it's ready to be colonized."

"Maybe. Or maybe the race as a whole is better off scattered across many worlds," Magnus said. Telisa could tell he was just challenging her thinking rather than truly disagreeing. It was how they examined multiple angles on their problems.

"Clearly we won't force them to do anything. Just inform them."

"Okay then. Inform the Admiral. There's nothing he can do about it; what you say, goes."

Telisa laughed. "Crazy, isn't it, how things have worked out?"

"Yes. Yes, it is."

***

Telisa and Magnus arrived at a small stateroom just on time. Inside, Admiral Sager and two other Space Force men waited at a dinner table, served by several small robotoids.

The Admiral and his companions rose. "This is

Admiral Akiyama, and this is General Trenton," said
Sager.

The group went through a tight series of salutes. In the
Space Force, admirals commanded starships and in-system
space forces, orbitals, and the like. A general oversaw
land, sea, and air forces planetside. Apparently, the Space
Force men ranked lower than an exalted Team Member.
Magnus felt embarrassment at the rank and the customs,
yet he valued the usefulness of it. With Shiny backing
them up, they would have what they needed.

Magnus took a half second to look over the two
commanders. Akiyama was shorter than Trenton, stocky,
with short black hair. Trenton had lighter hair a scar on his
face. Magnus wondered if it came from a combat
operation. What other reason to leave it there if it was not
a badge of courage? Despite the scar, Magnus's intuition
told him the men had not seen much action. He sent away
for their records in his link and resolved to scan them at
his first idle moment.

"Welcome to the *Midway*, ma'am, sir," Akiyama said
rapidly.

"Thank you," Telisa said. "It's an impressive ship."

"It's Akiyama's command, now," Sager explained.
"As the task force leader, I'm just squatting here."

Of course, what Sager says still goes.

"Would you like a report?" Sager offered.

"I think I'm up to date," Telisa said. "Let's talk about
what's next."

Magnus suppressed a smile. Telisa had adapted to her
new powers smoothly.

"Of course."

"The Destroyers will be back," Telisa said. "Your first

priority is to continue protecting the Celarans. It looks like you have what you need here to accomplish that, especially with the Celarans themselves resuming ship production."

Sager nodded.

"With your permission, I would like to land my forces and deploy for ground defense," General Trenton said.

"You have it," Telisa said. "Inform the Celarans first, and proceed at their convenience. Contact me in the unlikely event they refuse."

"Yes, ma'am."

"Secondly, assist the Celarans in re-establishing a safe economy."

Telisa paused for comments. Akiyama took the cue.

"I think we can feed them more raw materials from other sources in the system," Akiyama suggested.

"Exactly. Inquire as to their material priorities. Thirdly, I want you to learn from the Celarans. Exchange technologies. We'll hand off what we've learned to your experts. When the *Celaran* ambassador arrives, they should have what they need to get started."

The Space Force leaders nodded again.

"Shall we eat?" Telisa asked.

"Yes, let's eat," Sager echoed.

The group told the servant machines what they wanted. It did not take long for the food to arrive at the table. Magnus watched a Space Force robot place the food containers on the table, then move the contents to the plates like a Space Force General deploying his troops to planetside fortresses in ground assault ships. During the lull, his queries supplied him the verification he sought: the records of the two leaders at the table did not include much real action. The scar on Trenton's face, though, did come from a military training accident. Perhaps that was why the man had decided to leave it in place.

Everyone started to eat.

"May I inquire as to the PIT team's plans?" Admiral Sager asked.

Telisa stopped eating for a second and did not answer. Magnus was familiar with the behavior. Telisa was not afraid to pause while gathering her thoughts.

"We need to go find the other splinters of the Celaran civilization," she finally said. "I'm going to take the PIT team to their home planet. I want to know if there are any Celarans left there or if there are clues as to where these other sects went."

"Will we be deploying forces to these systems as well?" asked Akiyama.

"I sincerely hope not," Telisa said. "I hope to reunite the Celarans to strengthen them. I'd like to see them be able to take care of themselves, both to free up the Space Force and also to increase their strength as our allies. Either way, though, Terra will be stronger as a result. The Celarans possess technology beyond ours in many areas. What comes to mind first is their stealth technology. Has Ambassador Shiny offered any improvements to our ships in that area?"

"He has not," Sager said. "We've already begun studying the Celaran modifications to the *Midway*. So far, our experts are baffled."

"It's a steep learning curve," Telisa said.

They ate in silence for another two minutes.

"I believe there was something you wanted to speak to me about," Telisa reminded Sager. Magnus could tell by the Admiral's look that he had not forgotten about it.

"Yes. Did you take my advice about your team?" he asked.

"I did. I trust you had a good reason for me to tell them to be discrete about past... operations."

"The PIT team has built up more than a cult following on Earth. Ambassador Shiny has encouraged this, I think. At first, I thought most of the various stories were merely growing legends, made up tales and exaggerations. However, I've learned something disturbing—disturbing to me, at least—that shines a lot of light on why the PIT team is so well known and so widely idolized."

"Mind control?" Magnus asked.

"Ah, no, not that," Sager said. "There's no easy way to say this. Two weeks ago I talked to you, Telisa. You had just come back from the ruins of a major Vovokan colony."

Telisa and Magnus traded looks.

"Shiny has more than one of me active?" Telisa asked grimly.

"He has several PIT teams out gathering technology for him," Sager said carefully. "Duplicate PIT teams. He's taken snapshots of the crew from a certain time frame—I think from when you had been copied into those Trilisk columns. There are different crews deployed all over in various ships, mostly Vovokan ships, but not all of them. The crew of this ship was different than yours. Maxsym Kirilenko was on it."

"Earth knows about this?" Telisa asked.

"No. You see, to the Core Worlds, there's only one PIT team. But all the leaked rumors of all their exploits are rolled into one. Some team member appears at one place, mentions some alien race or encounter, shows off some artifact or other, then takes off. Later another PIT member is spotted somewhere else and new stories circulate. Some of it has to be false, but I've managed to verify enough sightings, besides my recent meeting with you, to get the big picture. My conclusions have been verified by Core World Security."

Magnus felt Telisa's turmoil rise even before she messaged him.

"Of course I'm upset... and yet... I'm not the original, either. I'm just another copy," she said to Magnus on a private channel.

Magnus would have reached out and put his hand on her shoulder, but he did not want to do that in front of the Space Force men.

"Thank you for informing us. We'll need a while to assimilate this," Magnus said.

"Yes. Thank you, Admiral," Telisa said weakly.

"All those copies are Trilisk host bodies," Magnus said. "That's reckless."

Sager shrugged. "I don't think they all are. The information available here is shaky, but I feel in my gut that the Ambassador has figured out how to make regular, accurate copies as well."

"He's ascending to godhood with all that power at his... legtips," Telisa said.

"That's the gist of it, and I'm sorry to continue..." Sager began.

"Yes?"

"It's not just you. Ambassador Shiny has almost certainly been duplicating himself, as well."

"I see."

Michael McCloskey

Chapter 24

Telisa was lost in thought in her quarters on the *Midway* when her door told her someone had come to see her. It was Lee, flitting about in the hallway outside.

An incarnate visit from Lee? Unusual.

Telisa told her door to open. Lee glided inside. There was no place to hang, so Lee floated in place in the center of the large room.

"Hello, Lee."

"I have some things I'd like to bring to a close with you," Lee said through the translators. She sent Telisa a pointer. Telisa accessed the data and found a list of tasks that Lee had helped with since they met. They were all related to the PIT team.

"What's up? I'm supposed to verify you did these things?"

"Yes. And evaluate me. This is my last day," Lee said.

"What?"

"I'm done with my post and ready to move on," Lee said.

"Oh! I'll miss you. What's your new job?"

"I could be a PIT team member now!" Lee said excitedly.

Telisa stared at Lee for a moment in shock. Lee probably did not grok the reaction since Celarans did not rely upon motions and expressions.

"Well... yes, you could be. Terrans—"

"Yes, I know, I need your permission to take this new position," Lee said. "Will you let me?" The voice's enthusiasm remained unabated.

"I'll clear it with the rest of the senior members of the

team," Telisa said carefully. She realized that meant only her and Magnus now that Cilreth was gone.

"Good! Please let me know when you decide."

"Sure. How long do I have? Will you be in trouble if it takes longer than a certain amount of time?"

"I won't get in trouble. If you take too long, we can just blame it on a cultural difference!" Lee explained exultantly.

Telisa smiled.

"Do you know our expressions? Do you see my smile?"

"Yes, but it's hard to notice. If your lips glowed, it would be clearer."

Telisa nodded.

"Some Terrans do use lip paint that can emit light patterns controlled by a link program. But it's mostly just for parties."

Lee flitted around the room. "We have parties, too. When we're ready to break into a nice fat juicy vine we haven't tried before."

Telisa bit her lip. She could not accept Lee's offer yet, but she could clarify a few things.

"Lee, there are some downsides to being on the team. While I consider your offer, let me bring them to your attention. My purpose is not to discourage, but to inform."

"Okay!"

"As you know, Terran ships are not hollow. So you'd live in a cargo bay," Telisa said.

"Okay!"

"You saw how dangerous it is. Aren't you afraid?"

"Yes. But it's dangerous everywhere now, isn't it?"

Maybe not on the Core Worlds. But that's no place for

Celarans.

"We're thinking about going to your home planet and trying to contact these other Celarans. We think that it might help if the fragments of your civilization are connected again."

"The home planet is said to be poisoned and unlivable," Lee said. "All space habitats there were destroyed."

"Well, we can go there to check it out. If the various Celaran factions don't want to communicate using the tachyon receiver bases anymore, maybe the Terrans could carry messages for you?"

"We're afraid," Lee said. "If Terrans go to all our planets, and they bring the communications bases with them, then maybe the Destroyers will hear them and find us everywhere!"

"We won't do that," Telisa said. "I'm sorry, I should have thought of that. I'll make sure and tell our new ambassador to the Celarans that this is an issue. As for the PIT team, we won't bring any TRB with us to your homeworld."

"Well, they already know about *that* place," Lee pointed out.

"Right."

Telisa got a reminder from her link.

"Excuse me, please," she told Lee. "I have to break some bad news to my team. I would invite you, but it's nothing to do with you, even if you join the team. Also, I'll mention your application to them and get their feedback."

"Sure!" Lee said. She told Telisa's door to open and drifted out. Telisa followed her out, then headed for the meeting room she had reserved. When she arrived, she found everyone waiting. She looked over the faces of her tiny team. They looked relaxed—happy, even.

"So how did you find your time on the *Midway*?" Telisa asked.

Everyone just blinked for a moment. They must have expected her to start belting out orders again.

I have gotten rather imperious lately.

"I'd forgotten what it was like to live around real people," Siobhan said. "Well, *normal* people... oh, you know what I mean."

"There were all these crazy stories about us," Caden said. "I think it must have something to do with—"

"Why the Admiral asked us to keep our mouths shut," Siobhan finished for him. She looked expectantly at Telisa.

Okay, they won't let me delay any longer. Dive in.

"Shiny has copied the PIT team many times from the Trilisk columns and sent them all to The Five knows where, all over the frontier and beyond," Telisa said in a single breath.

"What?" Caden spat.

"Frackedpackets!" Siobhan cursed.

Marcant said nothing. Telisa turned to face him. "As far as I know, there's only one of you, Marcant, since you probably were never copied into a column. It should be limited to those of us present when we met the UED unit, maybe up to the time we explored the space habitat with the Blackvines in it."

Caden's face changed as she mentioned that.

Of course. Arakaki.

"There are copies of us out there, doing work all over the place. Mostly tech recon and retrieval. The crews probably include Magnus and me, you two, plus Cilreth, Imanol, Maxsym, and Jamie."

"Jason?" asked Siobhan.

"I don't know," Telisa said. She tried to recall if Jason had ever been around a Trilisk column. Then she accepted they had no definite knowledge of what distance the Trilisk technology worked at; for all she knew Shiny did have copies of Jason, Marcant, and anyone else he wished.

"Is Shiny going to... *refill* our team?" Siobhan asked in dismay.

Telisa shook her head. "I don't know. We're just going to have to roll with whatever happens. Years from now, duplication may be common in our society. If Shiny releases the technology to the Core Worlders, who knows how things will change? It might be a revolution."

"I suspect Shiny may want to keep those special powers to himself," Magnus said.

"Are we going to work with the Space Force more now? It's interesting to be on the *Midway*," Siobhan said.

"It's tempting, I know," Telisa said. "I felt it, too. But we aren't a military unit. Stealth suits our purposes much better. I don't want to go looking for a fight with anyone."

"What can we do? The *Iridar* was destroyed," Magnus pointed out.

"Lee will take us to the Celaran homeworld," Telisa said.

"Take us as in..." Caden asked.

"Guide us. We have our choice of Terran starships here. We'll probably take a modest assault carrier, something designed for moving in and out of atmospheres quickly and stealthily with a good cargo capacity. I'll ask Lee to put in some Celaran stealth modifications as they did with the *Midway*."

"It doesn't sound smart to me," Caden said.

Siobhan looked at her boyfriend in astonishment.

"I mean we won't have supplies," Caden protested. "Weapons, robots, attendant spheres..."

Telisa nodded. "Shiny sent us a shipment of attendants with the fleet," Telisa announced. "I agree that we're running thin on a few other things and we'll miss the robots. But I have gifts for you all."

Telisa handed out small black containers to everyone.

"What are these?" asked Caden.

"Breaker claws. The Celarans came through for us," Telisa said.

"So slickblack!" exclaimed Caden, taking his out of the smooth case. It looked like a silver claw or talon, the size of a Terran's thumb.

"Careful, the breakers can cause explosions. Practice using them in our VR training first," Telisa warned.

I shouldn't treat them like green recruits. They all know that. Still, we've lost people to weird accidents...

"And these?" asked Siobhan, holding up a small metal sphere.

"When Lee produced these breaker claws, of course I was overjoyed," Telisa said. "And yet I had the audacity to ask for her to reproduce something else for us. My cloaking device."

"They already succeeded in fabricating another—" Siobhan disappeared. She reappeared after a moment. "Oops. Sorry. They reproduced another alien artifact!"

"Not exactly..." Telisa said.

"But it came from Shiny's vault on Vovok, right?" Caden asked.

"Yes. But when I showed it to Lee, she explained that it's Celaran technology."

"What?!" Caden gasped.

"Watch," Telisa said. She took out a Celaran lift baton and touched it to the sphere. They joined with a soft click. Joined together, the pieces looked vaguely like Siobhan's stun baton.

"Interesting," Magnus said, staring at his new devices. "I suppose it does seem like something Celarans would make if you think about it—they're good at evading attention."

No one said anything for a second, then Caden bit.

"So how did Shiny get one?" he asked.

Printed in Great Britain
by Amazon

50060344R00161